THE JUICY PARTS
AND OTHER QUIRKY STORIES

The Juicy Parts

and other Quirky Stories

A collection of short stories

by

LIBBY BELLE

Adelaide Books

New York / Lisbon

2020

THE JUICY PARTS AND OTHER QUIRKY STORIES
A collection of short stories
By Libby Belle

Copyright © by Libby Belle
Cover design by Matthew Bryer

Published by Adelaide Books, New York / Lisbon
adelaidebooks.org
Editor-in-Chief
Stevan V. Nikolic

For any information, please address Adelaide Books
at info@adelaidebooks.org
or write to:
Adelaide Books
244 Fifth Ave. Suite D27
New York, NY, 10001

ISBN: 978-1-953510-64-8
Printed in the United States of America

This book is a work of fiction. Names, characters, places and incidents either are products of the author's imagination or are used fictitiously. Any resemblance to actual events or locales or persons, living or dead, aliens or zombies included, is entirely coincidental. She apologizes in advance.

With much gratitude, the following stories
have been previously published:

"Twinkie in the Pantry," Woman's Weekly, UK

"Old Paul Elly," Woman's Weekly, UK

"Me and Shirley," Woman's Weekly, UK

"Aftermath," Adelaide Literary Mag NY

"The Gift," Adelaide Literary Mag NY

To my darling sidekick,

Robert Alan

Whose dedication to my imagination

brought these stories to life

Contents

Prop up a pillow, grab your favorite drink, and enjoy the ride! These stories are meant to entertain. You hold in your hand 22 delightfully quirky tales full of lovable, incorrigible, funny, and impulsive characters that you may recognize – some might even be friends or family!

In the story, *A Simple Lie* a divorcée struggles with love addiction. It's payback time in *Intruder Alert*! Tragedy in *Out of Luck* links a mournful songwriter to a charming Irish taxi driver. Meet two brave teens, a zombie and a couple of ghosts in *"Beyond the Wall"*.

The Bathroom Material section was created for those of you who like to read on the throne, with "shorties" like *Gertrude*, a zany gut-spilling massage therapist, and *It's Over*, where that four-letter word is mistreated, while *Ten Items or Less* rolls you down the aisle to an unusual grocery store scene. And there's more to enjoy.

Need a unique and fun gift idea? Wrap up a Libby Belle collection of short stories with a six-pack of toilet paper and a bottle of wine.

Cheers!

Introduction

My fertile body has been replaced by my fertile imagination. Growing up with four wildly different siblings and raising six strong-willed children of my own has given me an incredible source of material for my stories. Toss in ten delightful grandchildren, everyone I've ever met, even those in my dreams, and my imagination is continuously sparked.

What really started me writing up a storm was not just my love for the art form. I did it to heal my broken heart. Crazy thing to say, but it's true. You see, one of my beautiful children died, and I was out of my mind with utter sadness. I am still sad and will forever grieve. Writing has helped me move that energy another direction – away from despair.

I cherish my faith, and in order to strengthen it, I believe that we should do what we enjoy the most and do it well. Until the day we look back at our life, and we yell out to the world in all its glory, "It was good. I gave you all I had. I enjoyed the ride. What's next?"

I hope you, too, enjoy the ride and my quirky stories along the way. And if you do, please let me know. I write them for you!

Yours truly,
Libby Belle

Gifts come in a variety of ways. Some are ordinary,

some are extraordinary, some are meant to appease,

some are meant to please.

And some gifts last a lifetime.

The Gift

Gina would have jumped out the window and ended it all, only her house was a one-story, and crashing to her death just wasn't possible with a mere three-foot fall. Although, a few broken bones might take her mind off the real reason she is imprisoned in her own home. But in the end, all it would do is add to the medical bills that would never be paid in *her* lifetime – a lifetime shortened by this creepy disease they call cancer. It was a good thing she had decided early on not to bring any children into this cruel unforgiving world. They'd never have to know the shitty way their mother suffered.

The bald head was not a big deal, really, because Gina knew she had a very pretty face, tiny features, only a few wrinkles for a woman in her fifties, thin crow's feet that a good make-up could easily disguise, a full set of lips and exceptionally large eyes that appeared impishly cat-like when eyeliner was applied. Her hair had always been thin anyway, and when it fell out she was quite surprised to find that her perfectly shaped head had no lumps or dents. Not one. Altogether a miracle since she had fallen off the bed during playful hours of sex more times than she could count.

These days bound mostly to her bedroom, the vomit tray within reach, she spent a lot of time pondering the past and those crazy years divided up unequally between four husbands. Yes, she had married four times. Although, the last two really didn't count because she had given each of those husbands a six-month trial period during which they both failed miserably. And in both cases, she had filed for annulment, which technically meant she had only been married twice. "Well, you know what they say, third time's a charm," the men would quote, followed by a wink and another drink. Unlike, *married four times* which always got a stupefied reaction, as if she'd said, "Here, hold this stick of dynamite while I fish through my purse for a match."

One thought always led to another, and if she had enjoyed writing, Gina would have put all these tidbits down on paper. Instead, she'd just have to take them all to her grave.

It was a cloudless, sunny day and as always, Gina wrapped a designer scarf around her, smooth, hairless head and made up her face to absolute perfection. The nightgown she wore was stunning, and if a lover had of been in her presence, he would have told her so just before he ripped it from her body. Yes, ripped! Gina liked her lovers wild and daring, just teetering on the edge of cruel, and she especially liked them eager and greedy – never satisfied with only one orgasm.

So, where are all those exciting lovers now? Not one came to see her, not one called or sent flowers, or even a lousy three-dollar card. Her girlfriends were few, and most of them owed her money and stayed away in shame. She was sure that her co-workers thought she had died. And neighbors? No one likes to make friends with the only pretty single woman on the block, even if her days are numbered.

Her last hope was her favorite aunt who promised to visit soon after recovering from a bunion removal. "Sure, when will that be? At my funeral?" Gina had sarcastically blurted just as she hung up the phone, imagining the epitaph on her tombstone in a sad, drippy font, "Here Lies Beautiful Gina Who Died of Loneliness."

As for her best friend, Ellen, she was too exhausted from her own miserable life at home with her schizophrenic father, her divorced daughter and her ungrateful brats. And bearing the brunt of it all was Frank, poor, sweet Frank, the neglected husband who Ellen was gradually losing all desire for. Gina couldn't blame her friend for not coming around anymore. Seeing her sick like this just added to Ellen's misery.

Thank goodness for daily talk shows and old soap opera reruns and particularly those magazines pertaining to home design, as Gina loved to decorate – accessorizing her place with sexy lamps and rugs, thick window coverings to darken a room like a cave, and always a touch of leather. Men like leather. She found comfort surrounded by beauty, taking selfies dressed in her Scarlet O'Hara gowns, posing next to statues of naked Greek gods or lying on her plush bedspread laced in metallic golds and reds surrounded by a never-ending line-up of frilly throw pillows trimmed in feathers or tassels. She envisioned a new epitaph in a sensual gold font, "The World Less One Classy Broad!"

It wouldn't be the worst thing to die in all this lushness, she told her dog, Archie. She had rescued the little canine from her mean step-father who had planned to take him to the pound right after her mother's funeral. "People can be so awful," she warned the little terrier.

Archie was who kept her going. Archie was what kept her believing, because Archie cried when she cried, was happy when she was happy, and never left her bed like most of the men in her life eventually did. So, it wasn't surprising that Archie would grow to be over-protective and lunge after anyone who knocked on the door – the pizza delivery boy, always at the wrong address, or that UPS man with those chiseled calves and cute brown shorts. Archie tore through his thin black socks faster than a terrier could tear through a rat, clinging tightly to his ankle until the man kicked him loose. Gina had quickly scooped him up and admonished the driver for his act of cruelty, not only to the dog but to herself, "a very ill young woman on the brink of death!" The guy felt such deep sympathy for Gina, none for the dog, he dismissed the threat of a lawsuit and accepted a cup of coffee with her on the porch, while Archie watched him closely with beady-eyed anticipation.

That was six weeks ago – much too long for a woman with a fierce sexual appetite to be without a man to flirt with, toy with, kiss, or just to give him a taste of what she had to offer once that awful uninvited intruder was extracted from her body.

Gina sat alone at the window watching for any kind of life to remind her that she was still alive. The birds chirping and the smell of freshly cut grass used to heighten her senses. There was a time when the cool air sifting through the screened window would have made her feel light and hopeful. But not today.

That is, until she saw Frank's car in the driveway. She had known him since high school long before he married Ellen, and she had always been fond of him. Truth is, if Ellen had not taken Frank for her own, Gina might have. There was a delicate undercurrent of sexual tension between them that Gina thought Ellen detected, and even though nothing was ever said about it, Ellen made sure that the two were never left alone. Thirty years later, Gina still sensed Ellen bristle up when Frank talked to her, even if it was about something as simple as football. How exciting that he was here now, and without his wife.

Outside it was strangely quiet. She leaned in and stretched her neck looking for Frank, Archie by her side on alert. She heard the water turn on from the outside spigot. "What's going on out there?" she asked her furry friend.

Gina saw a stream of water squirting from the hose to the roof of her car. "Why look, Archie, Frank's washing my car." She caught her reflection in the nearby mirror, and the look of delight on her tired face excited her. "Oh, how sweet."

Knowing Frank would not want her to protest, she stayed hidden at the window and waited to see him as he approached the front of the car. She saw his hand first, grasping a big sponge, vigorously scrubbing the doors. Then, she saw his bare back gleaming in the sun, already sweating from removing weeks of filth from her vehicle. He has a beautiful back, she thought, focusing on the muscles moving with each sweep of his arm.

She was completely unprepared for what she saw next. When Frank came into full view she could not believe her eyes. He was without question, totally naked. Stark naked! No shorts, no shoes, no baseball cap on his head.

Gina dropped down to the floor on her knees and giggled. "Don't look now Archie, but Frank's outside washing my car in his birthday suit!"

When she eased back up, she saw that Frank was taking an exceptionally long time cleaning the side view mirror, feverishly removing the hardened dead bugs, his rear end muscles flexing with each small vigorous movement of his hand, the water hose held conveniently within reach between his thighs.

"Oh, my," Gina exhaled, her eyes half-closed with pleasure when he proceeded to the windows, and in slow, broad sweeping motions he wiped across the glass, pivoting in rhythm from one foot to the other. It was then that she realized the possibility that Frank was performing for her. She lured Archie to the guest bedroom with a peanut butter cookie and tiptoed out to the porch for a better view.

Frank just had to know that she was standing there, still as a deer listening for potential danger, her heart beating loudly in her chest. But he gave her no sign that he knew and continued washing her car, the spring sun warming his flesh, as he performed one of man's favorite weekend rituals just for Gina.

It was a beautiful thing and something she had never experienced, nor ever heard of anyone doing. She was so entranced by his movements, she had forgotten that she was sick and closer to death than she'd ever been. She swooned when Frank laid his chest across the broad hood of the Cadillac drenched in a sea of soap suds. Bent over, she could not help but see his testicles hard and swollen, his penis strong and erect. In her lifetime, she had seen many nude men, but nothing as sensual and exciting as this. When he moved to the other side of the car where he would be facing her, Gina decided to go back inside just in case they might catch each other's eyes and break the spell.

Back in her bedroom, she pictured a new epitaph, this time in a playful font, "Men Washed Cars in the Nude for Gorgeous Gina." In the excitement of the moment, she felt weightless; the constant dread lifted from her tired body. She fluffed the pillows, eased under the covers and waited to see what Frank would do next. It felt like Christmas day.

When she heard the water being shut off, she tensed, listening carefully for any other sounds. Then she heard footsteps on the porch and the screen door opening slowly. She grew excited with each creak of the hinge.

"Gina?" Frank called softly from the center of the living room.

"Yes, Frank. I'm in my bedroom," Gina answered in a meek voice.

"Can I come in and say hi?"

She considered asking him if he had his clothes on, but decided against it, since secretly she hoped he had left them off. "Come on in," she said, biting her lip to keep from giggling.

She heard his wet bare feet slap the tile floor as he approached her room. She sucked in a breath, picked up the magazine on the bed and pretended to be reading.

Frank entered one step over the threshold and stopped. Gina slowly tore her eyes from the magazine and looked up. There he was, like a man who had just gotten out of the shower after a pleasurable round of sex, standing there before her uninhibited, a towel flung over his shoulder, the tightness in his groin now relaxed along with his facial expression.

"How are you, Gina?"

"Well, Frank,…frankly, I haven't felt this good in a while. You do know you're naked, don't you?" she replied coyly, concealing a smile with the tips of her fingers.

"Yes. I do know that. I've been washing your car," he casually spoke.

"Well that was very nice of you. The old gal really needed a cleaning. I appreciate it a lot. But that doesn't explain why you're naked," she said, not scolding him but sincerely wanting to know what was on his mind.

"You watched me. I'm glad. I did it for *you*, Gina. It's my gift to you."

"I don't understand, Frank."

"Gina, I know how sad and lonely you are here. I know you miss your social life. I know how much you miss being sexy and sexual. So, I thought I'd remind you that you still are." His eyes left hers as he looked down at the floor, concentrating on what he was about to say next. Gradually looking up, he met her eyes again. "If you don't mind me asking…do you think *I* am still sexy?"

"Hmmm." Gina propped herself up higher on the pillow, raised her finger up in the air and motioned for Frank to come closer.

He slowly stepped forward until Gina signaled for him to stop right where a shadow was cast across the floor, the perfect soft light surrounding his body. She studied his torso, trying not to stay too long on the mid-section. When her eyes landed on his feet, baby white from years of wearing boots, she said, "OK, now turn around," still using her finger, like a trainer directing a seal.

Frank turned around and faced the door, dropping the towel on the floor. Gina studied his rugged back, bits of wild hairs scattered from his neck to the middle of his shoulder blades, the love-handles not as firm as they used to be, but darn cute, the tan line along his waist framing a very nice bottom, her second favorite part of a man. "OK, now turn back around."

She looked directly into his eyes and gave him a full report. "The way I see it Frank, you're still a darn sexy man, and I think you look gorgeous from head to toe. And by the way you moved out there on my car, it's very possible she's pregnant now."

They both laughed, a hearty laugh between old friends that would've, and maybe could've been more, but both had a mutual love for Ellen.

"I'd love to stay and visit with you longer, Gina, but the way things are sizing up," he glanced down at his groin, and quickly wrapped the towel around his waist, "I think it's best I leave now."

"Yes, I suppose you should." She looked away, and feeling tears welling up, she dabbed at her eyes with a tissue. "Frank, I have to tell you. That was the nicest gift anyone has ever given me. Thank you. I'll *never* forget it."

"And thank *you*, Gina."

"For what, Frank?" Gina looked confused.

"For being you."

When Frank walked away, Gina quickly slipped out of bed. "Wait, Frank, wait!" she cried out breathlessly, rushing toward him, clutching at her gown, the intoxicating scent of freshly sprayed Shalimar bursting from her pores.

Startled by how swiftly she had moved across the room and was now just inches from his body, he looked at her curiously, "What is it, Gina?"

"Will you, please, give me just *one* more gift, Frank?" she asked imploringly, eyelashes fluttering, her hands clasped together on her bosom, her top front teeth biting down on her lower quivering lip.

Frank's eyes grew wide with anticipation. A tiny drop of sweat slid slowly down the bridge of his nose.

Gina moved in closer. "Will you…will you wax my car?"

I've always loved the word "beyond".

To Infinity and Beyond! Beyond the horizon.

Beyond words. Far and beyond. Beyond the pale.

Beyond my wildest dreams...

Beyond the Wall

Haley's mother sighed heavily in reverence as they drove slowly past the wall. Below the eight-foot-tall structure was a small shrine where folks had left flowers, miniature statues, and stuffed animals of all kinds. On the wall's surface, the bold letters painted in bright red held Haley's attention. That one all-encompassing word meant more to her now than ever before.

She had the sudden urge to put her hand out the window. She took the bunny rabbit's glass eye from her purse, placed it in her palm, and with an out-stretched arm, Haley closed her eyes and reflected on the moment she had first set foot on that very corner:

School was disrupted that day – seems someone reported a bomb in the cafeteria, and when the coach ordered everyone out to the baseball field with his shrill whistle blowing above all the chatter and commotion, Haley and her friend, Delilah, decided to keep on walking. No one would miss them anyway, and besides, the same unwarranted scare had happened before. Ever since that new president had come into office and divided up the country in such a way, even outspokenly courageous Haley was apprehensive about expressing her thirteen-year-old opinion.

"Don't look back, Delilah!" Haley ordered her accomplice, who was walking with head bent, eyes darting from left to right and repeatedly reporting how afraid she felt. "If you do, they'll know who's playing hooky. This way, all they can see is our backs and those pretty legs of yours."

"Aw, Haley, stop making fun. I can't help that I'm bow-legged. My mama said it was because she had to bend over so much when she was carrying me in her stomach. Picking grapes while pregnant ain't an easy job," she said with a certain kind of pride in her voice.

"Probably not. But all that picking is what got my uncle drunk every weekend. He drank enough wine his lips finally turned purple. Last time I saw him they were nearly black, and his teeth were stained, too, and his tongue was blue. But he said his digestive system worked like a charm, and the doctor reported that his colon had turned a nice rich purple."

Haley knew that what she had just said went right over Delilah's head, but she hoped it would make her think of something else besides being scared. Even though the lanky, timid girl wasn't the best conversationalist, she was a true friend. Haley had many times protected her from the bullies at school, and the stuck-up girls who had no good excuse to pick on someone not as pretty or smart, or the same skin color, but they did anyway. It seemed lately to be a full-time job, and as long as she remained a student at Scarborough Middle School, Haley promised Delilah, "I've always got your back, little friend." In return, Delilah swore she'd always be her faithful sidekick.

Just as they turned the corner, Delilah, looking as befuddled as ever, glanced behind her. "Phew, that was a close one. I thought I saw my math teacher looking our way. She's got eyes like an eagle. I know cause there ain't no cheating in her class. Rylie Johnson gets caught *every* time." Finally letting her fists relax, she asked excitedly, "Where are we going now, Haley?"

"We're going to sneak around the back way to my house. If we walk down the main road someone will see us. Since my mother's at work, we can go in through my brother's bedroom window…he always keeps it unlocked. He sneaks out at night. And then we can eat the Fritos that he has hidden under his bed and steal a cola from my dad's little refrigerator in the garage. Soap operas are on tv, and I hear people kiss on those shows."

She looked over at Delilah who was clearly intrigued, a perfect opportunity for Haley to show off her acting skills. "Yes, kiss! Smooching, like this." She turned her back to Delilah, crossed her arms and walked her fingers up and down her sides, moving her hips seductively and making loud smacking sounds with her lips.

She could always make her friend laugh, and now Haley would make her do something even more daring than just skipping school. "Come on, we're on an adventure, and we're going down Bradbury Lane. Stay close to me and do what I say. No sudden moves. Just keep walking straight and in a normal stride. Zombies live on that street. My brother said he saw them, which probably means they're not real, but just to be on the safe side…."

Haley knew better than to take that particular route home. Bradbury Lane had always been forbidden by her mother, and even when her father was home, which was rare, he would remind her to stay on the beaten path. The stories told about that old street sent shivers up Haley's spine, but even so, today she felt exceptionally brave.

Delilah pressed shoulders with Haley as they moved deliberately but cautiously toward Bradbury Lane. The convenience store on the corner was also a forbidden place, so they walked around the back of it where a long chain link fence separated the nicer homes from the creepy street. Haley spotted a big feral cat standing on the edge of a dumpster trying to open the lid with its razor-sharp claws. The girls steered around it, not wanting to disturb the wild creature for fear it would jump on their heads.

As they walked down Bradbury Lane, the light quickly faded as if the sun had been held hostage behind a dark cloud, and everything seemed to be soaking in an ugly gray. Looking up they spotted an electrical line with six pairs of shoes hanging by their strings, and as they studied them, they nearly stepped on a man lying face down on the sidewalk. Haley jumped back, while Delilah stood frozen staring down at the lifeless creature. The man opened one crusty eye, glowered at Delilah and grabbed her ankle with his dirty hand.

"It's a zombie! Run, Delilah, run!" Haley screamed and took off running down the street. When she looked back, she saw that Delilah was still standing there, her mouth gaping, a silent scream stuck in her throat. Haley ran back and tried to pull her from the man's grip, who was now propped up on his elbow, a slimy malicious look on his grimy face. She yanked harder and as she did, she fell down, bringing Delilah with her.

The zombie began to crawl toward them; a gurgling noise pouring from his twisted mouth. Just then, a shadow fell over them, and when Haley looked up, there stood a tall man, thin and pasty dressed in all black, including a long flowing cape and a mask over his eyes – only the red Converse high-tops on his feet clashed with his impressive costume. "Unhand that maiden!" he demanded with a low, booming voice that surprised them all.

Letting go, the zombie fell back and covered his eyes, as if he were looking upon something powerful and magical. The skinny swashbuckler raised his cape over the girls and hurried them along. "You are safe with me," he spoke with authority.

As they moved quickly down the middle of the street, avoiding the filthy, cracked and uneven sidewalks, they saw men leaning against buildings, staring blankly straight ahead at nothing. A group of angry-looking disheveled people in tattered clothes walked toward them with sticks raised, and when their hero growled, loud and guttural, they scattered like flies. The girls were terrified and clung tightly to each other. Old hags screamed at them through broken glass windows of the dilapidated houses, and a mangy dog followed them, urging them to leave with his sickly yap.

They reached the end of the street where the sun began to shine again and rushed to the corner where they stood looking at one another in amazement. Catching her breath, Haley spoke first, "Thank you for protecting us. I'm Haley, and this is Delilah. I, I well, we aren't allowed to go down that street, but, well, we kind of skipped school today and…," she stopped short when she heard Delilah sobbing.

"It's okay, it's okay," said the cloaked man, his voice soft and kind. "You are safe now, and look," he pointed behind them, "the street is gone, disappeared, no longer there to frighten you. See, there's a regular old building there, vacant and harmless, but if you were to go through that door with the sign on it, you'd walk right back to Bradbury Lane."

Delilah, apparently afraid to acknowledge him, kept her head down while Haley looked back, and to her surprise, the street was indeed gone, and in its place was the building he had just described. She looked down at the weeds beneath her feet and beyond the sidewalk over at the telephone pole filled with hundreds of staples and thumbtacks holding pictures of missing pets, leaflets, handwritten pages advertising a garage band. Everything else around them seemed familiar. Then Haley turned to see the tall concrete wall behind them. It had a thick coat of white paint and the word "FORGIVE" written in red, inside the letter "O" someone had crudely drawn a peace sign. Below the wall, flowers were placed next to little stuffed animals faded from the sun, and drippy candles that had once been lit, and on the side of the wall was a stack of paint cans and dried out paintbrushes.

"I know, it all seems weird, doesn't it?" the man with the pale face and kind eyes, now looking much younger, smiled down at the dazed girls. "My name is Kalmin, and I have a purpose," and just as he said that, a car pulled up and a hand reached out through the opened window.

Kalmin looked at Haley and said, "Excuse me for a moment, please." He grabbed the edge of his cape and dramatically swooped it in the air as he walked over to the car. He held his hand over the extended hand, bowed his head and closed his eyes. Then he spoke something inaudible, a goodbye was said from within the car, and the driver continued on down the road.

Kalmin turned to see Haley looking at him in confusion. Delilah stood talking to herself in front of the shrine. "I give messages to people," he said with conviction. "Messages that they may already know but cannot seem to believe. Good messages, of course. Like that word right there behind you." He pointed to the wall. "But I must be going now. See you ladies again, I hope. But not on Bradbury Lane!" And with that, he turned and walked right through the letters painted on the wall and completely disappeared.

Haley grabbed Delilah's hand and pulled her away from the scene. Delilah jerked from her grip, ran back, snatched up a stuffed Koala bear and shoved it in her backpack. Instead of heading to Haley's home, as planned, they turned and ran down the main street toward school, not a single word between them. Somehow, walking into an empty house after what they had just experienced wasn't as exciting as they had thought. It seemed the best place to be at the moment was safe and sound among their schoolmates, even if there was a bomb scare.

Neither of the girls could sleep restfully with their secrets. At school the next day, Haley told Delilah that she wanted to go back to the wall, via the regular route, of course. But there were after-school duties she had to fulfill, and they would have to wait until Saturday before they could visit Kalmin again. Providing, of course, he would return. After seeing him vanish through the wall, who could be certain of anything. Skinny or not, behind that mask was a very fine-looking superhero, and Haley was anxious to learn more about him. Delilah reserved her own thoughts with nervous nods and cautiously hid behind her friend's enthusiasm.

Saturday finally came and not even an invitation to shop the mall with her mom could keep Haley from going to the wall. Delilah would come when she could, after helping her grandmother can peaches. Haley ran most of the way and when she got to the corner, she was disappointed that Kalmin wasn't there. Just when she sat down to catch her breath, a car pulled up to the curb.

The driver sat for a few minutes and then reached out the window as if to touch something. She held her arm in midair for a while before she let it dangle against the side of the car door. Then she opened it, and with one foot out, Haley could now see her strained face; on it a look of sadness that tugged at Haley's heart. She could see the woman hesitate in between long, drawn-out breaths. Believing that she was waiting for a message, Haley thought for certain that Kalmin would appear to deliver it. But he didn't show, and after a while, the woman closed the car door, rested her head on the steering wheel and began to cry.

Haley felt tears come to her own eyes, and what she did next completely surprised her. She rose and walked over to the car. She could only see the back of the lady's head, the long hair draped over her shoulder as she wept. She waited, still and patient, for her to look up. When she finally did, she jerked at seeing Haley standing there. Composing herself, the woman allowed her eyes to focus on the innocent face of the teenage girl.

Knowing what Kalmin would do next, Haley reached for the woman's hand. The woman hesitated. Haley turned her palm up and held it out closer, a trusting look on her face. Slowly, a slightly trembling hand came out from within the car, and long delicate fingers rested lightly in Haley's palm. She placed her other hand on top of the woman's, closed her eyes and waited, for what she was not certain.

Images appeared in her mind, things she could not understand. When she let go of the woman's hand, she stood paralyzed, as if in a trance, not sure why or if she should tell her the words that were whispered in her ear. The woman gazed at her in desperation, her eyes pleading. Haley glanced over her shoulder at the wall that seemed to be reassuring her. The words came easily when she spoke, "You must forgive her."

Fighting back more tears, the woman put the gear in drive and gave Haley a sad, but hopeful smile. Haley looked closer, and in her face she recognized Kalmin's smile: a small, but friendly overbite, a deep dimple in the left cheek, plump pink lips naturally outlined in a brownish, bloodstained red. Above her right cheek was a thin ragged scar, one that looked as if it had been with her for years. Before Haley could say anything more, the woman said, "I do, I do forgive her," and then she drove away.

Still somewhat dazed, Haley went over to the shrine and studied each of the items placed there. The wilted flowers looked sad against the white painted background. Nearby she spotted a shiny object sticking up from the dirt. It appeared to be a piece of jewelry etched with an inscription. Scooping it up she discovered that it was a necklace with the name "Cecilia" written in a fancy type font, caked in dirt, but still intact.

She looked around for other things she might have missed. She spotted a glass eye that had fallen off a stuffed bunny rabbit and put it in her pocket. Something else caught her attention, and it wasn't Delilah, who had been hiding behind the wall watching her. Lying on its back was a wooden cross. She lifted it and read the letters, RIP.

At that very moment, Kalmin came back through the wall. She held up the cross for him to see. She was reluctant to ask, but she knew she must. "This is for you, isn't it? I mean, you are dead, aren't you?"

"Quite, it seems. But *you* can see me, and…," he looked around for Delilah, "I hope that doesn't disturb you too much. I mean no harm, and as you know, I protected you from the zombies, so now we are friends, and you know my purpose."

"Well, at least that explains why you can walk through the wall…I guess." Haley rolled her eyes, uncomfortable with her ignorance. She wanted Kalmin to tell her more, especially now that the encounter she had just experienced may have been with his mother. Before she could share that with him, she had to ask, "How did you die?"

"I was killed on this corner, Haley. I was in my first year in college." When Kalmin slowly approached her, Haley constrained a nervous reaction to step back. She remained thoughtfully still and silent. "Anyway, it was Halloween, and my mother and I were on our way to a party. I was dressed like I am now… a young Zorro, I guess, is kind of what I had in mind." He let out an awkward chuckle and turned to face the street. "We were hit head-on by another car. Unfortunately, the driver was killed, and so was I. I'm very glad my mother survived, only, I know she is suffering. So, I began this mission to give messages to people as they stopped at this corner, hoping that one day she'd come, and I'd be able to give her a message I know she needs. One that will heal her heart."

"I'm so sorry you're…," Haley snapped her mouth shut and focused on his brightly colored tennis shoes to prevent herself from saying something stupid. "I waited for you today. While you were gone, a woman drove up in a maroon car. She stopped and reached out as if she wanted something. Then she cried. I don't know why I did it, but I went over to her, and she let me take her hand. I closed my eyes and heard a message. I gave it to her and then she left." Haley looked away, biting her thumbnail, still hesitant to suggest that the woman was his mother.

"Did your mother have a scar on her cheek?" she asked.

"Yes, yes, she did, on her right cheek." Kalmin's eyes opened wide in excitement. "She has long brown hair and beautiful hands. She plays the piano. I have her lips, and her dimple, the rest of me, including this lean body, is my dad's. Does that sound like that might be her?"

"It does," Haley said, watching Kalmin slowly drop to his knees, holding his hands to his heart, and although he was smiling, he was also crying. She went over and sat down across from him. She wanted to place her hand on his, but she was uncertain what would happen if she touched a dead person, a ghost, a spirit, so she resisted the temptation.

Kalmin looked up at her face, full of innocent curiosity, full of life. He wanted to touch her hand that had touched his mother's hand. He wanted to change places with her, he wanted to be alive, he wanted so many things he could not have. But more than anything, he wanted his mother to know he was safe, and then he could move on to an understanding. He was afraid to ask Haley what message she had given her, afraid it would not be the right one. He forced himself to ask, "What did you tell my mother?"

Haley shifted to one side and kicked out her legs in front of her. Just as she did, Delilah came out from behind the wall, inching her direction. Kalmin said a hello, and Haley welcomed her friend. Delilah offered a panicky smile and held up the Koala bear, now clean with a red ribbon wrapped around its neck. "It's for her," she said timorously, placing it next to the other stiff and dirty stuffed toys.

"Her?" Haley gave Kalmin a confused look. In return he gave her a simple shrug. While Delilah skirted around Haley, who was now looking up at her strangely, she moved to where Kalmin was sitting and nearly sat right on him. Kalmin laughed and scooted over. Haley let out a shriek, "You almost sat on Kalmin! Don't you see him?"

Delilah stood up quickly, looked around the spot and shook her head emphatically. Her face scrunched up as she whimpered, "Oh, Haley, I *don't* see Kalmin. I never have. I played along with you because, because, well, because of Cecilia. She's standing over there by the cross." She pointed, while peeking through her fingers. "Do *you* see her?"

Haley looked over and saw no one. "Stop that! There's no one there! Of course, you can see Kalmin. He saved you from the zombie. He talked to you. He consoled you. Didn't you see him talk to the person in the car? Stop fooling around and pretending you see another ghost!" Haley was very upset at what she thought was a lame joke.

Kalmin looked with concern at Delilah who was wringing her hands and pleading with her distraught friend. "I can still play the game, Haley. I can pretend just like before. Don't be mad at me. Show me where Kalmin is now, and I'll try to look harder." Frantic, her eyes searched in a tight squint. She so wanted to remove the scowl from Haley's face.

Next to Delilah, Kalmin looked as real as she did. He's standing next to her, Haley thought, and she still doesn't see him. I must be insane. Or is Delilah nuts? Is he really a figment of my imagination? Is Cecilia a figment of Delilah's imagination? The questions came from all directions, but one thing she knew for sure, she had definitely met Kalmin's mother. She opened her hand to reveal the necklace with Cecilia's name engraved on it. All at once, the missing pieces fell into place. In a new calm, she smiled at Delilah, moved closer to Kalmin and said in almost a whisper, "I told your mother that she must forgive her. It's Cecilia she must forgive, isn't it?"

"Yes," Kalmin said, his eyes closed in relief, and that dimpled smile Haley could easily grow fond of, crossed his young face. "The message you gave her was from Cecilia. She was the driver of the car that killed me. She is standing close by, just as Delilah said." Kalmin looked beyond Haley and gave a wink and a tender smile to Cecilia, a sweet sixteen-year-old. "She's very grateful to you, and so am I."

Haley tried to see Cecilia but couldn't produce even the slightest image. She sent a sorrowful look her direction and placed her hand on her heart in an expression of condolence. "Cecilia," she raised her voice higher, "his mother said she forgives you." Turning back to Kalmin, they shared a deep sigh.

"Now, if you could give my mother a message from *me*, she will know I am alright and that I love her and that everything will be okay." Haley nodded, and welcomed Kalmin's message.

"Tell her our favorite word, our secret word that we've shared since I was a child. It meant that we could do anything if we tried hard enough. Tell her the word, *Superman*." Then he turned, swooped the black cape above his head, reached out his hand and said, "Come on Cecilia, we can go now," and they glided effortlessly together through the wall.

Like a statue, Haley stood peacefully transfixed on something beyond the wall, other than Kalmin, now gone, and the word *Forgive* highlighted by a soft ray of morning sunshine. Then it occurred to her, "But I don't know where your mother lives," she said, her words barely audible.

It was too late. Only Delilah heard what she said while waiting impatiently for Haley to remember that she was still standing there uncomplainingly listening to her talk to no one. Bothered by Haley's silence and the puzzled look on her face, she spoke cautiously, "Cecilia told me to tell you thank you, and then she left through the wall. Is Kalmin still here?"

Startled by her friend's voice, she answered, "No, he left, too." They both blew out a breath at the same time.

"Hey, Delilah, I'm really sorry. I believe you, you know." Haley gave her the necklace, walked up to the wall and placed her hand on its solid surface. Sliding her fingers along the letters, her eyes lit up. "Of course!" she exclaimed. Turning quickly and grabbing her friend by the arm, she led her to the stack of paint cans.

With a familiar impish glint in her eye, Haley grasped Delilah's boney shoulders. "Alright, my brave little friend, if you've never done graffiti before, well, here's your chance."

"Really?" Delilah tucked her chin in and kept it there.

When Haley stuffed a paint brush in her hand, Delilah's big brown eyes shifted from left to right, and then a naughty grin gradually lit up her mortified face. "What are we going to write, Haley?"

"Just one word…one very important word. *Superman*!"

"Be careful what you wish for…"

Any Attention

The voices in the dark are laughing. They've been chatting about a co-worker, a woman whose uniform was too tight for her big, bazooka breasts. They don't seem to care if I hear them, or anyone else for that matter. Although there is no one around, except those driving slowly by stretching their necks my direction to see if they might recognize the disheveled woman in the back seat of the police car. I wish the darn cop had turned the cab lights off, but NO, he left them on, shining brightly in my face to make sure that everyone passing could see the criminal he had caught. Criminal! That's what I am now, a blankety-blank criminal! I never did learn to cuss.

Imagine a comfortable, predictable marriage of twenty-four years with three adequately healthy children, a dog that survived being run over twice, a turtle and a parakeet that will outlive me, a nice home, a boat and a successful business, twenty-two vacations, four broken bones, a funeral for my uterus and one for a gerbil that experienced such a tragic death I will never look at those sticky mousetraps ever again! And out of the blue you're plucked from this typically safe life and find yourself handcuffed, trapped in the back seat of a police car, all alone with only your menopause and your memories.

Our last child waved goodbye as she rolled out of the driveway, the car full of her belongings, on the back a ten-speed bike and on the roof, several boxes of things she just could not live without. I was still upset that she chose to go to school ten hours away, when her brother had selected a community college in a nearby town, and the oldest sibling had moved a mere fifty miles down the interstate with her English Professor. I tried not to show my disappointment and smiled wide, mimicking my husband's big grin as he stood three steps below me robotically waving his arms. As soon as she turned the corner, he dropped his shoulders and his fake smile, patted me on the head and went inside.

I stood there looking at the empty driveway and both of our cars squeezed into the cramped garage that also stored boxes full of our lovely children's collectibles, a rusty exercise bike, and way too many bags of coffee beans labeled *Beano*. Fixated on the baked oil stain from where my daughter parked her car, I felt sadness like no other. A strange kind of melancholy. A loneliness. I trembled at the thought and stood there awhile trying to get a grip on this feeling that I had kept bridled inside me anticipating an empty home with just me and Ben.

My husband has never really been a sensitive man, but I liked that about him because it kept me from thinking too much. He's practical and self-assured, like his mother who was one of the few female taxidermists in the country. And like her, he achieved great success, only not with the dead, but with a franchise of coffee shops scattered throughout Austin. Our children grew up working for him and experienced the retail world from behind the counter serving hot java to lines of impatient people needing their daily caffeine fix. I stayed as far away from the little stores as possible and now spend most of my days working part-time at the local community playhouse. Being a former Thespian in college, it is the closest to acting I will ever get. Besides, it gets me out of the house, and now with the kids gone, it is all I have. Sometimes I wish for more. More? I'm not sure what that means.

"Ben," I called out, hearing my voice return to my ears in the emptiness of the living room. Being it was about lunch time, I expected to see my husband leaning into the refrigerator. I bent over the kitchen sink, looked out the window and saw only his feet crossed at the ankles as he sat idly at the picnic table. I wondered if he was feeling anything like I was at that moment. More likely he was worried about our little girl heading west at eighteen years old all by herself. Slowly opening the back door, I went outside to find out.

"What are you doing out here?" I asked, gingerly approaching him and then sitting down on the far end of the bench since he had his arms spread out across the table and a beer can resting in his hand, looking as if he had no intention of letting me enter his space.

"Just thinking," he said, staring at the tire swing that for years had delighted our children – now full of water from the last rain with a spider web stretched across the center. The old oak that it hung from was finally dying. It was beautiful and sad.

"I hope she remembers to call us when she gets halfway there," I said.

"Oh, yeah. I think she will. I'm not worried. She's smart, she'll be alright."

Comforted by his assurance, I decided to share my thoughts. "Well, I guess we need to figure out what we're going to do from now on, since we're now, well, empty nesters. Seems like every time I bring it up you don't want to talk about it. Is now a good time?"

"Becca," my husband said, turning to look at me, "I don't want to do the same thing anymore."

"What do you mean? You want to sell the coffee shops?" I had always hoped that someday he might grow tired of the smell of coffee like I had.

"No, they're thriving nicely, no need to do that. What I mean is, I want to do something different. Like travel more, see the world, take a cruise, eat fresh avocados in Maui."

"Oh, you do?" I asked, cocking my head and seeing my husband in a different light. He had never expressed adventures like this before. Everything was always about the business and our annual vacations that he meticulously planned after every Christmas. I was amused by his new ideas and felt a smile light up my worried face.

"Yes, I do. But," he paused and looked down at his feet, "I want to do it alone."

My smile dropped, and my face suddenly felt very heavy. "Alone? What do you mean?"

"I want to experience these things by myself. I mean, without you," he said, still looking at his feet. "I just, I just…." He shook his head and looked away.

I was dumbfounded, sitting there looking like a stupid chimpanzee wondering where the banana went. Several awkward minutes passed until I finally unzipped my lips and forced another question, "I don't understand, Ben. What are you trying to say?"

He looked up at me, his eyes slightly glazed. Were those tears he was holding back? I had not seen him cry since we sang, "America the Beautiful" at my son's graduation, who like our firstborn, flew the coop the very next day.

41

"I'm trying to say," he swallowed hard, releasing the beer can and folding his hands together, "I want to be free."

I let out a small, nervous chuckle. "Free? You want to be free? You mean like, get out of jail free? Speak English, will you?" My voice hardened by sarcasm could not hide the unexpected anger building up inside me.

"Becca, don't be cocky," he scolded. "I want to separate. I need to experience time alone. We've been married for so long, I've forgotten who I am. Do you understand?"

"WHO YOU ARE?" I stood up abruptly, jolted by my sudden outburst. "You don't know who you are? You're the husband of a good woman with fat ankles that stood by you since college. A father who raised three beautiful and strong-willed children. A successful businessman! Why, you even built our home, you raised money for our church, uh, well, until you recently became a non-believer, and you were a Boy Scout leader, you...."

"I know all that, Becca. I know *all* that. But, I need to experience just ME. There isn't much more I can say about it. It's really that simple." Ben dropped his head to his chest and muttered, "I didn't think you'd understand."

"But, but, what about me?" I whimpered like a sad child being left out of a game. When he didn't respond, I asked the question every woman is afraid to ask, "Are you saying...you don't love me anymore?"

Ben kept his head down and didn't say a word. If I didn't know better, I would have thought he had fallen asleep. I waited. I waited for what felt like all afternoon. The silence was unbearable. Give me an answer – a simple no, a deadly yes! I wanted to cram the words in his mouth, stuff them letter by letter through his tight, thin lips – lips that I had kissed, lips that I had watched move when he used to pray or give lectures to our children, lips that had said, I love you. I couldn't find the strength or the will, and I knew better than to speak for him. His silence said it all.

I dropped my head and walked slowly back into the house toward our bedroom. It didn't feel right in there, so I went to the guest room, shut the door, and threw myself onto the bed that hadn't been slept in since my firstborn visited just long enough to get over the English Professor who left her for "some grad student with a double D." I heard the garage door open, Ben's car starting and when he backed out, a weak hello to the next-door neighbor.

It is very hard to describe the loneliness I felt that week walking through our empty home with reminders of all the deserters that had jumped ship. Every night since Ben left, I slept or tried to sleep in the guest room on top of the bedspread under an old soft corded sofa throw. I don't remember doing it, but I called into work and said I was sick with the flu. I only know that because later I found it written ten times on a piece of paper, as if I had to rehearse the lie. When our daughter called to report her safety, I was relieved that she rushed the conversation and said that she would call another day when her dad was home and not running errands. Yes, I lied to my child. So, sue me!

No one else called, not even Ben. By the third day, I wished that someone, anyone would give me some attention. I even considered calling Wally, an old friend who often asks me to leave my husband and run away with him, usually when I'm alone at church, which has been a lot lately since Ben decided, with no given reason, that he's an atheist. I wish I had more guts.

On the fourth day, sleep deprived and exhausted, I walked out to the garage and sat in my car contemplating the worst. As I sat there hugging a decorative pillow, one that Ben often used to prop up his feet, I imagined myself dead, slumped over the wheel, drool dripping from my mouth and who would find my lifeless body first. The only comfort I had was that the kids would not be here to discover me. Chances are it would be Ben. He would have to come home eventually – after all, he left his precious golf clubs.

Of course, I really didn't want to die. I just wanted, for some pathetic and pitiful reason, to pretend to off myself. Perhaps it was the latent actress in me that wanted to act it out.

I hadn't realized how hungry I was until sitting there with half-closed eyes, listening to the uneven sound of my engine and wondering if I needed a tune-up, I heard my stomach grumble. Oh, what I wouldn't give for a greasy burger with fries and a freezing cold soda.

The car smelled like coffee. Everything always smelled like stinking coffee. I shoved in a Van Morrison CD and went straight to *Into the Mystic.* Placing the pillow over the steering wheel, I rested my head and imagined myself dead. Then, without meaning to, I fell asleep. I slept peacefully without moving and had a weird dream about singing on stage in front of a huge audience. Only, after a few notes, my voice sounded laughingly atrocious, like…like Florence Foster Jenkins?

A squeaky high-pitched note jolted me awake. I opened my swollen eyelids, and tried to lift my head, but my neck was so stiff I could barely move it. The CD player was dead, and when I pressed on the horn, it eked out its last toot. I tried to start the car. Nothing happened. I realized then that the engine and the battery had died, and I had not.

Collecting my wits, I looked at my watch. I had slept for two hours! I started laughing. I can't imagine why, but I laughed until I peed, which made me laugh even more. Did I really consider killing myself? How brave, how bold, how STUPID! Am I nuts? Thank heavens I have a bad habit of waiting until the car's on dead empty before getting gas.

I hauled myself into the house and studied my face in the bathroom mirror. A pillow crease was indented in my cheek. My hair was stuck to my sweating forehead, and a long crusty drool line ran from the corner of my mouth to my chin. I looked like I had been on a three-day drunk. "Snap out of it!" I yelled.

It was the yelling that brought me to my senses. I needed to switch gears, get out of the slump, get mad! And I did. I got so mad I took an icepick and jabbed holes in the seat of every pair of pants and underwear Ben owned. I spared the ties that I had bought over the years, but with a pair of scissors, I went feverishly after his striped Geoffrey Beene dress shirts that didn't look nearly as fancy without their sleeves. I yanked the sheets off our bed, no, *my* bed and stuffed them in the garbage can. I took every picture of Ben I could find and shoved them in the back of the hall closet. I kept one out and drew horns on his head, blacked out one of his teeth, and wrote "COWARD" on his forehead. I stuffed it in my purse. I called AAA for gas and a battery jump.

While I waited, I opened an expensive bottle of Cabernet Sauvignon that I had been saving for something special, like when I set my uterus free. I poured myself a glass, and took it and the bottle to the shower with me.

Most women keep a sexy "impulse buy" dress in their closet that she may get to wear "someday." Digging through the rack of untouched clothing, all neatly lined in their dry-cleaning plastic,

I got excited when I found mine. Red! Yes, blood red! Dressed and wearing my old faithful string of pearls, I met the Triple-A man at the door with a big smile. He looked curiously at me and past me. Normally, I would have told him to wait outside for my husband. Instead, I led him through the house and to the garage, sauntering slowly enough for him to notice that I wasn't wearing any stockings. Yep, bare legs for me! Closely shaven bare legs and shaved all the way up to my thighs. Something I hadn't done since I was in my twenties.

After I blamed my kids for the car's condition, the mechanic had it ready to go within minutes, and I was once again behind the steering wheel. As I backed out, I threw Ben's pillow out on the front yard, hoping to lure the neighbor's dog that left daily piles of poop on our beautiful, manicured lawn. I threw the depressing Van Morrison CD out, too. Not sure where I was heading, I turned on a station that my daughter always listened to when she rode with me to the mall. I found myself tapping my fingers on the steering wheel to Coldplay.

All dressed up and nowhere to go. Then I remembered a great jazz bar that Ben and I had frequented years back. It was the perfect place to meet men, I remember telling my newly divorced neighbor before she moved. Gorgeous men in suits. Men with money and hungry for women. The women were dressed to kill. None of them had to buy their own drinks – the men generally had one in front of them before they could even survey the room. Ben and I used to watch them and bet on who would end up with whom. Tonight, I'd be one of them. I was too mad to be scared.

I parked my car as close as I could get and walked five blocks to Sullivan's. The place was nearly full and there was only one empty bar stool available between a large man in a polo shirt and a thin woman in a glittery backless dress. I slid onto the seat and hung my purse on the hook next to my knee. I love the practical person who came up with that clever idea. I saw my reflection in the mirror behind the bar. I looked pretty, but tired. When I smiled and opened my eyes wider I seemed to look livelier, so I tried to maintain that pose.

"Any Malbec you have will do," I said to the bartender, looking over at the other drinks lined up in front of the patrons: martini's, tall fancy glasses of beer, a champagne and one red wine down at the end. I should have been hungry, but I didn't feel the pang, so I drank down the glass and ordered water next.

"I haven't seen you here before," the man to my left said.

"Probably not. It's been quite a while since I've sat at a bar. Do they still serve cigars?"

"Oh, yes. Look up at the fancy ventilation system. It's the best in town. My company installed it," he said boastfully.

"It really works well. I don't smell a thing." I observed the two men at the table behind me, each smoking a long cylindrical roll of cured tobacco leaves. "I'd love a thin one dipped in Courvoisier Cognac." I hoped I'd said the name right. "We smoked those in college."

"Well, let me do you the honor. My name's Ted." He reached out his hand and I shook it.

"Becca."

"And may I suggest a B & B with that cigar, Becca? They go beautifully together."

"Great," I said, smiling and feeling rather sexy, not about to let this guy know I didn't know what a B & B was. Before I knew it, Ted was clipping the cigar and lighting it for me. It tasted marvelous, and even though I didn't inhale, I had to swallow a cough before adjusting to it. "This is lovely, just lovely," the words squeaked out.

We talked for a while about simple things at first, and then it came out about Ben leaving me, and I felt myself fighting back tears. I think my speech was starting to slur, and I was talking much too softly as the man kept asking me to repeat myself and then finally moving his stool closer to me, we were talking head to head. He patted my hand and told me a long story about his own divorce.

I appreciated the attention, but his story was much, much too long. His voice began to fade. I looked at the mirror and scanned the room in its reflection. I noticed first a plate of appetizers, and just when I thought I should order one to alleviate the increasing nausea, I spotted Ben sitting in the corner with a woman in a green dress. It was thin and tight, and I could see her bra clasps poking into the stretched fabric. Her long hair was in a ponytail that hung over her shoulder with a beaded clip securing it. She wore black glasses. Ben was laughing, his hand placed on top of hers, a cigarette held unnaturally in the other. He hates cigarettes!

His hair was loose, and he had a five o'clock shadow. He looked much too relaxed.

The man next to me was still talking. I interrupted him, "Excuse me, I'll be right back." I extinguished my cigar in the shiny gold-plated ashtray and picked up my purse. Now, quite awake, I can't explain the kind of strength it took to walk over to Ben's table at that very moment, and the fact that I wasn't even slightly nervous is even harder to fathom. I suppose my queasy stomach masked the fear. But, I did, and I did it without a plan.

He didn't even realize I was coming his direction, and when Ben finally looked up and saw me standing in front of him, he jerked back and quickly let go of the woman's hand. "Well, hi there, Becca," he casually said, his eyes scoping out my sexy red dress.

"Well, hi there, Ben." Looking over at the woman, her eyes trained on Ben, I suddenly recognized her as our old neighbor, Laura, who had moved because she divorced and couldn't afford to live in her house at the end of our block.

"And hello, Laura," I said rather coolly. I pulled up a chair and sat down. I plopped my big purse next to Ben's glass of beer, nearly knocking it over. The effect of that near mishap startled him. "Are you going to buy your wife a drink?" I asked.

"Uh, well, sure. I guess you want a Malbec?" he said sheepishly, trying not to look at Laura who was staring at him dubiously.

"Oh no, I would like something a bit more exotic. How about a martini?" I waved at the waitress nearby. She batted her fake eyelashes and began suggesting a long list of memorized versions, until I finally settled on a Dirty martini.

Ben looked at me curiously, knowing I had never in our lifetime together ordered anything *dirty*.

"So," I intentionally stalled, remembering that's how I began interrogating my teenagers after finding a dent in the car or a bad report from their teachers. Matter of fact, it felt just like that, watching the two cheats sitting in front of me attempting to act as if everything was normal. "I thought you moved to Florida, Laura. What brings you back?"

"Well, I actually didn't move after all. I'm still here in town."

"Apparently." Looking over at Ben, I asked, "So, is this what you call "alone" time?"

Ben wouldn't speak. He just looked at me with an expression hard to describe. I would like to say it was like a man who had been caught with his pants down. But it was too smug to be that. I turned back to Laura and cut to the chase. "How long has this been going on? I think I deserve an answer."

She looked down at her folded hands and then up at Ben for guidance. I started to ask the question again, but the waitress sat the martini down in front of me. The two olives got my attention, and I pulled them off the toothpick and ate them quickly before I took a drink. Both hitting my stomach at nearly the same time, I felt a cramp followed by a wave of nausea. Ignoring my uncomfortable state, I said, "Laura, I think I deserve an answer. I recall that your husband left you without answering that very same question. Give me the decency, please."

Ben interjected, "She doesn't have to answer that. It hasn't been going on at all. We're just old neighbors talking. That's all."

Her mouth askew, Laura seemed clearly disappointed in his answer. I was determined to hear her out. "I believe I directed the question to *you*, Laura."

"Nearly a year!" she said, almost triumphantly.

"WHAT?" Ben pushed his chair back and rubbed his hand through his hair. "I, it, we...." He clamped his mouth shut, seeing Laura's stern brown eyes glaring at him.

Looking back and forth at the two, I was flabbergasted. "Nearly a year?" I choked on the words. Hoping to force back any tears that would naturally follow after discovering your atheist husband had led a double life for that long, I closed my eyes, tossed my head back and laughed. I felt like a complete fool, and all I could think to do was take another drink of the martini. So, I did and right when I swallowed I burped up the wine, the B & B, and the olives, followed by a puff of tobacco smoke. I slung my head toward Ben and vomited right onto his chest. He jumped up and fell against the wall, his hands raised in the air, looking aghast at the putrid fluid dripping down his shirt. I grabbed one of those silky black cloth napkins that Sullivan's offers their fine guests and dabbed my mouth.

"Well, I don't know about you, but I feel *much* better." Ben apparently did not share my joy.

I turned to look at Laura whose eyes were stuck wide open, and her bottom lip hung like a largemouth bass. I stood up tall and said, "He's all yours, neighbor. I'm afraid he's a little used up, and there might not be much left of him by the time the divorce is over, but you're welcome to all the coffee beans you want."

Walking away, I looked back at Ben, who was now accepting napkins from the others seated nearby. I cupped my hand around my mouth and yelled, "Buy some nose plugs, sweetie. He lets out foul smelling gas in his sleep that would knock a bull over. Oh, but of course, you already know that." The couple at the table next to me bent their heads in laughter. The waitress gave me the thumbs up.

Back at the bar, my drinking buddy was in a serious discussion with the woman in black sequin, who looked mildly annoyed. I whispered in his ear, "Thank you for the drink and the cigar. Nice ventilation system, but you really talk too much about your divorce. Get over it." I must have smelled bad, because he pulled away and looked at me like he'd never met me. I made my dramatic exit just when the band began to play. It felt like a scene from a third-rate movie.

Stopping outside Sullivan's big plate glass window, I took one last sober look at my husband still wiping his shirt while his mistress shamelessly sulked from behind tightly folded arms. In the city's dark shadows I braced my back against a brick building and tried catching my breath, until someone next to me spoke in a harsh whisper, "Got any change, lady?" So wrapped up in the moment, I wasn't even frightened by the tattered and dirty man sitting against the wall next to me. I pulled out some bills and stuffed them in his rough and shaking hands. Waking up to the reality of where I was, I hurried back to my car.

On the way home I took the time to grab that great burger I had desired earlier. It never tasted better, but it wasn't enough to stop the tears.

When I turned the corner on my street, I had forgotten about the cop that sits there on Friday nights, hoping to catch the tired residents driving in from an evening out with their kids. With no other cars in sight, I did a slow Texas roll through the stop sign and there he was, on my tail so fast, I started digging through my purse for my driver's license before I even turned off the engine. "Oh, now what?" I yelled to the heavens, the anger from earlier returning. "This day can't possibly get any worse."

Finding the license, I reached in the glove compartment for my insurance. The light from his flashlight came through the window before I could find it. "Just a minute sir, I'm getting my insurance."

"Open this window now!" the young officer yelled in a cracked voice that sounded like my son's when his older sister used to hold him in a half nelson.

"OK, OK," I answered haughtily. "Don't get your panty hose in a wad!" I've always wanted an excuse to say that. Lowering the window, he shined the light right in my eyes. I squinted and turned my head.

"Have you been drinking, ma'am?"

"Please move the flashlight away from my eyes, Officer. I can't see."

"Have you been drinking, ma'am?" he repeated, now shining the light on my cleavage.

"I, uh, well, yes, I had a little something earlier. But, I just live two blocks from here. I'm fine, and I'll be home in a second."

"How many drinks did you have?" he demanded.

"Well, let's see. One at home, one at Sullivan's...oh, but they're not in me now, they're on my husband," I chuckled. Noticing that he didn't appreciate my humor I straightened up. "Sir, I'm not drunk, I'm mad and maybe sad, but I'm not drunk. I can't imagine what would make you think that." I glanced at my face in the rearview mirror. Mascara had dripped down my cheeks, and I looked hideous. I grabbed a tissue from the side of the car door and feverishly wiped my eyes, brushed off a french fry stuck to my chest, and smiled innocently. He snatched the license from my hand, shining the flashlight back and forth from me to the license to determine if we were one and the same.

"I can assure you that's me, Officer. I'm just a few pounds lighter now, and I've let my hair grow out since then. Mostly because my son said I looked like a butch."

"Stay here. I'll be right back. Get your insurance card out now." I did as I was told, reluctantly, I might add. As I sat there waiting for him to return, the last four days passed before me. It was all a blur, but clearly surrounding it was the one thing that I had never considered – Ben, leaving me for another woman. I didn't think he had it in him. The anger inside me rose to another level and here was this snotty amateur policeman pulling me over, not for speeding, not for reckless driving, but for rolling through a stop sign that I had stopped at hundreds of times. I couldn't believe this was all happening to me. I wanted to get out of the car and walk home. What the hell was taking him so long? I had no record of any kind, unless the time I got a warning for parking on the grass at a football game. I racked my brain trying to remember if there was another offense that might be on record. I wondered if it's illegal to vomit on someone in public.

"Step out of the car," the officer spoke, startling me out of my current state of mind.

"Sir, I am two blocks from my home. Please let me just drive home and end this day. I am a mother of three, a good citizen, why I was once nominated for the president of the PTA. My kids are all gone, and…and…my husband ran away with my skinny neighbor. I just want to…."

"Step out of the car NOW!"

"Oh my God," I said, dragging the word "God" out as if it would make him change his mind.

I opened the door, and up walked another man in a uniform. "Thanks, Terry," he said, "I'll take it from here."

The officer taking charge was tall with a large belly that looked like a balloon full of water hanging over his thick belt. He had a scar on his left cheek that ran from the bottom of his eye down to his chin. He looked as though he had seen a lot of action, but his lips were deep red, almost like he wore lipstick. I started to tell him he had lips like Elvis until he spoke again, this time with much more authority than the officer standing in his shadow. "Lady, stand at the back of the car. I'm going to give you a sobriety test."

"You've got to be kidding!" I gasped, looking up at him the way I looked at my daughter when she told me that she wanted a tattoo of Jim Morrison on her thigh. "I've done nothing seriously wrong except drive through the stop sign without a full stop. If you ask me, I think you should put your efforts somewhere else where it really counts."

"I didn't ask you, lady." He pulled out a tiny flashlight. "Now go to the back of the car."

"But look," I said, reaching through the window into my purse and pulling out the picture of my husband that I had desecrated with a black Sharpie. "My atheist husband left me the minute after our last child drove off to college. I've been terribly upset, sleep deprived, and ….."

"You've got two seconds to move to the back of the car." With his hands on his hips and his fingers tapping nervously on the gun holster, as if we were in a shootout, I thought maybe I should cooperate.

"Now, I want you to follow this light as I move it east to west. Don't move your head, just follow it with your eyes," he instructed.

"Well, sure. It is dark out here, though. I'll do the best I can." The officer moved the light back and forth, back and forth, and continued for the longest. I actually enjoyed the game. It calmed me down listening to the night and the cars slowly passing by. I felt as though I was being hypnotized. I don't know what he was looking for, but he kept the test up for much too long.

"Did you find any cataracts?" I asked facetiously.

He ignored my ridiculous question with a grunt and pointed to the ground. "He's going to place a white line right here, and I want you to walk it with your hands straight down by your sides."

The young officer followed the order without hesitation and stepped back in the shadows. I could barely see the line in the dark with the lights from the second police car blaring at us. "It's hard to see, and besides that, I couldn't do this even in the daylight. I'm wearing what they call bifocal contact lenses, not to mention these heels."

"Lady, just do as I say and walk the line. Keep your arms by your side, and put one foot in front of the other. Walk to the end, turn around and walk back the same way."

"Without my arms? This seems ridiculous!" He said nothing more but stood there waiting for my performance.

55

I took a deep breath and gave him everything I had. The second I put my foot in front of the other one, my arms instinctively flew out beside me.

"Put your arms down!" he ordered.

I put them down, and when I took the next step, up they went.

"Put your arms down!" he yelled again.

I did exactly that, and the next time my arms sprung up, he didn't say another word. I felt certain that I had passed the test and the officer was impressed.

"OK ma'am, the next thing you need to do is blow into this." He held out a long plastic tube and shoved it toward my face.

"Oh no," I said, "I have read that you should *never* blow because it is an inaccurate measure of alcohol content. Isn't that why I shouldn't?"

"Either blow, or don't," he barked back.

"Well, I don't know if I should." I had no idea what the repercussions were for not submitting to a Breathalyzer test. I thought at that moment the officer would write me a ticket, and I would drive home facing court in the next few weeks. I wish it had been that simple. But, no, of course not. He read me my rights, just like in the movies, and within seconds, my hands were behind my back. Before I knew it, I was handcuffed and in the back seat of his car. He turned on all the interior lights that blared down on me like the bright bulb in a refrigerator. I felt the handcuffs rubbing against my wrists. They were too tight, and although I told him so, he said nothing, but got out of the car and greeted another officer that had showed up at the scene.

Now, there were three cars, three officers and the intersection was lit up like baby Jesus in the manger scene in front of our church. I listened quietly to their stupid conversation. When I closed my eyes, they sounded like my kids talking in the next room while I prepared dinner. Thinking of them made me cry again. I shouldn't have gone out. I should have called my mother and told her everything. She would've made me feel better and said something ingenious in her monotone voice, a cigarette dangling from her mouth. Something like, "Ben's always been a schmuck. You've wanted to leave this damn cedar infested town anyway. Now's your chance." Mother was an army brat and had learned early on how to cuss.

Too much time had passed, and the officers were still in rapid conversation. The neighbors drove slowly by, staring open-mouthed at the Treasurer of their homeowner's association handcuffed in the back seat of a police car.

I saw my Suburban being hoisted onto the back of a wrecker. "Can't you just drive it home?" the words squeaked out of my mouth. "I just live two...."

At that moment, I felt a panic attack coming on. I forced myself to breathe evenly. Like a bizarre sort of bliss, I surrendered to the reality of my situation. Having my hands locked behind me felt almost liberating. Somehow it gave me a willingness to accept my fate, a life without Ben, without coffee beans or my children.

This is temporary. Everything is temporary. Who am I to think I'm exempt from life's misfortunes? Kicking off my heels, I slumped down in the seat. My eyelids grew heavy welcoming slumber, and the last thing I mumbled was, "Any attention, any attention at all."

Aftermath

She walked barefoot along the boardwalk, as she had done many times as a child, and now an adult, she saw things much clearer. The roughness of the planks beneath her feet had become that way naturally from the sun's constant heat but remained dry and brittle from neglect. The ugly debris huddling around the base of the pier knocking against the battered and beaten wood made her feel vulnerable. No longer white, the sand was stained from the spills of alcohol and other man-made products that carelessly loosened from the fingers of those disregarding the others who would inherit the aftermath of their thoughtlessness.

Although Maggie was disenchanted returning to her childhood neighborhood in such a state of disrepair, the incredible body of water that lay before her was still as mesmerizing as ever. Seven years away may have taken her heart and mind captive, as places like Paris and Ireland will do, but her soul remained with the Texas Gulf Coast and its endless shoreline. Traveling as a professional cello player brought many new friends and lovers her way and in the most beautiful European settings. Yet, in all its splendor, she had longed for the simpler things – a fishing pole in one hand, a book in the other, an unpretentious life with a family that she adored. *I'm home. I came home.*

As the night approached, the water began to lap more aggressively against the pier. A sense of wildness filled the air and creatures that hid while it was light slowly moved closer into shore. Maggie slipped on her shoes and watched the sun worshipers drag their burnt and sweat-soaked bodies back to where they came from, leaving the beach to the thinkers, the poets, the philosophers, those who wanted to visit with the ocean and all its inhabitants. Maggie was one of them, knowing that if she remained after dark, she would hear mysterious and private conversations drifting in and out of the waves. When she was younger, the voices followed her to bed. They became familiar, but rarely understood. They brought a sense of hope or despair, depending on her mood, and always there was the final voice, the voice of reason that guided her to sleep. She needed to hear that voice now, more than ever. *I am so looking forward to sleeping in my old room under an open window.*

She inhaled the last draw from a cigarette, a habit she had picked up in Amsterdam, and as she carefully extinguished it in the water, depositing the butt in her pocket, her thoughts turned toward Monte. *Ah, Monte, steadfast Monte.* The man she had wanted to marry if she hadn't been lured overseas. Unlike her, he had no desire for adventure and remained loyal to the Coast, still teaching Creative Writing in the same khaki pants, cotton shirt, loosened tie and worn-out sneakers – wide-eyed students under his spell. He was the perfect mixture of old-world charm and an overload of cuteness. Yet, she never regretted leaving him, until lately. But soon it would get too dark to see, and since the bulb in the overhead lamp appeared to be broken, she thought better of staying much longer. There would be plenty of time to think about the aftermath of earlier choices and Monte.

Maggie's family had gathered in the house only a few blocks away, cooking up something marvelous for their family reunion. Aunt Chelsea came early to prepare some of the fancy dishes she had learned to cook after the many culinary classes she had taken at Le Cordon Bleu. Maggie's mother loved surrendering the kitchen to the capable hands of her sister and humbly offered to serve as the dish washer. The twin cousins along with their wives had arrived that morning, while everyone waited as usual for her brother Ryan's "fashionably late" debut. His divorce had been finalized and according to the family, he was seen often with a new girl in tow. Maggie hoped that he would come alone.

Then there was Emily, the baby sister; the 'uh-oh' they called it, when a couple goes through their mid-life crisis and thinking they can turn back the hands of time accidentally conceive in a wild night of passion. As it often happens, the parents, growing older and less motivated, were more lenient with the headstrong daughter, and when Maggie and Ryan gradually moved out, the unruly teen spent her adolescence without the wisdom of the older siblings. Shortly after barely graduating from high school, Emily ran off with a band called *Louie's Lump*, later changed to *Scum of the Earth*, and finally settling on the name, *Toasted*. Since that abrupt career move, she had hardly spoken to the family, but before the night was through the impetuous twenty-two-year-old would soon be landing at their door, full of bizarre stories that would age her parents instantly. *Brace yourself family, a storm is on the horizon!*

Back at the house, Maggie stood at the gate before entering and listened to the hustle and bustle within the walls of her childhood home. Someone, most likely her brother, had put on a Elton John album, and she could hear her aunt barking orders from the kitchen. It sounded like the cousins were attempting to keep up with Elton on the piano, and she pictured her brother sitting near the speakers with his hand over one ear, trying to drown them out. She heard her father yell, "Where is Maggie? It's getting dark. One of you boys go out and find her!"

Maggie stalled before entering – waiting for him to say that famous line he used to yell when they were kids. *Go ahead, dad, say it.* "She'll get taken by the Beasley brothers' whale if she doesn't get back soon!"

Laughter filled the living room as everyone recalled the story of the two old fishermen, Horace and Harold Beasley who for many years had spread a whopper of a tale about nearly being eaten alive by a whale that popped up near the pier where they were fishing one early morning before sunrise. They claimed that on the back of the whale was a man with a trident, like Neptune, the Greek god of the sea. He spared their lives, making them promise to never spit or pee in the ocean or pollute it in any way, to never kill a fish bigger than they were, and to spread the word to the residents to do the same. To remind them, the ocean god gave both brothers a whale's tooth and a scar on the back of their legs from his trident, which they proudly showed to everyone, including the vacationers and anyone who would listen thereafter. *I wonder if they're still alive, or did they become Moby Dick's last meal?* It was a fond memory, and she enjoyed listening to her family talking over each other, enhancing the story with their own lively narratives.

She decided it was probably time to make her entrance before her dad really started believing the Beasley brother's tale and called the Coast Guard to search for the remains of his oldest child.

"Maggie, my dear," her father bellowed across the room, followed by cheers from the rest of the family who were

watching her timely entry through the front door. She surveyed the room, like one would study a Norman Rockwell
painting, acknowledging each character before she responded
to the headmaster, himself. "Dad, I told you I'd be back before
dark," and anticipating his next question, she said, "and no, I
did not see a whale or Neptune!"

Upon hearing the commotion, her mother came rushing
in, drying her hands on her apron with the most wonderful
fresh-baked smile on her face. "Oh dear, I thought you were
Emily. Well, I'm glad you're back. I need you in the kitchen,"
she said, taking Maggie by the arm and leading her past the rest
of the family. Leaning in, she whispered, "It's your turn with
Aunt Chelsea. I'm exhausted. You'd think we were cooking for
the whole island!"

The kitchen looked like one in a movie restaurant scene.
Her mother had taken out every piece of cooking and baking
kitchenware that she owned. Aunt Chelsea was busily using all
of them. "Kiss your favorite aunt and then throw those rolls
in the oven," she ordered, feverishly stirring the sauce that she
had just painstakingly concocted.

Maggie did the perfunctory kiss thing on her aunt's glistening forehead and at the same time swiped a sample of the
sauce with her finger. As usual, it tasted divine. So divine, she
gave Aunt Chelsea another kiss, this time on the cheek and
without being told to. The kitchen smelled heavenly, and any
feelings of dread that she had felt earlier were put in the oven,
along with the rolls. She caught her mother smiling at her,
her hands coated in soap suds. Knowing her mother sensed
her delight, she blew her a kiss, too. *Oh, mom, it's so good to
be home!*

Savoring each scrumptious bite, dinner was a huge success, and while the men had seconds, the ladies retired to the

living room with tall glasses of Long Island Tea. Just when they all sat down, the front door flew open and Emily boldly entered. The room was silent for the first time that evening.

"Well, I'm here! Is everybody glad to see me?" Emily dropped her duffle bag onto the floor and stood stiffly, her tattooed arms held tightly to her sides.

"Oh, my baby girl!" her mother cried, rushing toward her prodigal child with arms opened wide. The cousin's wives shrank deeper into the sofa. Aunt Chelsea hid behind her glass of tea, while Maggie stood waiting to greet her sister. *What the hell has she done to her hair?*

Avoiding everyone else in the room, Emily expressed her urgent need for food and barged into the kitchen, brushing past her father and the others that had filed into the living room. A few eyes rolled, and an official deep sigh was heard from someone anticipating what was coming next. "I'll help her, mom," Maggie said, patting her mother's back. "Sit down and enjoy yourself." Relieved, she nodded meekly and did as she was told.

When Maggie entered the kitchen, Emily was digging into the refrigerator, pushing items to the side and grumbling to herself. She looked over her shoulder and asked Maggie, "Don't you have any beer in this stale, old house?"

"Hi little sister," Maggie said sweetly. "It's been awhile. How about a hug?"

Emily turned and leaned against the refrigerator door. "I didn't recognize you without your dummy by your side. Is he here?"

"You know darn well Monte and I broke up years ago."

"Oh, I guess I forgot that. What happened? Couldn't compete with that big-ass cello of yours?"

"That's enough of that nonsense. Now, get over here and hug your sister," she urged, motioning with her hands, worried that Emily would reject her, as she did the rest of the family. "I haven't seen you in so long."

For a second, Emily's cold eyes softened. She took one step forward and stopped in her tracks, lifting both arms robotically. "Hurry up, I have a low threshold for mushiness these days, and hugging has been off my list for a long time."

"Oh stop, you goof!" Maggie pushed forward and wrapped her arms tightly around the annoyed sibling. "It's so good to see you kiddo." She felt Emily go limp; her cheek pressing against her neck.

"Yeah, you, too," she muttered, quickly pulling away and turning back to the refrigerator. "Now where's the beer in this house?"

Maggie sighed. *Well, that's a start.* "Don't think dad has any left. But there's plenty of food. Let me fix you a plate."

"Crap! What else is there to drink?"

"Here, drink my Long Island. I'll make another one later."

Emily stared at her sister's hand reaching out to offer her the glass. "Man, you're getting old, Mags. I can see the veins through your skin. What are you, about forty now?"

"Not quite," Maggie groaned, thrusting the glass toward her. *Although, sometimes I feel like it.* "And honey, if you insist on being rude, please just practice on me. The others don't deserve it, especially mom and dad. OK?"

"OK," Emily relented, "I'll try. Now, aren't you going to fix me a plate?"

The sisters sat mostly in silence. Emily ate fiercely, as if she had just finished a three-day fast. Maggie studied her face: the black lipstick matching her black-chipped fingernail polish, the tiny rhinestone pierced in her small upturned nose and the gorgeous long eyelashes coated in thick mascara. The hair, well, it could be salvaged. She let her eyes only glance at the tattoos. *Thank God they're simple music notes and not skulls or snakes.* She thought if only she could cradle Emily in her arms, the innocent smile she knew so well would return. Now was not the time, and any questions would be saved for later after the family had gone to sleep.

The conversation in the living room came to a hush when the sisters entered. It seemed as though everyone was afraid to engage the tyrannical offspring, except Ryan. His role as the peace-loving brother who loved listening to music more than people helped him avoid the family exchanges. It was amazing how a pair of ear buds could keep him out of unnecessary arguments. He pulled one out and said, "Hey, sis. How's that singing career going?"

Emily took another long swallow of tea before answering and reported in rapid succession, "Let's see…I got kicked out of the band, I wrecked my car, I'm without a job, I'm out of hair dye, I'm broke, I've got cancer…and, I have a P.I."

Everyone sat frozen, as if they were holding their breath, including Maggie. Emily's father looked up from the magazine he was scanning and pulled his readers down to the tip of his nose, "What did you say?"

"Yes, what did you say?" her mother repeated, her eyes opened so wide you could see the whites all the way around.

Ryan followed up with, "What's a PI?"

"Oh my God! You're all a bunch of imbeciles!" Emily threw the empty glass into the fireplace and fled the scene.

Emily's mother pleaded through the wide open front door, "Please honey, don't go. We're here for you. Talk to your family!"

Maggie gently moved her mother to the side, "Let me handle it, mom." And to her father who was perched on the edge of his chair, she ordered, "Dad, stay here. I'll bring her back." Avoiding the rest of the family's faces and her brother who was questioning a cousin about the meaning of PI, she turned quickly to chase her sister down. *Oh, good Lord, is this why I came back?*

Scanning the yard, adjusting her eyes to the dark, Maggie instinctively headed for the pier. Like her, Emily had spent hours fishing in that area when she was a child. Maggie could hear the restless waves racing to the shore. Above, the clouds gathered and darkened, along with gusts of wind that weren't there earlier. Wrapping the sweater tightly around her, she reached the foot of the pier and looked for signs of life.

Only one lamp was left to light the entire area, and she couldn't see more than ten feet ahead. Walking to the end of the pier at night had been forbidden when she was a child. The stories of lives swept away came back to her, and there was her father's voice again, "The sea creatures lie patiently waiting for their next victim."

Inching ahead Maggie hesitated with each step. Between the billowing clouds the moon was waxing nearly full, sporadically lighting the way just long enough for her to see a small figure huddling a few feet from the end of the pier, unidentified until she heard familiar wailing. Emily had learned on a camping retreat the art of chanting and whenever she felt overwhelmed, she'd sit cross-legged, close her eyes and repeat loudly, "Eeeooowah, eeeooowah, eeeooowah."

Maggie slowly approached and stood quietly behind her. She visualized the letters from the sacred song dancing overhead in the misty air. An overwhelming urge to join in coaxed her to sit down beside Emily. Without acknowledging each other they lifted their faces toward the moon, and what started out as chanting turned into a familiar tune about the old man and the sea. When the singing stopped, she put her arm round her sister and pulled her close.

Emily dropped her head onto Maggie's shoulder and cried. She cried hard and long, not moving her head once to either wipe her eyes or say something derogatory. Finally, with a frail whisper, she said, "I'm done."

"Em, it's getting pretty rough out here. The waves will be over the pier soon. Let's talk about it at home."

"I don't want to go back. I want the ocean to take me." Emily sat up abruptly, facing the water. "This cancer thing, well, they're not sure it's curable."

Uncertain how to respond to the disturbing news, and assuaging Emily's fears would only aggravate her even more, Maggie chose a more direct and honest approach.

"OK, so you think you're going to die. I get it. But don't you think it would be great to spend the rest of your life happy? I mean, happy with us, your family who loves you?"

"And make everyone miserable like I have the past few years? I doubt they want that."

"Of course, they don't want the angry you, but I know they want the Emily they raised…the lovely girl who came at the most unexpected time and brought such joy to our lives. It was boring before you came. Can you imagine growing up with just Ryan?"

Emily managed a chuckle, giving Maggie a sense of hope. "Look, I know we're year's apart, little sister, but the time I had with you was wonderful. And when I started traveling and being away for so long, I missed you terribly."

"You and Ryan deserted me." Emily said this with her head between her knees and the words came out choppy.

When Maggie finally deciphered what she had said, she took a bold leap.

"Listen, I won't go back to Europe. Truth is, I need to be home for a while, too. And besides, we've got a lot of catching up to do." *I can't believe I'm about to say this.* "We can both move in with mom and dad. It'll be fun."

Maggie could only guess what Emily was thinking and thought better of saying more.

"Maggie," Emily said, shakily, "I lied. I don't have cancer."

"WHAT? Then why would you say you did?" Maggie was aghast. She tried to look into Emily's eyes for some explanation, but they were empty, lost in the dark of the night. "That's alright, I'm just relieved you don't have it. The family will be, too."

"The truth is, I have something worse…something you will not understand. And when I tell you, don't ask me why. OK"?

"What?"

"Promise, or I won't tell you."

"OK," Maggie agreed, half-heartedly.

"I don't want to live anymore. I want to die."

"Oh, Emily, no…" Any questions that gathered at the tip of Maggie's tongue were swallowed whole. Even if she wanted to, she couldn't form an intelligible response to such a dire statement. Pulling her closer, the words found their way out naturally through her own tears. "I may understand more than you think. We'll help each other, sis. Please stay with me."

Emily's body stiffened, but her voice softened, "Tell you what…while we're sitting here, if that whale the Beasley boys bragged about shows up, I promise I'll stay."

"And, if not?"

"Just let me be. It's my life, not yours."

As the waves lapped harder against the creaky old pier, Maggie held her sister tighter and prayed fervently for the Beasley brother's whale to be real.

Siblings - Melody, Me, Bill and Marshall in the 60's
This is a story started by me and finished by my brother,
Marshall, aka Corky. I thought it would be fun to put two
writer's heads together and see what they come up with.
Maybe you can tell where I ended and where he began.

Fear 101

Sheldon and Amy (not to be confused with the fictional couple from the *Big Bang Theory*) had met in a jazz club one night and ended up closing the place down after a long discussion about each other's mental conditions. When the owner finally insisted that they leave – the staff gone and the band loading up – Sheldon and Amy advanced to the nearest park bench where they continued their conversation until the sun rose in front of them.

Departing separate ways, Amy went home, her head and her heart spinning. She climbed into bed and thought about everything she and Sheldon had shared. She found herself extremely attracted to the reserved, but handsome man and felt very sad that they ended their meeting both realizing that their disorders would prevent them from seeing each other. Tears kept her awake until she eventually fell asleep and dreamed about bungee jumping, falling just inches from Sheldon's outstretched arms.

Sheldon walked into his apartment and poured himself a glass of milk and took the last Girl Scout cookie to wash down three ibuprofen tablets that he hoped would ward off an impending headache. He had never felt so strongly about a woman before and it pained him to think that he wouldn't see Amy again. Wrapped inside two blankets, face down, his feet hanging off the twin bed, he covered his head with a pillow. He whispered softly, feeling his warm, milky breath return to his face, "If I should die, before I wake, I pray the Lord my soul to take." As he did nightly, he repeated it over and over until he drifted off to sleep.

Later that day, Sheldon and Amy woke up to their regular Saturday afternoon routines. Amy ate a hearty breakfast of bacon and eggs on a soft tortilla with a glop of avocado on top. She poured her second cup of coffee and munched on a half-eaten cinnamon roll that had since dried on the kitchen counter. The weather threatened a storm and she grew excited about experiencing it. As soon as the sky blackened, she slipped into jeans and a sweatshirt, pulled on her thick rubber wading boots and picked up her camera by the door. She didn't take the time to brush her hair; certain that she'd be drenched by the time she got home.

Sheldon sat erect at the kitchen bar of his apartment and read the daily paper as he slurped down a bowl of bran cereal. He shook his head at the current news – the bombings, the bank robbery, a senator being scrutinized after an affair – and then he finished off with the obituaries. He painstakingly read each and every one and studied their pictures as if he might be meeting them someday and needed to remember their names and faces. Tears gathered at the rims of his eyes and his breathing became sporadic. Seeing from the window dark clouds rolling in, he frantically ran around the apartment and turned on every lamp in order to keep the rooms brightly lit. When the first bolt of lightning struck nearby, he panicked and climbed back under the covers where he repeated his nightly prayer. He didn't want to think about it, but the memory of the time he got struck by lightning while burying his pet snake, Alfred, still haunted him. The details of that horrible day blazed before his eyes with each terrifying bolt.

He was returning home from a business trip and upon entering his apartment door he stepped right on Alfred's head. The rest of the poor reptile's body was twisted around the os- cillating fan that he had left on to circulate the air. It seems the lonely and bored snake had taken a joy ride on the steel cage and stuck his head where it didn't belong. Sheldon was shaken and immediately placed Alfred's body parts into a shoebox, grabbed a garden spade and proceeded outside to the small courtyard area beyond his porch.

Unaware of the dark clouds quickly forming overhead, he walked to the very end of the fenced yard where he would bury the snake in an area that the maintenance crew mowed

around, right under the City's electrical pole. When he finished digging a hole, he said a little prayer before tossing the
dirt onto the grave. He had made a small sign that he attached
to a metal clothes hanger that read, *Here lies Alfred Hitchcock,
a good serpent and friend.* Just as he shoved the sign into the
ground, lightning struck the electrical pole above him with a
deafening boom that knocked him flat on his back. Shaking
so violently his watch fell off, he stumbled into the safety of
his apartment. His teeth hurt and there was a continuous shrill
in his right ear. His fingers tingled. He looked at himself in
the bathroom mirror and saw that every hair on his head was
standing straight up. Dark circles were appearing around his
widened eyes, and he was as white as a ghost.

"I'm dead, I'm dead!" he screamed, not knowing how loud
he was yelling. "Good Lord, I'm dead."

The over-friendly, very nosey, and unattractive neighbor
next door – an unemployed nurse with a massage therapist license, who had tried often to get Sheldon's attention – heard
him screaming and ran to his aid. When she saw the awful
state he was in, she coaxed him into her apartment where
she insisted that he could rest quietly on her waterbed and
where she could apply her highly trained skills. Stunned, and
still in a state of shock, Sheldon didn't have the capacity to
argue. Unaware of what was happening, he let the whistling,
wanton woman undress him, wash him and have her way
with him. As he began falling into a deep disturbing sleep,
he knew for certain that not only was he dead, he had gone
to Heaven.

When he awoke the next morning and opened his eyes
to her shameless smile, he realized just the opposite – he had
gone to hell and had taken the ringing in his ear with him. He
knew then that he would never be the same.

While Sheldon hunkered down under the covers, Amy stood outside very close to where the first lightning bolt had struck. She thrilled at the familiar tingle of hair rising on her arms. "Darn, I missed it!" she protested and continued walking down the middle of the street with the camera turned on and ready.

She had been struck by lightning once before while playing golf with her last boyfriend. Fortunately, the strike was weakened by hitting a tree limb first and then arced from there to Amy's shoulder where it entered her body and came out her toes. Also, fortunately, she managed to crawl to the clubhouse where she was immediately attended to by two doctors who had had the good sense, like everyone else except Amy, to get off the course at the first sign of the storm. Everyone present was amazed by her instant recovery, but surprised by her reaction to the near-death experience, as Amy stood up on her scorched feet and said cheerfully to her boyfriend, "Ready to finish that round?"

A changed woman after the freak accident, Amy spent the following years expecting death, nearly asking for it. Subsequently, Sheldon spent the following years terrified of death. While he took unnecessary precautions like driving only in the right lane, Amy drove wildly over the speed limit, changing lanes every time there was an opening. Sheldon gave up all sports and traveling on airplanes and took up chess where he played safely in quaint little coffee shops within walking distance. Amy had kept only men friends and couldn't resist accepting their challenges, like sky diving, whitewater rafting, mountain biking and axe throwing. She even took up skateboarding until she twice broke the same arm and while convalescing, she became addicted to the video game, *Final Fantasy*.

So, this is how the two became members of two different self-help groups representing two different disorders that were oddly related. Responding to ads in a natural health magazine, they began attending group meetings for their kind of disorders that were ironically caused by narrowly escaping death from God's own finger. Sheldon found a group called F.O.D.S. (Fear of Death Syndrome) and Amy found a group called S.O.D.S. (Sure of Death Syndrome). The groups ranged from thirty to sixty-year-old members and each had their own stories to tell.

Sheldon was not uncomfortable about sharing his lightning bolt story, but more concerned about telling the others in the group how he finally realized that he needed help when he stood frozen on the sidewalk after he witnessed an elderly lady being hit by a car. Fearful that he, too, would be run over if he crossed the busy six lanes to assist her, he cowardly turned around and walked the other direction. Shame followed him all the way home and he decided right then and there that he could no longer live with himself and his dreadful fear of death.

And then, there was Amy.

Shame, too, was the reason why Amy sought help. When she got swept away by rushing water after attempting to cross a river over slippery rocks on one of her many hiking trips – even after her friends begged her not to try – she landed battered and bruised, wedged between two huge boulders and was barely rescued just when the water rose an inch below her chin. Not only was she ridiculed by her colleagues, who nearly drowned trying to save her, she was told that her recklessness was unacceptable and that she would have to risk her life without them. Losing her thrill-seeking buddies like that, she had no choice but to find a way to change her behavior.

Oddly enough, one night the F.O.D.S. and S.O.D.S. groups got together for a mixer. The members were encouraged to interact; hoping they could learn more about themselves by sharing with others who lived their lives in fear in completely opposite ways. Amy had not seen Sheldon standing in the corner, but when Sheldon spotted her he almost choked on a pimento cheese wedge, spraying the chewed-up pieces onto a nearby woman's steel-toed boots.

Hoping she hadn't noticed, he bent down to wipe them clean with the small decorative napkin that had held the tiny sandwich. When Sheldon stood up, his eyes met hers and he instantly knew that those wild flickering eyes belonged to a member of the S.O.D.S. group. Avoiding an awkward conversation, he excused himself and slid behind a sizable man eating a plate full of olives, sucking the pits out one by one and placing them in his pocket.

Amy was busy conversing with two men, one wearing an Evil Knievel jacket, the other in a wrinkled business suit. Sheldon immediately noticed that she had changed her once blonde hair color to brown. It wasn't near as exciting, but it softened her face as it swept around her chin. He liked what he saw and although he knew better, he was hoping that she'd recognize him.

As he stared at this exciting, dangerous and forbidden woman Sheldon pondered the words he had heard from a guest speaker at his last F.O.D.S. meeting; words from a soft-spoken psychiatrist named Dr. Wendall Wibbly, founder of a mental health treatment center known as Legacy 101. Dr. Wibbly spoke on a topic that seemed bizarre to Sheldon: Embracing Your Fear.

In a gentle, almost hypnotic manner, Dr. Wibbly had told his edgy and resistant crowd, "Fear is not our enemy. It is one of the most powerful forces endowed in us to protect our very lives. It is there to shield us from the forces of life that may bring us harm. It empowers us to see and sense when danger is afoot. Without it, our kind would not have survived."

As the crowd became more restless, and some began
inching toward the exit doors, the doctor quietly surveyed the
situation, stepped down from the podium and walked into the
midst of his skeptical audience. He scanned the room, looking
into the eyes of all around him, and suddenly exclaimed in a
loud voice, "And when the master spoke, the people cried in a
thunderous voice, BULL SHIT!" Then he smiled and returned
to the podium.

Sheldon remembered being transfixed, flummoxed, completely off balance, and he was not alone. This strange man
stood there for what seemed like an eternity, but was less than
a minute, with a serene look that conveyed sweet compassion.
Returning to a soft voice, he said, "Now that I have your un-
divided attention, let me tell you about my mission, the small
mark that I hope to make in a very confusing world, the legacy
I hope to leave behind."

He told them the challenge before them was not about
ridding their lives of fear. It was about understanding the na-
ture of fear, the purpose of fear, the power of fear, and the harm
that comes only when it exceeds the limits it was designed for,
when it becomes a destructive force that threatens the life it
was intended to protect. He compared fear to a great wall we
build around our lives to protect us, only to find one day we
have built it so well that it has become a prison that denies us
access to the world we live in. The safety has become an illu-
sion. In exchange for what we made to protect us, we have lost
the contacts and experiences that bring the joy, the purpose,
the excitement that comes in sharing the great adventure of a
full life.

He explained that they had experienced a very promising
response from a new course called "Fear 101". The mission is
to understand what allows fear to become a destructive force

in our lives and that there is a kind and loving way to approach this beast within, to guide it, nurture it, embrace it, and make it a powerful, positive force in life. The program is but the beginning of a life-long process. Graduation comes when our life journey ends, and all that remains in this world is our legacy. Still, as promising as those words were, Sheldon had not taken the course. Yet, remembering them again seemed to somehow bolster him.

Completely absorbed in his reverie, Sheldon did not notice that Amy had seen him, and she was walking, hesitantly, toward him, confused by a mixture of hope and doubt that seemed so foreign to a woman who approached the perils of parasailing, bungee jumping, and even javelina hunting in Mexico with fearless abandon.

Startled when he realized she was coming to *him*, he frantically searched for the right thing, the profound thing, to say to this alluring and frightening woman he was so attracted to, like a moth drawn to a flame. Unconsciously a beautiful smile broke his serious expression – a smile that for a split second melted Amy's confused heart until of all the words that tumbled through Sheldon's fevered brain only one came out as a simple, "Hi!" He was mortified over his loss for words.

Even so, when Amy looked into eyes that evoked feelings she thought had been suppressed, even killed, in her frantic life as an adrenaline junkie, around him she felt a calmness, a peace that was foreign to her, even disturbing. In a life where she always felt in control, she suddenly felt out of control. In a life where she had concealed fear and doubt, she heard voices that said, "What am I getting into? What if I am misreading this...what if he does not really want me?" She felt like a teenage girl desperately hoping that a boy would ask her out. And to her deep surprise, it felt strange, right, and good, all at the same time.

Overwhelmed, the tears she thought had long abandoned her, now filled eyes that silently pleaded, "What is happening to me?"

Sheldon studied the wild range of emotions etched on Amy's face and realized it was now his move, and he was startled that things seemed so clear to him, when only moments before he was paralyzed by the fear that had dominated his life.

Almost in a trance, he heard himself say, "Amy, I am not a poet, I have no words of eloquence, but I know now that I love you, and I have loved you from that night we had our long talk. I can't explain it Amy, but I want to be with you, and I refuse to let my fear protect me from facing the possibility of your rejection. For the first time in my life I will not run from something I have so deeply feared, commitment. Amy, will you share your life with me, warts and all, an imperfect man, but a work in progress, a man who loves you and seeks your love in return?"

Amy looked deeply into his eyes, as if probing for something intensely profound to say. For a fleeting moment Sheldon felt doubt and fear creeping into his mind. He flicked them away like they were annoying little gnats, and he waited for her to speak.

"That is the most beautiful thing I have ever heard, and I never dreamed words like that would be directed to me. You want an answer? Let me state this in my most eloquent way. Why the hell have you waited so long to tell me this Sheldon? I feel the same way about you, but until this moment, I was afraid to admit it even to myself. Do you hear me, Sheldon? I was *afraid,* and it scared me so much I did everything I could to tell myself how hopeless it would be, what a foolish notion to even *think* that a kind, gentle and loving man like you would ever want to be with a confused and frantic soul like me. Please tell me, Sheldon, are those words really from your heart, or have you taken up drinking? You think you're the only one with warts? Welcome to the club. I can match you, wart for wart. Are you ready for this journey? Are *we* ready for it?"

Sheldon decided that enough words had been exchanged. In a move that surprised him, he embraced Amy and kissed her with a passion he had never felt for any woman; a passion he had long dismissed as unattainable in his cautious, lonely and fear-driven life. Like Kryptonite, the kiss weakened Amy and she was putty in his arms.

Startled by a burst of applause, they both looked up and realized everyone in that room had been silently watching their drama unfold. They were deeply embarrassed, but as they gazed around them, they saw only smiles. No frowns, no derision, no judgment.

The sound of a spoon tapping on a glass brought silence to the room. Sheldon heard a soft, gentle and familiar voice speak.

"Ladies and gentlemen, my name is Dr. Wendall Wibbly, founder of the Legacy 101 Institute. Many of you have been students in my Fear 101 class which is why I was invited here tonight to tell you about a new program we are launching next month called "Partners 101." This program departs from our usual emphasis on the individual and addresses the needs of two persons in a committed relationship who are searching for a way to strengthen their bond without losing their personal identities. I was concerned about how to present this to a group for the first time, but my task was preempted by these two beautiful people whose passion and focus overcame the things that were keeping them apart and allowed them to find the truth in a crowded room of onlookers. They also made my own message seem like a foot-note to what we all witnessed."

As Dr. Wibbly approached the couple, he said, "In the hope that I have predicted the outcome of this magical moment in their lives, I offer to Sheldon and Amy a full scholarship in our first "Partners 101" program, with the profound belief they will bring more to our table than they will take away. That is how it should be."

He looked at Sheldon and Amy, who were clinging to each other in a state of elation, yet quite dumbfounded. They could not speak, but they each mouthed an inaudible, but unmistakable, "Thank you."

Wibbly turned to the crowd, held up his water glass as if giving a toast, and announced, "Here's to these two brave souls and their life journey together, and to their wonderful legacy that has begun right before our eyes." The room erupted into a loud cheer. The women and men in leather jackets hoisted the couple onto their shoulders and the focus of everyone's attention was on Sheldon and Amy gliding through the sea of believers, proud, content, and for the moment, unafraid.

The Juicy Parts

"My mother just isn't the same," Cherisse said to her friend who was sitting on the floor fanning her freshly painted toenails while chewing aggressively on a big wad of bubble gum.

"How so?"

"I can't explain it really, except lately when I'm talking to her, she just looks away as if she's seeing through the wall."

"My stepfather does that all the time, but he's an actor. I think they're supposed to do that," Ginger said, just before she blew a huge bubble that she kept alive until it finally burst and stuck to her face. "Oh, man!"

"So, does your stepfather rummage through your brother's closet for something to wear? All of a sudden my mom's taking an interest in my style of clothing. How weird is that?"

"Oh, *that.* She's just going through what the psychology books call a mid-life crisis. That's all," Ginger surmised with an air of confidence.

Frustrated, Cherisse dove onto the bed and buried her face in a pillow. She noticed immediately the strong smell of the cheap cologne that Ginger doused herself with every morning before school. Feeling a sneeze coming on, she pinched her nose and said nasally, "Mid-life? Just what does that mean?

She's nearly fifty years old! Does that mean she's going to be like this until she's a hundred?"

Lying on her back, peeling gum fragments from her lip, Ginger attempted to explain what little she had learned about the mid-life crisis period while Cherisse stared blindly up at the ceiling. "It's kind of like trying to regain your lost youth. Just be glad she didn't get a facelift like my aunt. She looks like a pancake now." When Cherisse didn't laugh, Ginger looked concerned. "Are you *really* that worried?"

"Yeah, I think so. She's acting so weird. I don't know why it's bothering me so much. Shoot, I'm about to graduate! Shouldn't I be worrying about other things, like a date for the prom, if my nose will stop growing, sex, college, stuff like that?"

"Speaking of sex," Ginger rolled over onto her stomach, raising her heels in the air, "my mother just recently gave me the birds and bees talk. A very different version from the one I got when I was fifteen. She was pretty cool about it." She stuck her head sideways under the bed that was propped high on an antique metal frame. "Wow, you should see the stuff under here!" She drug out a crumpled box full of Barbie dolls stacked on top of each other and a beaded jewelry box that she had made while in Girl Scouts. She dug deeper for more treasures, while Cherisse studied the bottoms of Ginger's white, freckled feet that were now sticking out from underneath the bed.

"Look what I found!" she yelled excitedly. "That old swimsuit magazine with the half-naked dudes we used to look at in the tenth grade. Pull me out, I'm stuck!"

The girls flopped down on their bellies, thumbing through the pages of men in body-hugging swimsuits flexing their smooth and oily muscles underneath tight, hairless young skin.

"This is kind of silly, isn't it?" Cherisse said, turning over on her back, bored with the magazine. "They all look the same…like Ken dolls."

"Yeah, you're right." Ginger stuffed the magazine under her pillow and flipped over, lifting her toes in the air to see how the bright red nails looked against the white ceiling.

"So, what exactly *did* your mother say about the birds and…?"

The gentle knock on the door couldn't be Ginger's brother – he would have burst in unannounced – and her mother was out for the day, so the girls lay silently, mouths tightly shut, wondering who it could be.

"Aren't you going to answer it?" Cherisse whispered.

Ginger rolled off the bed and opened the door just slightly. When she saw who it was, she opened it wider.

"Hi, Ginger. I just thought I'd drop by and tell you something interesting," Edward spoke as soft as his knock on the door. The girls had befriended him a year earlier when he enrolled as a new exchange student from London. He turned out to be quite the prize, often running errands for them, helping with their homework and practically anything else they asked him to do. He was a different sort, quite timid with other girls, and he didn't play any sports, preferring band and chess, but they both agreed he was as cute as a bug. Cherisse and Ginger adored his cockney accent and on occasion would call him *Jeeves*, their own personal butler.

Cherisse pulled herself up on her knees and straightened her skirt. "Hi Ed."

"Oh, hi Cherisse. I didn't know you were here." Edward stepped back into the hall as if he should leave.

Ginger curtseyed and motioned for him to enter. He searched the cluttered room for something to sit on and settled on a crunchy bean bag, awkwardly shifting his body back and forth, his long legs sprawled out in what little space he had. He eyed Cherisse nervously.

"So, what's the latest news? And don't leave out the juicy parts," Cherisse urged, hoping he had discovered something cool to share and yet at the same time, she wished he would stop looking at her in that strange way. Ever since they kissed in a Romeo and Juliet skit, and it was barely a kiss and on the sides of their mouths, as their teacher instructed, there was a silly awkwardness between them.

"I, I don't think I should tell you, now that *you're* here." Edward peered over his Buddy Holly glasses at Cherisse.

"Well, that's kind of rude, isn't it?" Ginger frowned.

Cherisse jumped off the bed and tripped over a box. She landed just inches face to face with Edward who had broken her fall by grabbing her waist.

"Wow, that was close!" Edward grinned, lifting her to her feet with ease.

Exasperated, Cherisse firmly removed his hands and re-positioned the headband that had fallen toward her forehead. "Don't worry, I'll leave if you have something you need to say to Ginger that doesn't involve me."

Ginger spoke up, "Now wait a second, you're my best friend. If you have something to say to me, Ed, Cherisse can hear it, too. You have a problem with that?"

"Umm, well, sort of," Edward squirmed.

Cherisse sat down in a huff, double knotting the strings of her sneakers, ready to leave at any given moment should Edward insist that he couldn't share his news. *But, why wouldn't he? After all, it was me who convinced Ginger to bring him into our circle of friends. And wasn't I his first American kiss…sort of?*

"I don't know," Edward began. "It's something I was going to tell Ginger first and then let her decide if she should tell you."

"Oh really!" Cherisse sat up erect, chest out, hands on her hips. "Well, now I'm not leaving at all. Speak up, man!"

Edward looked at Ginger for help. "You know she's as stubborn as a mule, Edward. You might as well start spilling your guts."

"Well?" Cherisse waited.

Edward cleared his throat and spoke only to Ginger, avoiding Cherisse' glare. "I saw Cherisse's mother kissing another man that wasn't her husband."

"WHAT?" Cherisse shrieked. "My mom kissing another man that wasn't my dad?"

Edward scrunched up his face and nodded.

"Where?"

"In the little park behind the drug store where I work. I had to take out some boxes to the dumpster, and I saw them leaning against your mother's car."

"Are you sure they were kissing? I mean, maybe they were talking, or he was helping her put boxes in the car or…." Cherisse stammered, pleading for a different answer, hoping that Edward's imagination had simply run amuck.

Ginger interrupted in her softest voice, "Edward, this is huge what you're telling us. Are you really sure that's what you saw?"

"Look, I wouldn't be here if I assumed this. You know I'm not a troublemaker, and I've never told anyone all the secrets you two have shared with me. Not even the time you poured ketchup on the coach's knickers to make her think she had started her menstruation. I could've spread that one all over campus."

"OK, OK!" Cherisse groaned. And at that moment she remembered another reason why they had befriended Edward

– his respectable use of the language, like the word *menstrua-tion* instead of something vulgar like *on the rag*. She lowered her voice and tried to soften her tone. "You're right, but this is really bad. What'd the jerk look like?"

"Well, he was kind of dark skinned, maybe a tennis player. He had a ponytail and a really cool t-shirt – looked like *The Grateful Dead* was on the back. Your mum's arm was in the way, but I'm pretty sure I saw the word *dead*."

"Oh, this is awful, just awful," Cherisse shook her head in embarrassment.

Attempting to console her, Ginger said, "Well, you told me earlier that your mom was acting strange. This could be one of the reasons why, and it does fit the mid-life crisis thingy I was telling you about."

"Is that supposed to make me feel better?" Cherisse threw her body back on the mattress, curled up into a ball and began rocking back and forth, trying not to imagine her mother kissing some stranger.

Edward reached out and touched her knee. "I'm sorry. I honestly thought you should know, but not necessarily through me." He drew in a long sigh and sunk back into the beanbag.

No one spoke until Cherisse finally broke the silence. "You know, I could get all weird about this and let it mess me up in the head. I know already that there's no way I'd tell my dad. It's kind of hard to explain, but I would feel like I was betraying my mother…being a female and all, you know. We can't betray our own. Besides, what good would it do? Ruin their marriage, my family, my life?"

"Good point," Ginger agreed. "So, now what? You think you can look at your mom the same way and pretend nothing's happened?"

"No."

"Well, my friend, I think you should confront her. I remember my dad was always mad at my grandfather because when he would get drunk he would say horrible things to my dad, and he'd forget the next day what he said. My grandmother would always take up for her husband and say he just had a bit too much to drink and didn't mean any of it and begged my dad not to confront him. But one day, my dad had enough, and he visited my grandfather on a Sunday morning when he was sober and his likable self." Ginger paused, considering what she had said. "I don't think drunks get drunk on Sundays. Well, anyway, he told him, 'Look old man, if you weren't my wife's father, I'd have beat the shit out of you by now for all the rotten things you've called me. But let me warn you, I will not put up with it anymore. You are quite capable of controlling your booze and shutting your mouth in front of your family. Do you have any idea how much you hurt all of us when you do this? Especially your daughter!'"

Ginger was now standing up, her hands rolled up in fists, pretending to be her dad. "Well, you know what happened because my dad told him the truth?"

"What?" Edward and Cherisse asked at the same time.

"He quit drinking. My mom explained it to me. Seems my grandmother was what they call a textbook enabler. It didn't mean she was bad, just protecting him from getting hurt and all the while, keeping him from being responsible for his actions. It makes sense to me."

"That makes sense to me, too," Cherisse said, impressed by her friend's evaluation. "But, I'm afraid if I tell her what I know she'll be really mad at me and things won't be the same."

Ginger put her arm around her best friend. "Things aren't the same, Risse. Your mom's changed, and it makes you feel crummy, like she's not a part of you. This takes guts, but I think it's the right thing to do."

"Blimey!" Edward blurted out from across the room. "This doll doesn't have any nipples." Slightly repulsed, he turned the naked plastic Barbie toward the girls.

Both girls started laughing. Ginger reached over and handed Ed a pen. "Here, draw some on. That's always bothered me, too."

"And while you're at it…here," Cherisse tossed a Ken doll at Edward's feet. "See what miracle you can perform on him!"

That night at the dinner table, Cherisse had a hard time enjoying the meal, even though it was her favorite dish. She usually liked slurping the long spaghetti strands and wiping her plate with French bread, and now that she was eighteen, her dad would pour her a glass of wine. "In preparation for adulthood," he would say. "Learn how to drink responsibly, and you'll enjoy it the rest of your life. Alcohol has a mind of its own, sweetie. Don't take it for granted."

She found it hard not to gulp it down, thinking it might give her more courage for that talk with her mother, who was sitting at the table mindlessly twirling pasta in circles instead of eating it. Then she thought about the story Ginger had shared earlier and felt better about her decision.

"I'm going to the library tonight, Keith," Maryanne nonchalantly said to her husband while clearing off the table.

Cherisse quickly spoke up, "Perfect! Uh, I'll go with you, mom. I need a book for school."

"Oh?" her mother seemed surprised. "Don't you have a project to finish?"

"I finished it," Cherisse lied. "I really need this book for tomorrow, and if it's not there, I have to find one like it."

Before her mother could protest, her father saved the moment. "I'm glad you're on top of your assignments, honey. It's so easy to wait until the last minute. I learned that early on in college, and it sure made those four years a lot less painful."

Cherisse excused herself from the kitchen. "Be ready whenever you are mom!" she yelled from the hallway.

Minutes later, Cherisse saw the lights of her mother's car backing out of the driveway. "Well, darn it! She left me!"

"Dad," she said, pecking him on the forehead with tight lips, "mom forgot me, so I'm going to drive myself to the library."

"Oh, that's too bad, honey. She has been a little forgetful lately. It's hard turning fifty. I remember it well. You get a little squirrely about it."

"You mean you were strange when you turned fifty? I guess I didn't notice. That was about four years ago wasn't it?"

"Yes, it was, and I was acting weird at the time. Your mother helped me through it, though. Catch up with her and see if you can talk her into getting something worth reading other than those romance novels she's been bringing home lately. It doesn't do a woman going through a mid-life crisis any good," he laughed. Looking up from his book, he caught his daughter's frown, "Don't worry, it's a natural stage in life. You'll understand someday."

In the library parking lot, Cherisse had a strange feeling come over her when she discovered that her mother's car was not there. She parked under a tall lamp post. The light beamed down on the dashboard. "A little squirrely?" she spoke to herself in the rear-view mirror. "Did dad actually say that? And would he think that his wife kissing another man would be just a little squirrely? I think not!" She turned the car around and drove determinedly toward the drug store where Edward worked.

"I get off in twenty minutes," Edward said to Cherisse.

"I'm actually not here to visit, Edward. I was wondering if you could take me to the back of the store out to the dumpster."

"What?"

"Yeah, I just want you to show me where you saw my mother the other day."

"Morbid curiosity?" Edward looked slyly over his shoulder, placing the last box of denture glue on the shelf.

"More like, natural instinct," Cherisse said. "Hurry, before I chicken out."

"OK, but it seems a little silly."

"You mean it seems a little squirrely," she laughed and rolled her eyes.

"You Americans, always using creatures to describe things. Chicken-out, squirrely, dog-tired, mad as a hornet, fat as a cow, dumb bunny, pussy-whipped. Ha, ha ha," Edward slapped his knee jokingly.

"Funny guy you are. That's why Ginger and I keep you around. You're like our little pet."

As they entered the warehouse, Cherisse stopped to look at all the boxes stacked up against the walls. "Wow, *that* is a *lot* of toilet paper. My brother would be in hog heaven if he saw this. He wraps a cheerleader's house at least twice a month in this stuff."

"See, there you go again…hog heaven?"

Cherisse laughed. "OK, OK, you've made your point."

"I have to hold the door, or it'll automatically lock from inside. Make it quick, will you?"

Cherisse timidly stepped into the dimly lit alley. She'd never been in the back of a store before, and she felt as if she was doing something illegal. Running her hands along the side of the cold, metal dumpster, she stopped at the end and peeked around its edge. A small parking lot was neatly carved into a wooded area that served as a greenbelt between the strip center and a neighborhood. Cherisse leaned out further and squinted. Just when she thought the lot was vacant, she saw headlights pop on and a car moving slowly from underneath the trees. Instinctively, she walked out from behind the dumpster and stood in the path, barring the exit. The car came to a halt, just ten feet away, the lights so bright, she had to cover her eyes.

"Are you daft?" Edward hissed from the doorway.

"Go back to work," Cherisse ordered. "I'll see you later."

"OK, but just remember, curiosity killed the cat."

Cherisse suppressed a nervous giggle, walked to the passenger side of the car, and opened the door. "Hi mom. I think we need to talk."

The shadows couldn't hide the fact that her mother had been crying, and when she saw her daughter's concerned face, she burst out crying some more.

Cherisse slid onto the front seat and put her hand on her mother's hand tightly gripping the steering wheel. "Mom, I know what you're doing, and I think I understand."

Her mother dried her eyes with a wadded-up napkin and looked at her daughter. "You do?" The look on her face was like a small child's, and Cherisse suddenly felt like they had swapped roles.

"Yes, more than you can imagine. Where's your friend?" Cherisse asked, looking over the back seat for any sign of another car or person.

"My friend? What do you mean?"

"Mr. Ponytail." Cherisse turned off the car and pulled out the keys.

"What are you…?"

"Mom, please don't lie to me. I'm not here to make you feel worse than you already do."

"Oh dear," her mother moaned and covered her face with her hands. "I'm so sorry, I'm so sorry." Looking up through her fingers, the tears glistening on the tips of her eyelashes, she asked meekly, "You haven't told your father, have you?"

"Of course not! I don't want to hurt him."

"Neither do I," Maryanne said, reaching over and pulling Cherisse toward her. "Neither do I, honey. I love your dad." And when her mother buried her head into Cherisse's shoulder and began sobbing, Cherisse wanted to cry, too. She caressed her mother's fine hair and had never felt closer to her. She recalled at that moment walking in on a similar scene – her mother holding her own mother, gently consoling her as she wept.

"Does this mean you're not going to. . .well, uh. . .do *this* anymore?" she asked.

Her mother sat upright and blew her nose. "Yes, that's why I've been crying. I feel so stupid. I didn't want this to go any further than, well…flirting." She looked sheepishly at her daughter. "And it didn't, I promise. It's just that…I'm about to turn fifty. Fifty!" She pounded on the steering wheel. "I feel so old and undesirable. And frankly, I'm scared. I haven't had a period in three months. I'm in menopause. Like an old lady!"

"No more periods? Wow, that must feel fantastic! Just think, mom, you don't have to worry about getting pregnant anymore. Ginger's aunt told her that sex actually gets better when you don't have to worry about getting pregnant."

"Why would she tell her niece that? That's awfully personal," Maryanne protested, moving right back into her mother mode. Catching herself, she snorted, "I guess that sounded a bit silly, didn't it?"

"Well, yes, but I understand. It's hard letting us grow up." Cherisse stopped short of making the moment about herself. "I think I'm trying to tell you that you're not getting older, you're getting better. That's what dad told me when we were pulling weeds out in the yard the other day."

"He did?" Maryanne's face lit up.

"Yes, and he also told me that you were having a mid-life crisis and that you might be acting a little different for a while until you figured it out."

"He did?" her mother's voice lifted a notch higher. "It seems everyone knows what I'm going through but me."

The car was filled with silence as mother and daughter sat still thinking about the father, the husband, the king of the castle.

"Your dad is very special," Maryanne said, reaching out to touch Cherisse's hand again. "Just a few years ago your father went through a similar thing. He told me that he felt old, and when he started playing tennis again and took that membership to the gym, I knew he was trying to make himself feel better. By the end of the year, he seemed more relaxed and settled back into his life. He finally stopped sucking his stomach in every time he was in front of a woman."

"That's weird. Actually, I kind of remember dad doing that. I just thought he had indigestion. But honestly mom, if dad had the guts to tell you how he felt, then you should do the same. It might take some of the pressure off. You know, kind of like talking to a priest."

"Well, you might be right, only I don't think people need to tell *everything*. There are some things you do in life that are yours, and yours alone. There's times when you should probably keep the juicy parts to yourself."

Cherisse decided she'd have to think a little more about what her mother had just said and tucked it away for the time being. "I suppose we should go home now. Take me to the front of the store, please. My car's there. Oh, and one more thing...I lied to you earlier about finishing my project. I'm sorry."

Maryanne moaned, "I lied to you, too, honey and worst of all, I left without you. That felt pretty bad, and I don't ever want to do that again." She reached for her daughter's chin. "You were amazing tonight, Cherisse. I'm really proud of you, having the courage to confront me. I don't know if I could've done that at your age. You don't hate me do you, honey?"

"MOM, I could *never* hate you. But, it would be nice to have *you* back again."

"I think you'll see a lot more of your normal mother from now on. This talk really helped. I didn't know you loved me so much." She smiled crookedly, biting her bottom lip to keep from crying again.

"Oh good, there's Edward." Cherisse pointed toward the storefront, relieved for an excuse to break free from any more crying scenes. "I'll see you at the house later."

"Well, how'd it go?" Edward asked, propping himself up on the hood of his car, as Cherisse approached him.

"Bloody fantastic! And you know what else?"

"No, what?"

"If it weren't for you caring enough about me to tell me, this might have turned into a real fiasco. I want to thank you."

"You're welcome." Edward slid off the hood and opened his arms wide for a hug.

"No, you deserve more than a hug, my friend." Cherisse wrapped her arms around his neck, stood up on her toes and kissed him right on the mouth.

She let her lips linger longer than she expected and when they broke apart, Edward pulled her closer and kissed her again, this time slowly and sweetly.

"Wow," Cherisse crooned.

"Yes, wow." Edward reluctantly released her. "That's the best bloody thank you I've ever had."

"To tell you the truth, I wanted to do that when we played Romeo and Juliet," she said coquettishly, followed by a wink. "See you at school tomorrow, Edward."

Edward stood motionless, completely spellbound, watching Cherisse drive away. He leaned against the fender, arms crossed, and said dreamily to the moon, "Fickle women, kind of like a pack of wildebeests, you never know which way they're heading."

Cherisse entered the house timidly. When she came to the living room she saw the back of two heads touching in her dad's recliner and the faint sound of *Touch of Grey* by the Grateful Dead coming from the big corner speakers. She turned to tip-toe out, not wanting to disturb the sweet scene when her father looked over his shoulder and said, "Hey kiddo, don't forget to kiss your old parents goodnight."

"Who are you calling old?" Maryanne lightly elbowed her husband. Cherisse moved cautiously to face the couple, hoping that her dad wouldn't say anything about the library. She didn't think she could handle two lies in one day.

When she leaned over to kiss him first, she noticed a book opened between them. She walked around to kiss her mother and leaned in closer to see what they were reading. She recognized the title, *Bridges of Madison County*. She stood up and looked at her dad curiously. "I thought you didn't like romance novels."

"Well, your mom thinks that you can't teach an old dog new tricks. I'm proving her wrong."

Cherisse laughed, and for more reasons than one. When her mother said, "He's just wanting to relive his midlife crisis with me. I hear they can be lots of fun if you go through it with the one you love," she added a wink to assure her daughter that everything was fine between them.

"You two look like a pair of doves," Cherisse smiled, again amused by the comparison. "Happy as a clam, I'd say."

"By the way," Maryanne asked, "do you have a date for the prom?"

Cherisse caught an impish gleam in her mother's eyes. "I just might, after tonight. Goodnight mom and dad."

"Goodnight, honey. Sleep tight, don't let the bedbugs bite."

Under the covers, Cherisse mulled over the last twenty-four hours. Somehow, she felt older, as if she had learned some valuable lessons. It dawned on her that this would be the last year living at home with her family, and she felt closer to them than ever before. As she contemplated her loved ones, Edward's face kept popping up, and she caught herself reliving their sweet kiss more than once. She thought about telling Ginger. But remembering what her mother had said earlier, she decided to keep the juicy parts to herself.

Do you ever wonder what would happen

if you'd just let go?

A Tepid Man

The day was without pretense and was just as ordinary as the one before. No clouds in the sky to help create a mood, no wind to bring back memories, neither hot nor cold…tepid. Matter of fact, lukewarm was exactly how Harris felt these days as he stood in front of his apartment building trying to remember a time in his life that made sense, when he had a purpose – a time when he enjoyed waking up to a new day. Nothing came to mind.

"It's a nice day out there," someone said, interrupting his worthless thoughts. Harris nodded and opened the door for the man he'd greeted often who generally arrived just as he was leaving. *Darn, what is his name? Jack, Jim, Jerry, something with a J. Hmmm, doesn't really matter.*

"Yeah, it's another doozie," Harris responded disingenuously and let the door close behind the old man, relieved to avoid another lame conversation about the weather.

Harris walked away quickly, not sure where he was headed. Just when he bent over to tie his shoe, a black bird swooped down from above and dropped something hard right on his head. It rolled down his neck and into his shirt that was neatly tucked inside his casual jeans. He reached with his free arm to feel it lodged underneath his belt, large enough to make him aware of its presence, small enough to leave there until he could find a private moment to remove it.

A woman wearing a vibrant smile walking toward him said in passing, "I saw that bird drop something on you. You do know that means good luck, don't you?"

Harris was surprised by his jovial response. "Didn't know that, but I sure could use some. Thanks." He watched her walk away, her smooth stride and slow, rhythmic hips swaying gently in a delicate rotation. She turned around, smiled at him and gave him a friendly thumbs up. For a split second she reminded him of his lost love, the woman who broke his heart. But he was cursed, and it seemed like every female reminded him of Vickie.

He noticed the woman's hands were free, unencumbered by a purse or bag. She had a thin leather pouch around her tiny waist and nothing in her flowing hair. Harris thought that she must be in her forties, but her walk in bright green tennis shoes was like a young girl's. Captivated, he stood in the middle of the sidewalk watching her as she stopped in front of a bookstore, placed her hand against the glass and leaned in to read what was on display. It held her attention for some time, and Harris found himself wishing that she would look his way again. When she didn't, he had a sudden urge to walk toward her, but his feet felt cemented to the ground.

"Mr. Harrison! Mr. Harrison!" a woman yelled from behind, running excitedly toward him, waving a magazine in the air, her heels clicking noisily on the hard pavement.

Harris couldn't begin to imagine who would be openly yelling his name on an early Saturday afternoon and with such gusto. He covered his eyes from the sun's glare and peered in her direction.

"Oh, Mr. Harrison, I'm so glad I found you. How are you?" the female asked enthusiastically.

Harris' face drooped when he recognized the woman from the Private Detective Agency that he had not seen since he stopped investigating Vickie's disappearance. Those visits had cost him a hefty fee, to no avail, and here she was, a reminder of why the investigation had failed. He greeted her apathetically, "Hello, Millicent. I'm just fine."

"I'm glad to hear that," she said, looking at him dubiously. "Well, I need just a minute of your time, please. How about right over there?" She pointed at Caroline's Café. "Shall we get a coffee?"

Harris glanced back at the bookstore to see if the woman he had been admiring was still there. She was not. Disappointed at missing the opportunity to meet her and blaming it on the animated little female standing in front of him, he stammered and tried to create an excuse to leave. But Millicent was not taking *no* for an answer and grabbing him by the shirt sleeve, she pulled him toward the café.

When they entered the door, she pointed at a table in the far back. "I'll be over there waiting for you. A Cappuccino would be awesome."

"Sure, of course." Harris was glad for the excuse to delay what was most likely another solicitation to hire her firm for another year. While the barista meticulously prepared the coffee, he thought again about the woman he had briefly spoken to just a few minutes earlier. He was surprised by his immediate attraction to her. Deep in thought, he poured too much cream in his coffee and cursed under his breath.

Sitting down across from her, Harris thought about how many times he had sat impatiently in front of Millicent in her dingy office, trying to avoid looking at her ugly, polyester suits. But here in the soft light of the cafe with the view of the street behind her instead of a US map, she looked rather nice. He realized seconds later what was different about her. Her hair was down and flowing past her shoulders instead of piled on top of her head.

She caught him staring and said, "I guess you never thought I had long hair or owned a pretty skirt." She tugged at the full fabric and wiggled her hips in the chair. "I actually have a life outside the office. A good one, too."

"That's nice to know," Harris said with little sincerity, looking down at her hands holding the magazine, her index finger bookmarking a page. "What is it that you want to tell me?"

"Well, I'm no longer with the Agency, so I can talk to you off the record now." She removed a wad of gum from her mouth and stuck it to the saucer. "As you know, since Vickie took all her credentials and personal things with her when she left, we couldn't really consider this a missing person's case. I'm so sorry that in all that time we couldn't find her and give you the break you needed. But today, while I was in the book store, I picked up this magazine and found this." Turning it around, she flattened it out on the table, leaned back in the chair and crossed her arms, waiting.

"What'd you think? Is that her?" she asked, excitedly.

Harris dropped his head and looked closer at the picture of a couple standing amongst several dignitaries; men and women posing with rehearsed smiles on their faces. The woman he recognized was dressed in a tailored suit, her hair up in a twist and around her neck a choker that he had given her. His heart began to beat loudly in his ears and he felt his face flush with heat. Nodding his head slowly up and down, with lips tightly shut, he murmured, "Uh huh." He let out a quick breath, realizing that it had been lodged in his chest.

Excited, Millicent slapped her hand so hard on the metal table, coffee spilled over the edge of her cup. "I knew it, I just knew it! I've carried that face in my head ever since we opened this case. After we closed the file, I refused to give up looking. Go on, read the article," she insisted.

He needed more time to digest the fact that Vickie was actually alive and obviously not alone, locking arms with another man.

"Go on, read it. I can't wait to hear your response." Millicent smiled wide, like a woman who had just given a birthday present that she would have bought for herself.

With creased forehead, Harris squinted to read the fine print. He was told he would need reading glasses by the time he reached forty. He was now two years beyond that and determined to get by without them.

Millicent took notice and tossed her reading glasses across the table. "They help, you know."

Harris picked up the flowered, plastic half-moon glasses and handed them back to her. "Not sure I want to be seen in those, but thank you."

"Suit yourself," she teased. "That crease between your eyebrows is becoming quite impressive looking. Before long, you'll have one big man brow."

"Thanks, I'll take that chance." He continued reading, and when he finished he sat back in his chair and ran his fingers through his hair.

"Well?" Millicent asked, leaning in toward him.

"Well, there you have it. It looks like she's now with a big businessman named Kertan Olonaglu from Istanbul."

The silence that followed was clearly driving Millicent to the brink of hysteria. Staring at him impatiently, she rapidly tapped her fingers on the table as if he had missed something.

"What is it? You seem to be disappointed in my reaction."

"Well, I thought maybe you'd throw the coffee cup across the room, or flip over a chair and run to the restroom to splash water on your face. I mean my goodness Harris, you spent a whole *year* looking for her."

"Yes," he said sluggishly, "yes, one year too long. I almost hoped she was dead, and by the look in her eyes," he paused to glance at the photo, "she doesn't look all that happy. Perhaps she *is* dead."

Clearly dismayed, Millicent stood up and announced, "Well then, case closed." She reached for the magazine.

Harris held it tightly to his chest. "May I keep it?"

"Are you sure?" she asked, with a curious raised eyebrow.

"Yes, I'm sure. And by the way, thank you. I imagine you're relieved as well." She had been overbearingly positive to the point of annoyance during the entire investigation and just as disappointed as he was in the end.

"I am, Harris. I truly am." Millicent leaned over and kissed him on the forehead. "Get on with your life," she said, holding his chin in her hand. "If you weren't so much older than me, I'd help you get started." Then she winked, turned on her heel and sashayed toward the door. Harris chuckled when she lightly lifted her skirt and curtsied. "Good luck!" she said before she exited the room.

"Hmm, good luck, again?" Harris muttered. *Since when have I had any of that?* The day was beginning to tug at his emotions – emotions that he hadn't felt in quite some time. *Get on with my life, yeah right.* And at that very moment of self-awareness, he felt bad for not inquiring about Millicent's wellbeing, for not remembering the friendly neighbor's name, for the wasted months he had spent looking for a woman that didn't love him, and finally he felt sad about missing the opportunity to get to know an attractive woman in green tennis shoes that smiled at him as if she knew his heart.

He didn't know how long he had sat there staring at the photo, reading the article over and over as if he had missed something in between the lines. Remembering the engagement ring he had given Vickie, he wondered if she still had it. He had yet to get over spending most of his savings, nearly fifty thousand dollars on a diamond. *I must have been nuts. Completely nuts!*

He picked up the magazine and held it up to the light. He did spot a ring, a huge emerald, almost the size of a blueberry on Vickie's loose hand. "She did well," he scoffed, rolling up the magazine and tucking it under his armpit.

Entering the bright sunshine, he glanced at his watch. He had wasted nearly an hour in the cafe reminiscing, and now his head felt heavier than ever. He decided to walk off the impending headache and turned the opposite direction of his apartment building, still uncertain where he was headed.

The park was just blocks away. If he had any so-called luck, it might not be crowded with children and he'd have a bench all to himself. As he approached the corner and saw the little people running all over the grounds, chasing balls and yelling at the top of their lungs, he made an about-face. Children made him nervous. He didn't know why.

When Vickie announced that she didn't want children, he was relieved. It was the perfect relationship. She wanted everything he wanted – so he had thought. What a fool he'd been. It would take him at least another five years to save up what he had spent on her and with his stocks continuing to fall, he felt insecure and unattractive. The thought was so unsettling, he decided to step into the nearest bar and get a drink to calm himself down. He knew exactly where to go.

Inside the bar was so dark when he entered, he had to stop and wait for his eyes to adjust.

"Mr. Harrison," a familiar voice yelled from across the room, "long time, no see." He recognized immediately the bartender's good-natured chuckle.

Harris blinked several times before the friendly Asian with the Cheshire grin came into view. "Hello Ming. Yes, it has been awhile," he said, slowly moving toward the barstool.

As if it were a current event, Ming blurted, "Did you find the girlfriend?"

"Well, yes and no. I see you didn't find your lost tooth either."

"No, and too big expense for a new one." He held his crooked smile in place, revealing a missing front tooth. "But someday, new tooth for me, new girlfriend for you. You will see."

Since Harris had spent many an hour crying in his beer at this cozy little neighborhood bar, he felt at ease placing the opened magazine in front of Ming. He put his index finger on Vickie's face and tapped it.

"What is this? Oh, I see…new man." Ming said, shaking his head, as he studied the picture. "You need nice drink on me."

"What do you have in mind?"

"A special I make just today. It cures what ail you … leave no overhang."

"Hangover, Ming, hangover. Sounds perfect." Ming's misuse of the language never failed to amuse Harris. He laughed openly.

"I could use one of those overhang drinks, too," a woman's voice came from behind.

"Ah, Mrs. Livingston," Ming greeted her. "Good to see you."

Harris turned to see the woman he had briefly connected with on the sidewalk. He felt a slow smile light up his face.

"No, Ming, not Mrs. Livingston for long. Mr. Livingston is living in Europe now with his lovely assistant. I prefer Ms. Green."

"Oh, yes," Ming said, leaning over the bar. "Green, like your shoes."

She laughed and greeted Harris with a friendly, "Hello, I'm Victoria Green." It took her a few more seconds to recognize Harris. "Oh, how nice to see you again. May I join you?"

"Of course, please do." He tucked his knees back under the bar and said to Ming, "Put her drink on my tab, Ming." *How funny that her name is Victoria*, Harris chuckled, thinking about coincidences. *Just when I finally let go of Vickie, she pops back into my life twice in one day.* "Humph!"

"Fill me in on the inside joke," Victoria said, "but first, your name would be a good start."

"Oh, I suppose it would. I'm sorry, I'm Harris Harrison."

"That's a fun name. Do you go by Harry?"

"Ha, good one," Ming chimed in, placing the tall drinks in front of them. He stepped back and studied Harris. Stroking his small goatee, he mused, "Harry. Yes, I like it."

"Yeah, right." Harris looked askance at the cockeyed bartender. "Don't even think of it, Ming." While he rolled up the magazine he asked, "Do you go by Vickie?" He hoped she didn't.

"Please, no, my mother would have a fit, and I might, too. So, Harris, you were chuckling about something earlier. Care to share?"

Knowing he could have said anything but what he was really thinking, Harris surprised himself with his answer. "Why not, Victoria." Her name rang nicely in his ear. "It's been awhile since I told my story. Matter of fact, the final chapter ended just today."

Ming nodded supportively with a saddened face.

Harris shifted his body away from the sensitive bartender and faced his guest, his elbow casually resting on the bar. She was easy to talk to, and before he knew it, he had told her everything from when his fiancé disappeared, up to his earlier meeting with Millicent. He deliberately left out Vickie's name.

"Wow, into thin air, just like that." Victoria snapped her fingers. "Without even a note." Clearly engrossed in his story, she eyed the rolled-up magazine lying near Harris' arm. "I bet you feel really weird about this. I mean, I've never heard of anyone doing such a heartless thing."

"Weird, glad, sad, stupid, you name it…I feel them all."

"What will you do now?" she asked, curiosity and concern in her voice.

"Well, nothing. She's with another man and in another country, and that's that." He shrugged and took the last gulp of his drink.

"You want another?" Ming asked, before Harris could set the drink down. "I see it good for you."

Harris chuckled, "It is calming me. Or maybe it's being in the presence of this charming and beautiful woman." He gave her a most amiable smile. It had been too long since he flirted with anyone. He enjoyed watching Victoria blush.

Appearing delicately flushed, Victoria stretched out her legs and took in the compliment. "Tell you what, you get another and so will I. I may need a little extra shot of courage to tell you *my* story. I'm not near as calm as you."

"Good choice all round," Ming said, leaving to prepare their concoctions.

Harris wanted to know more about this intriguing woman, so he posed a leading question. "I heard you say that Mr. Livingston is in Europe with his assistant. I'm assuming you meant he's with his new, uh, woman?"

"Assume no more, you are right. Except, she's not exactly *new*. I found out that she's been more than an assistant for quite a while."

He wasn't sure how to react to her candid remark. "Bastard!" would have been a friend's natural reply. Until he knew her better, he offered a weak, "That's too bad, sorry."

"Yes, it is too bad. I knew when I married him that it'd be difficult. He traveled a great deal, and I couldn't go with him much. I have my practice here and just can't up and leave like that. I'm a counselor for abused women, and unfortunately, the numbers have risen in the past year. We're thinking the recession is the cause. But, anyway, it's important enough for me to stay close right now."

"So," Harris paused, knowing he should ask more about her interesting profession, but not wanting to miss out on the essentials, he asked, "when are you officially divorced?"

"As far as I'm concerned, I already am. But, legally on paper, well, hopefully this week. It's been a long process, and I've had to fight like a dog to get mine. Makes it harder because my ex is always in London, and things keep getting delayed. His company moved their headquarters and his assistant there about nine months ago. How convenient," she snarled. "Oh, but enough of this nonsense."

Victoria lifted her glass to drink and when Harris mirrored her, she spotted the magazine again. "Is that the magazine with the picture of your ex-fiancé in it?"

"Matter of fact, yes, it is. I should probably throw it away," he sighed and rolled it up tighter while looking around for a trash can.

"Don't do that yet. Can I see who the vixen is?"

"Morbid curiosity?"

"I'd like to see what kind of woman could do something that rotten."

Harris opened the publication to the correct page and handed it to her. "I think it's been photo-shopped. Looks like her horns have been removed.

Victoria flattened it out on the bar. "There," he pointed, "the woman in the blue suit. That's her."

She looked closely at the picture, and then looked up at Harris, her eyes and her mouth equally wide open. "Oh, my God," she said slowly. "Oh, my God!" she repeated louder.

"What is it?" Harris asked, tapping her arm. "You look like you've just seen a ghost. What is it?"

"That man standing next to your fiancé is my husband."

Harris grabbed the magazine and held it at just the right distance to focus. "Which one, to the right or to the left?"

"The man on her left, the one holding her arm. Her name is Vickie, right?"

"Yes, yes it is, how'd….uh." The rest of the words clogged up his throat.

Victoria held a stiff one-sided smile on her crumpled face. "This is unbelievable, simply unbelievable," she gasped, leaning into Harris' space, pressing against his arm to get another look at the couple.

"I thought your husband's name was Livingston?" he said, his nose just inches from hers.

Victoria scooted back to her seat. "It is."

"But, it says Olonaglu. See?" He handed her the magazine.

"No, that must be the other couple. Look, here." Victoria pointed at the name Livingston mentioned within the article, but no mention of the woman next to him. "This is obviously an error. But that *is* my husband, excuse me, ex-husband. I can tell you that for certain."

"And that is my ex-girlfriend," Harris confirmed. Together they experienced an inexplicable discomfort, and then the absurdity of the bizarre coincidence hit them all at once, and laughter seemed to be the only solution. They cut loose with hearty guffaws.

"Of all the gin joints in all the towns in all the world," Victoria mimicked Bogart from the famous Casa Blanca scene.

Ming appeared in front of them, smiling curiously. "What so funny?"

"Oh, just Victoria here trying to imitate Humphrey Bogart. That's all." Harris waved his hand nonchalantly.

"I do that." Ming said, and when he repeated the famous line, his toothless grin beaming for approval, their laughter accelerated.

"That bad?" Ming asked.

"That bad," they both blurted, doubling over, wheezing and snorting at the expense of the naive bartender.

No longer amused, Ming retreated to the other end of the bar, mumbling to himself, "I never understand Americans."

After several gulps of breath and a couple of stifled chuckles they sank into silence — gazing dolefully at their former mates displayed in one silly photo in a stupid magazine.

Turning the magazine over, Harris said with softened eyes, "I hope this doesn't have any adverse effect on my next question."

"I won't let it, if you won't," Victoria said, sitting up straighter.

"Would you like to have dinner with me sometime soon?"

"I would. Yes, I'd like that a lot. So would my sister. She has been all over me about dating again."

"Does that mean she has to come, too?"

"Ha, ha, I doubt you can handle *two* Green women. But, there *is* something I'd like to ask you," Victoria faltered, "if you don't mind."

"Shoot."

"John flew in today for business and to finalize the divorce. I was told that he's brought Vickie with him." She paused to study his face. "Would you like to see her again?"

Caught off guard by her question, Harris sat perfectly still, profoundly contemplating his answer. "I don't know, truthfully. I don't know. I suppose I would like to have some kind of closure. But, how?"

"I can make it happen for you, if you'd like. There's a company dinner tonight, and since I'm still on the board, I am expected to be there. You could come as my date." She lifted her eyebrow slyly. "I'm betting John will bring Miss Priestly with him. Might make for an interesting evening."

Miss Priestly? Is that what she calls herself now? Harris knew her by another name. He tucked that tidbit away for later. "I'm not sure what I'd say to her, even though she does owe me an explanation. Would her answer make me feel any better? I don't know." Then Harris considered that he would want to know why she left him shortly after he gave her the ring. He'd always thought that he'd been swindled. He wouldn't mention this to Victoria, either. It would make him sound cheap to have wanted the ring back. The previous anger toward Vickie returned, and he realized that he might not ever have this chance again to get this off his chest.

"Let's do it. I'll know what to say when the time comes." He reached over and placed his hand on Victoria's arm. "As for you, how do you feel about meeting your replacement, or have you met her before?"

"I've only seen her picture. Actually, now that I met you, I feel okay with it. Isn't this almost like serendipity?"

"It's pretty wild, that's for sure."

"Speaking of such," Victoria grabbed his shoulder, "this all started, you know, with the bird that dropped poop on your head."

"Oh, yes, it did. But I don't think it's bird feces. It's too hard, probably a stone, and it's still in my shirt. I forgot all about it."

"Bring it with you tonight." Victoria beamed. "I believe it's our good luck piece." She jumped up from the stool and put her arms around Harris' neck and kissed him on both cheeks. "Pick me up at seven o'clock sharp." She wrote the address on the back of her card. "I don't live far from here."

"Yes ma'am," Harris said with a soldierly salute, watching her once again walk away. When she reached the door, this time she looked back and smiled at him.

Ming strolled over and startled Harris from his trance. "See, Harry, I told you my drink make things better. But what is this about bird poop and good luck?"

Harris tried to explain in a hurry what he himself didn't even understand. He left poor Ming perplexed, as usual.

When he walked out of the windowless room into the bright sunlight, he felt a change in the air. A change he realized was way overdue and desperately needed. *Harry? Hmm.*"

Looking forward to a soothing, hot shower and a nap on clean sheets, Harris couldn't remember the last time he had felt so alive. Even slipping off his shoes and socks felt good. When he loosened his shirt tucked deep inside his pants, he felt something scratch his skin. "Ow!" Arching his back, he pulled the shirt over his head without unbuttoning it. Then he heard a little clink as something hit the hard tile and bounced under the freestanding sink. He twisted his body around to see a scratch, tinged with blood. "Some good luck piece," he grumbled. He stepped into the shower before it warmed and let the cold water revitalize him. He felt like a kid under a yard sprinkler.

When the hot water heater finally kicked in, he stood with both hands braced against the tiled wall and let the massaging spray soothe his shoulders. He summarized the day and began imagining what it would be like to see Vickie again. Would he smile, would he be cold, would he stand back and watch her? What will she do when she sees me? No one in the room but the three of us will know the truth. Will Victoria tell her ex-husband? He decided not to let the questions rushing at him interfere with the lighthearted and rare mood he had been enjoying. They would have to wait until later.

Harris slept longer than he had planned and when he awoke, he only had fifteen minutes to dress. He hurriedly brushed his teeth and slipped into one of his nicer suits. Realizing that he hadn't dressed up since he proposed to Vickie, he got excited about wearing his fancy clothes. He searched frantically for his gold cufflinks and Rolex watch, and not finding them, he settled for a simple pair of silver cufflinks and left his everyday watch on the nightstand.

Just before he turned off the bathroom light, he remembered that Victoria said to bring the good luck piece. He got down on his knees and searched under the sink. Running his hand along the base of the pipe, he felt a tiny sharp object and squeezed it between his fingers. It was dirty and hard with an oblong shape. Smiling, he considered it might be a chunk of rock or a bead from some cheap, costume jewelry. He chuckled thinking about what Victoria would say when he presented it to her. He dropped it in his pant pocket, adjusted his tie, and ran out the door.

Victoria was waiting on the front step of her home when he arrived. She was wearing a tight red evening dress, accentuating her lovely figure, but hiding all the female parts accept for her tan legs from the knees down. Even her arms were covered by the long slender sleeves and the soft layers of fabric gathered around the neck brushed loosely just under her chin. She wore her hair up with a gold, butterfly comb and her tiny earlobes held round gold studs with a small ruby in the center. There was no doubt in Harris' mind that she looked beautiful, but there was a professional look about her that made him want to stand up taller.

"I'm so sorry, I'm usually ten minutes earlier," he apologized, when she got to the end of the steps.

Victoria waved him off, appearing to be a woman on a mission. "Not to worry, but let's get going. We still have time to position ourselves. I'd prefer to get there before they do."

Fortunately, the traffic was light and the ride to the event was quick and easy. The valet took the car and Harris took Victoria by the elbow. She looked up at him startled. "Oh, I'm sorry. It's been awhile since I've had the luxury of a man escorting me."

"Or, the luxury of a fine female to escort," he added, placing her arm on his. Then he stopped and looked seriously at Victoria. "Does this work for you, or would you rather appear without a date?"

"It's good for me, but you may want to be discreet until you know how you will handle seeing Vickie."

"Perhaps you're right. Plus, we don't want to add any extra tension to your divorce, especially since you're just hours away from signing."

Victoria looked disappointed at their practicality and gently pulled away. Without looking at Harris, she turned to acknowledge a couple that was calling her name. Harris stood there uncomfortably waiting for her to introduce him.

When she didn't turn around, he understood and walked past her to enter the building alone.

There were at least fifty tables covered in starched and ironed white tablecloths scattered throughout the spacious room. In the corner a jazz band was tuning up, and a large man with a head full of dreadlocks was cleaning out the mouthpiece of his saxophone. Harris recognized him at once. He was the musician from his and Vickie's favorite restaurant and where he had proposed to her. At Harris' request and on cue, the sappy song he had selected was the background music when he presented the engagement ring. The memory was dismissed when he saw Vickie come through the door.

She was alone, with no sign of her lover nearby. He hadn't expected the overwhelming sadness he felt at seeing her in the flesh. He knew then that he wasn't ready to approach her and slipped behind a large pillar. Peeking around it, he saw her being escorted close to the podium at a table designated for the upper echelon, where she was seated with her back turned toward him.

Victoria walked in with several people, all happily chatting and being shown to their tables. She spotted Harris and excused herself.

"Mr. Harrison," she said, holding out her long graceful arm.

"Ms. Green," he smiled and took her hand in his.

"Would you like me to seat you?" she asked. "Somewhere where you can observe and not be noticed?"

"I think that would be wise for now. You read my mind. Our friend is over there," he pointed. "The one with the Scarlet A on her back."

"Ha," Victoria laughed. "Glad to see that you're keeping your sense of humor intact. Oh, and look, my ex is entering the room now." She took Harris by the elbow and said under her breath, "Come with me, I have the perfect seat for you," and led him to the table in the rear, practically hidden by a statue and a large vase of flowers.

"Where will *you* sit?" he asked.

"Unfortunately, I will have to sit at the table with other members of the board. I'll be directly across from Vickie, so I can make her as uncomfortable as possible. How are you holding up?"

"I really don't know how to feel right now. But seeing her has made my stomach hurt."

"Might as well make this worthwhile, Harris. They'll be leaving in a few days and won't come back here for a long time. This may be your only chance to get that closure you think you need."

"I agree. Let's see how it goes." It seemed like the perfect time to kiss his co-conspirator on the cheek and pay her a compliment. "You look amazing, by the way."

"I look like a bloody sausage link," she said, returning a kiss on his cheek. "Have a drink, it'll settle your stomach. I'll see you in a bit."

As if she had summoned him, the waiter walked by with a tray of champagne-filled glasses. "Let's make that two," he said. It would take much more than one glass of the silly bubbly to keep him calm. Courage was another story.

When everyone was finally seated, the President of the Board stood up at the podium and spoke. Harris was surprised by John Livingston's commanding voice. It was deep, with tones of clarity that didn't match his small frame and weak chin. He observed Victoria watching her ex-husband expressionless, while Vickie stared at him with a practiced smile of admiration.

With the formalities over and dinner being served, the music finally began, and the lights were dimmed. Harris felt much more relaxed and even braver in the low-lit setting and he easily motioned for another glass of champagne. When the band played a slow, melodic song, several couples advanced to the dance floor. Vickie hadn't left her seat once, nor had she barely moved a muscle; neither leaning over to talk to those at the table or getting up to powder her nose. Harrison guessed that the "Scarlet A" must be on the front of her dress, as well. Mr. Livingston sat next to her and jovially talked to those around him and others that stopped by to whisper in his ear. Victoria did the same, stopping periodically to stare at Vickie in her attempt to unnerve her. Harris caught Victoria's eye more than once, and they smiled across the room at each other.

The sax player moved out into the audience. When he finished the song, he spotted Harris and lifted his eyebrows to acknowledge him. Excitedly, he turned to tell the band what to play next. The band looked over at Harris all smiles, apparently remembering the night they had played his request. "When a Man Loves a Woman" began, just as it had when he placed the ring on Vickie's finger. There was nothing he could do to stop them.

Harris didn't know what came over him, but he knew right then what he needed to do. In a trancelike state he walked over to Vickie's table and tapped her on the shoulder. When she looked up, the surprised expression on her face was anything but welcoming.

"May I have this dance, Ms. Priestly?" he spoke gently, but firmly with his eyes.

Vickie looked over at John Livingston with a nervous smile. He didn't say anything, but merely stared at her, clearly unsure of her suitor's identity.

"Oh, darling, you must," Victoria broke in. "This is Harris, my guest. He would be terribly insulted if you refused him. Now, go on." She practically pulled the chair out from underneath Vickie.

John quickly spoke up, "Perhaps she doesn't..."

"Now, John," Victoria chided, "jealousy does not become you. How about you and I take one last round on the floor for old time's sake?"

"Yes, do John. Be a good sport," the others at the table joined in.

"Of course," he said, "the President of the Board should have the last dance with the resigning board member."

"Don't count your chickens too soon," Victoria warned.

Harris stood watching the exchange. Seeing Victoria handle John so skillfully, he took Vickie by the arm and led her to the dance floor. He could feel her body tense up when he took her hand in his.

"You're shaking, Miss Goodman, Miss Priestly, whoever you are. What's the matter?" Harris asked, pulling her closer.

"What are you doing here?"

"Not sure. Serendipitous, isn't it?" he said, and twirled her around. "Do you have anything you'd like to say to me?" He maneuvered her into a position where she was forced to face him. Vickie stayed tight lipped.

"Do you realize that for nearly a year I thought you were dead?" He tried again to force an explanation out of her.

"Well, as you can see, I'm not. Matter of fact, I'm quite alive, which is much more than I could say while I was with you."

"Oh, really? You certainly seemed happy enough, especially when I gave you the ring you had insisted would seal our love forever. By the way, what happened to it?"

"I made my life better with it. Don't you think I've done well?" she said smugly, looking over at John who was dancing awkwardly with Victoria.

"Good Lord, Vickie! Aren't you the least bit sorry? Do you even have a clue how much you hurt me?"

"You look fine to me. What is your point?"

Harris abruptly stopped dancing and stared hard at the cold, distant woman that had ripped out his heart. He didn't know her at all. A burst of anger shot through him, and his body started to tremble. Alarmed by his sudden demeanor, Vickie stepped back.

Having kept a keen eye on Harris, Victoria rushed toward him with John in tow. "Excuse me darling," she said, stepping in between the two and speaking directly to Vickie. "I think your lover would much prefer to dance with you, and I know mine is dying to dance with me." She stood up on her toes and kissed Harris right on the mouth. "Am I right, sweetheart?"

Before Harris could answer, Victoria grabbed him around the waist and moved him backward across the dance floor. "Down boy," she whispered in his ear. "It's not worth it, for either of us."

"I almost made a fool of myself...again." Harris looked past the crowd and saw John angrily pulling Vickie toward the exit door. "What did you say to him? He looks upset."

"Oh, not much, really...he has a terrible jealous streak. But look, they make a great couple, don't they?"

"They deserve each other." Harris tore his eyes from Vickie and focused on his dance partner. "Well, at least I have some kind of closure. Thank you for that, and thank you for intervening."

"You're welcome. Gave me an excuse to get out of that awful dance. I've always hated this song," Victoria said, rolling her eyes.

Harris agreed, "So do I." *I do now, anyway.*

Grabbing his hand, Victoria pulled him from the dance floor. "How about we escape this scene and head over to Ming's. I could use another one of those magical drinks he made us."

"Great, I can't take another champagne. Makes me act like a girl."

❧

At Ming's bar, Harris pulled off his tie and Victoria kicked off her shoes while they recapped the evening.

"I just wish I had walked in arm-in-arm with you tonight," Victoria confessed. "But, I honestly didn't know where you were headed with Vickie. I actually considered that after she saw you, she might want you back."

"To tell you the truth, I didn't know either. It worked out the way it was supposed to. She made it easy." Harris hesitated before sharing the next bit of information, but now he thought Victoria deserved the whole truth. "She is more of a cold-hearted woman than you know. I didn't tell you this before…I guess I didn't want to look like an idiot. But she has a good portion of my savings and it's all my fault. I let her talk me into buying her things that set me back quite a bit. And while I was dressing tonight, I discovered my gold cufflinks and my Rolex are missing. Last time I wore them, I was with her."

"Well, that stinks!"

"And, by the way, her last name was Goodman when I knew her."

"Goodman, Priestly, hmm. And you know what else? You said she left you in December, well, John moved her to London in February. She had time to re-invent herself, or maybe she had been with you both at the same time. Sounds like she might be a black widow. I suppose I should warn John, even if he does deserve that." Victoria winced and changed the subject. "Hey, where's your good luck charm? Was it a seed, a button, a stone?"

"Not sure," he said, standing up and fishing through his pocket. "Here," he placed the dirty chunk in her hand. "I didn't have time to clean it…whatever it is."

Victoria asked Ming for a martini glass. "Half water, a splash of dish soap and no ice, please." She dropped the dirt-caked object in the glass and like a curious child, she placed her elbows on the bar, rested her chin in her cupped hands and watched the grime gradually dissolve. Ming joined in, equally curious. Harris sat back observing in amusement. A couple of minutes passed when Victoria fished it out and rubbed it thoroughly with a napkin. She held it up to the light.

"Hmm," she said. "Hmmm," she said again. On the third "hmm," she started giggling.

Harris and Ming couldn't take the suspense another second. She had them under her spell. "What is it?" they nearly demanded.

Victoria handed the shiny thing to Harris. "I think you just got some of your savings back."

He rolled the sparkling gem gently between his fingers, until he realized what he held. "Is this what I think it is…a diamond?"

"Yes, and a darn big one. I told you it meant good luck."

"No, it's you…*you* are good luck," he shouted excitedly. "This would still be behind the bathroom sink if it weren't for you." Effortlessly, he picked up Victoria from the barstool and pulled her into his arms. Ming slid the tip jar closer to his favorite customers.

Several months later, Harris Harrison met with Salem Jewelers and had an engagement ring made from the prized diamond the bird had gifted him.

At the very same time, Ming was taking a leisurely walk through the park when a large crow swooped down from a tree and dropped something on his head. Ming yelled at the bird and shook the thing from out of his shirt collar. He bent down to pick it up and saw that it was a shiny white tooth. "Ah, how nice," he said, "just what the plumber ordered."

And just when he said it, a woman jogging past him said, "You know that's good luck, don't you?" teasing him with a wink and a smile.

"Good luck?" he yelled after her. She stopped and turned to face him. They exchanged smiles. Ming looked up to the heavens and back down at the tooth in the palm of his hand. Shaking his head in awe, he muttered, "Americans, ahh, now I understand."

Intruder Alert!

I'm out of the loop now. The truth be known, I don't believe I was ever even in the loop. I see me watching the people in my life like a lost dog watching a family of raccoons raid a dumpster. I'm beginning to feel like a stray sock stuck to one of those ugly Christmas sweaters stuffed in the back of the drawer. I can tell you how I got here, but I can't tell you how it will end. Not yet, anyway.

Let's start with *the pool*. The dreaded *pool* that I didn't want, but my new husband's one and only precious daughter in her final year of high school just had to have. After all, it was the least we could do since I wrecked her life by marrying her dad. My vote didn't count and frankly, it hasn't counted since I married Mitch. For the first five months of our marriage, my main purpose in their lives was to oversee the installation of the pool. Only when it was completed did his daughter finally talk to me, and mostly about adding items to the grocery list and when I could pick up her acne medicine from the pharmacy. I'm blessed with an occasional "uh huh" when asked if she wants breakfast or a grunt when she enters the room. She treats me like I'm leaving at five, with dinner in the oven, the house cleaned and returning the next morning to do it all over again.

This has gone on for much too long, and what's even worse is that Mitch has joined her side. So, now I'm not only feeling like the hired help, I'm feeling like an intruder in this place I'm supposed to call home.

Now, add our neighbors, Laina and Milton to my lot in life. They moved on our block shortly after we did, and being the newbies in the community, they gravitated toward us. Since then, every, not every *other* weekend, but *every* weekend like clockwork has been dedicated to outdoor bar-be-cues with this couple and always at our home because we are the only ones on the block with the *pool*.

It's another typical Friday, and the inevitable phone call will come in. Five-thirty. Mitch happens to arrive home from work at that time, the cell phone cradled between his ear and shoulder as he heads directly to the bathroom. I hear muffled words and laughter from the other side of the door, but no flushing.

Meanwhile, in the kitchen, I pour myself a glass of wine and stare out the window at the glistening giant bowl of water that set us back forty-nine grand and took the place of our honeymoon. 'We just have to have the waterfall, it's so romantic,' I can still hear his daughter's whiny plea. But just as I predicted, she spent only two weeks with her friends in the pool until she started dating a boy whose family's home took up an entire street with a swimming pool the size of Rhode Island. That's where she spent the rest of the summer, and that's also when Laina and Milton so conveniently entered our toxic lives.

There they were, at our front door, cheery as a Girl Scout mother and daughter selling those marvelous Thin Mints that I eat so quickly, I will never know if they really do freeze well. "It's a sign! We're both new in the hood!" Laina shrieked, thrusting a bottle of cheap wine in my face, as Milton offered Mitch a premium cigar from his Havana Club collection, followed by a friendly buddy punch on the arm. I stood speechless observing Mitch nodding excitedly through their long-winded stories as they meandered throughout the house scoping out our belongings and ending up on the patio, gazing in awe, coveting our precious *pool*.

"Your pool is fabulous!" Milton proclaimed. "We're planning on building one too, and it will be great to experience yours first."

"And isn't it amazing," Laina squealed with delight, "that we have the same initials? M and L?" She was so excited about befriending us, I didn't have the heart to tell her that my given name is Elizabeth, and Liz is merely a nickname.

So that's how it all began; me not having the heart to say or do anything to displease not only Mitch and his tyrannical offspring, but now, our new cheery best friends – a childless couple with the same initials, on the same block and still, four months later, without a pool.

"I'm home," my husband reported, flicking at the tight bun neatly piled on the top of my head and waking me from my trance at the window. He went straight for the beer, and I went straight for the freezer, knowing the next thing he'd say without even asking if I agreed, "Get out the steaks, Laina and Milton will be over around seven."

"Well, at least someone's using the *pool*," I sighed into my empty wine glass.

Mitch oblivious to my remark, pulled a bowl from the cabinet to begin preparing his favorite dip that our playmates could not live without. "Milt said he's got preliminary plans for their pool he wants me to look over."

"No kidding?" My mood slightly lifted, but my crummy attitude pushed it right back down. "So, they're *finally* going to build one? Whatever will we do now? Oh wait, I know! We can siphon our water over to their pool, fill ours up with rocks and hang out over there every weekend."

"What?" Mitch turned to look at me, his flattened lips moving toward a crooked frown. "You never have liked the *pool*."

I leaned against the counter and crossed my feet at the ankles. I don't know why I said that out loud. I've kept my rotten thoughts to myself lately since we've been disagreeing on everything. And with Mitch looking at me so smugly, daring me to start another fight I knew I could not win, I felt my body shrinking. Lucky for both of us, my rebuttal was stifled by the loud, unpleasant ding-dong of the doorbell.

"Oh, sure. Come on in. I'll start up the oven now," Mitch said to whoever was needing to use our appliance.

"Is Liz here?" Laina asked, following closely behind Mitch, a tray of appetizers in her hands, the sound of flip-flops slapping the heels of her feet (a sound by the way I can't stand). I visualized fragments of dead skin from her recent pedicure sloughing off in her tracks.

"Oh, hi Liz," Laina said, a tinge of disappointment in her tone. "These are for the party, but our oven broke. Now, they need to bake for at least forty-five minutes on three-fifty. I know I'm early, and I hate to bother you…"

"It's no bother at all," Mitch answered for me, turning the oven on. "Wow, they look wonderful! Yummy! Want a glass of wine?"

Mitch's syrupy voice and Laina's squeaky vocal chords made my teeth hurt.

"Oh sure, I'd love one. What a day, what a day!" Laina began, while I finished off my second drink. I don't think I heard a word she spoke, given that this was not the first time I've heard her complain about her job. Instead I studied the sheer bathing suit cover that rose above her swimsuit line and revealed a fleshy mound of white bottom when she bent over to put the tray in the oven. It reminded me of the packaged biscuit dough squeezing out of the tube when you whack it on the edge of the counter. Mitch, of course, stared too long behind his beer can, and I doubt he was comparing her cheeks to a can of biscuits.

When Laina announced that they would have to postpone installing a pool until next year, and Mitch consoled her with a promise to keep ours available to them indefinitely, I forced back my groans and excused myself to the bedroom to struggle into the ugly one-piece bathing suit that was still hanging stiffly on the closet doorknob from last weekend when the four of us gathered around the chlorine-saturated pool at, well you guessed it, exactly the same time, with exactly the same drinks, the same meal and the exact same conversation.

I donned the mu-mu I had bought from Hawaii when I was single and in between husbands and let my hair fall to my shoulders. There was no escaping the full-length mirror where I stood posing in different positions, trying to find *me* in all that fabric. It's no use. I'm stuck. I'm stuck with lame excuses, these crazy neighbors and that blasted pool! I'm stuck in *Groundhog Day!*

I threw myself onto the bed and listened to the cackling downstairs. *No pool till next year.* A dull ache filled my head, and I was unaware that I was falling asleep.

I dreamed I was in the eye of a hurricane, looking all around me at my life spinning out of control. I saw my stepdaughter sneering at me, snorting through her tiny pinched nose. I saw Mitch diving into the pool, reappearing at the other end, shaking water from his bald head, as if he had hair to shake. And then there was me, lying on the grass beside the dead oak tree that we sadly had to cut down to make room for the concrete deck. I was looking up at the cloudless blue sky when without warning, Milton's face appeared before me. He smiled down at me and reached out his hand. I didn't want to take it, but he grabbed my hand anyway, and before I knew it, I was standing in front of a closed door with Milton by my side. He whispered, "Open it. Go on, open it."

With the slightest touch, the door opened in slow motion. *Dorothy Gale, please let it be Oz.* The first thing that appeared was a pair of bare feet; brightly painted toenails suspended in mid-air pointing toward the floor. As the scene panned before me, I saw that the feet belonged to a woman in a thin, transparent gown lying face down on a bed, her arms still, next to her body. Above her was a naked man dangling from a trapeze, a ping pong paddle in his hand. I didn't recognize him, as I rarely put familiar faces on the naked characters in my dreams. He swooped down and spanked the woman on her rear end. She laughed, a hideous laugh and then pulled herself up on her knees. I immediately recognized Laina's plump cheeks pushing their way out of sheer panties.

The nude man swooped down from the ceiling again, and it was then that I knew it was Mitch, howling in laughter, as Laina lifted her bottom higher.

I felt my chin being guided toward Milton's fading face. "Are you ready?" he spoke, his eyes widened with lust.

I didn't know what he meant, and before I knew it, his mouth was on mine and we began to slowly spin around the room, as if in a waltz. I opened my eyes only to see Laina's lips on mine, not Milton's.

'Stop it, stop it!' I heard my scream inside her cavernous mouth, growing so large I thought she would swallow me whole. "Wake up! Wake…"

"Wake up, Liz. Liz, wake up. You're dreaming. Wake up, honey," a familiar voice came from above.

"Mmmm," I groaned and slowly opened my eyes to Milton hovering over me.

"Oh my god, what happened?" I sat up so fast, my head hit his front teeth.

"Ow!" Milton yelled, stepping back in pain and covering his mouth with one hand, balancing a drink filled with ice in the other.

"Ohh, I'm sorry. I was dreaming, I…what are you doing in here?" My anger took him by surprise.

"Liz, calm down. The steaks are almost ready, and we haven't seen you for over an hour."

My lips were buzzing and when I touched them, they were wet. I swiped my tongue across them and tasted liquor. My eyes went straight to the glass in Milton's hand.

"Milton, did you, did you *kiss* me?"

He stepped forward and placed his hand on my knee. "I couldn't help myself. You looked so lovely lying there in that sexy Hawaiian gown. You looked like Sleeping Beauty waiting for her Prince Charming." He looked ridiculous batting his eyelids with that goofy grin.

"Sleeping Beauty wouldn't be caught dead, much less asleep in this thing!" I huffed, pushing his hand away.

"Oh, come on. Let me be the prince." His eyes widened.

"This isn't funny, Milt." I stood up, both hands pressed firmly on my hips. "Go back downstairs. I'll be there shortly."

"You won't say anything, will you? You know, about the kiss?"

I glared at Milton until he apparently felt so uncomfortable, he left the room.

Hypnotically, I brushed my hair and went downstairs as if nothing unusual had happened, except the taste of Milton's kiss remained on my lips.

The evening went along as it always did, me stretched out on a lawn chair accepting Milton's refills until my mind went blank. Later, I opened my eyes to the emptiness of the backyard and the sound of insects being fried in the bug zapper. Even the house was lifeless; Pandora, frozen on the computer screen, silently asking if we were still listening.

Knowing where they most likely had gone, instead of going directly to bed, as I usually did, I slipped on my shoes and headed down the sidewalk to Milton and Laina's home. When I entered their ugly brightly painted front door, a futile attempt at duplicating the official UT burnt orange, I heard music coming from upstairs instead of in the game room where Milton and Mitch had spent hours challenging each other to Ping Pong on nights when I stayed home and read a book. I stood in the hall shadows and listened. Like my recent dream, the voices hooted and hollered. If I had not recognized my own husband's annoying laugh, I would have turned around and gone home.

If you've never walked up a dark stairway toward a light underneath a bedroom door, unannounced, knowing you were trespassing, not knowing what to expect, let me tell you, it's an eerie feeling. But Mitch's laughter urged me forward, and before I knew it, I had my hand on the doorknob. As if in my dream, it was not Milton telling me to open the door, but me, all alone with my morbid curiosity. It felt oddly symbolic, as if I was opening the door to a new life, a life I had been expecting, but was afraid to acknowledge. Perhaps even, a life without a pool. Again, my mind whispered, "Oh Dorothy Gale, please let it be Oz."

I stopped the door from opening all the way and peeked around it. What I saw might have made another woman charge into the room in sudden rage. Another woman might have fainted. Me, well, I became instantly nauseated by the three of them dancing in the nude to, of all things, Barry White music. Psychedelic lights from a disco ball plastered dots all over the room and on their quivering bare butts; their reflections in the wall-to-wall mirror creating a party of six. If both men had not been sandwiching Laina, the scene might have been funny. I slipped back into the hall and braced myself against the wall, waiting for my legs to stop shaking before heading down the stairs. When the laughter stopped, that was my signal to leave.

Mitch didn't come home that night, nor did he arrive in the morning. Later, around dinner time, he stumbled in wearied, but lacking humility. "Too bad you slept through the party." His insincere tone kept me from quizzing him. We ate in silence, ended the evening in silence and more silence when the sun rose. It was not an awkward silence, but a demeaning silence that had been strangling us long before this happened.

Monday came, the same routine. Mitch kept his secret and his schedule, and so did I. After work I attended the Conversational Spanish class that I had been taking in preparation for the aborted honeymoon to Puerto Vallarta. He spent his evenings at the gym. The rest of the week passed quickly, and on time, as if cued, Laina called, Mitch answered, and steaks were pulled from the freezer.

I'm not sure about the courage it took for me to sit in that lawn chair weekend after weekend and watch our neighbors take over my life. I think the wine helped a great deal. Strangely enough, it occurred to me that Mitch was the happiest when with his buddies, so who was I to take that from him? And honestly, was it really courage, or denial, or pure laziness that let me sit there passing judgment, feeling sorry for myself, my own pathetic life stagnant in a stopped-up toilet? Where's the plunger? Shouldn't one of us be fighting for this marriage or at least ending it? A marriage of convenience, a marriage that shouldn't have happened. A rebound, when after a couple divorces, the dumpee is scared to death to live alone and quickly seeks out another dumpee. And is it possible the rotten stepdaughter was right, that Mitch married out of revenge? It was true that when her mother remarried shortly after the divorce, Mitch rushed into his second marriage with me. Argh!

I was lost in thought, not noticing Milton making feeble attempts to get my attention while Laina and Mitch played water volleyball. Finally, he dragged his chair up next to mine and apologized again for the kiss, and in the same breath asked me if I liked it. When I didn't answer, he asked if he could take me to dinner. "I understand Mitch will be gone a few days this week, and Laina will be at a convention. Wouldn't dinner with a neighbor, a good friend, be a nice change?"

I looked at him with a straight face and asked, "Will you be bringing your whip?"

His eyes opened wider and a nervous smile curled up on one side of his mouth. "Oh, so Mitch shared, did he?"

"Shared what?" I asked most innocently.

"Well, about my whip, and…how did you know?"

"I didn't. Just guessing you might be into that sort of thing. Just giving some spice to the conversation."

"Oh, ha ha!" He faked a laugh and took a swig of his drink. A slightly confused look remained on his face. "Well, anyway, you know I speak a little Spanish. We can go to a Mexican food restaurant and teach each other words. *Por favor?*"

"No, gracias," I whispered and moved in closer. "But I'm sure we'll see you here by the pool next Friday. Bring your whip and show me how it works. But don't tell, Mitch. Let it be a surprise." And with that, I got up, and walked inside, swishing my bottom more than I ever have in my life.

What am I doing? Well, surely you don't think I'm going to rot by the pool the rest of my life.

Back in the middle of the bed where I hide out fighting sleep, I heard the partiers outside mosey on down the street to start another party...without me.

Mitch and I played the silence game the rest of the week, and I found him every morning asleep on the sofa, stripped to his boxers, ice melting in his Whiskey glass. I wondered how long we would be able to keep this up, and it occurred to me that it took over a year before my ex-husband and I admitted we had grown apart; me ignoring his indiscretions, sulking around waiting for him to come to his senses, which he never did. I was the perfect martyr, and I played the part well. And here I am again, repeating the same scenario. It was then that I realized I was not willing to spend another precious day pretending, and what I decided to do next took a set of balls the size of King Kong's.

Friday night, again. I'll skip the boring details and cut to the chase. Mitch and his daughter were due to come home after a three-day trip visiting her new college campus. He had called earlier, and I let him know that I was already preparing for Laina and Milt's arrival. Naturally, he was pleased.

Drinks all around, and I was in a particularly good mood. Even our guests were excited to be there. Mitch was running late, so I entertained the couple in the kitchen, refilling their drinks before they even were emptied. Milton watched me closely, like a wolf stalking a lamb for his next meal, while Laina talked on and on about the girl in her office that she so casually fired. By the time Mitch arrived, the neighbors were lit and ready to party.

"We have the house to ourselves?" Laina asked, when seeing Mitch enter the house alone wearing a restful five o'clock shadow, toting his expensive luggage and without his daughter dashing past us in fear that if she even glanced my direction she'd throw up.

"This isn't my week. She's at her mother's and by now she's probably already in her boyfriend's pool," he said.

"Great!" Milt raised a toast. "Now maybe we can finish the party off *here* for a change." He looked over at me and winked.

Mitch gave Milton a look that said, "Shut your pie hole." Laina leaned against the counter, arms folded tightly and giggled.

"Yes, let's do." I raised my glass high. "Let's whoop it up!"

That gesture got everyone's attention, except Mitch looked as if I had announced I had leprosy. "Well?" I scanned their eyes. "I'm in! Let's have some fun!"

"Not likely. You're a lightweight." Mitch scoffed and brushed passed me toward the wet bar.

If he only knew how that remark emboldened me. Instead of responding to it sourly, I fortified myself with another pour of wine and waited patiently for Mitch to gulp down his drink before saying the words I'd been practicing all day long. "Steaks are marinating, let's go skinny dipping!" I grinned so wide, my lip stuck to my front teeth.

"Skinny dipping? Sí sí," Milton smiled wickedly and began unbuttoning his shirt. "I'm all for that!"

Laina looked at Mitch questioningly and then over at me. "Are you kidding?"

"Of course not!" I said convincingly and began slowly slipping out of the floral beach kimono I had sworn I would cut up into dinner napkins every time I put it on.

Everyone's eyes widened watching me undress. I couldn't tell if it was lust or shock, but Laina, clearly not wanting to be upstaged, ripped off her flimsy cover-up and stripped out of her swimsuit as quickly as a three-year-old removes her panties while rushing to the restroom.

Eyes all turned her direction and within seconds, everyone was buck naked, standing awkwardly under the bold fluorescent kitchen light looking ridiculous.

"Last one in is a rotten egg!" Milton yelled, grabbing Mitch's hand, who quickly grabbed not my hand, but Laina's, and when Laina reached out for mine, I took it and pranced with them out the door toward our fabulous pool.

As soon as we reached the outdoors, Milton stopped in his tracks at the edge of the pool. I slipped from Laina's grip just when she and Mitch collided with Milton. Everyone stood frozen looking down at the pool. The beautiful glistening water was gone. It was completely drained, and written in bold red paint were giant letters glaring back at the confused and nude onlookers: ADIOS!

When they turned to look at me, I was nowhere to be seen, but having locked *all* the doors behind me, I rushed to my car neatly packed to the ceiling, slipped back into the kimono and drove away from the sound of the house security alarm blasting its loud annoying signal to all the neighbors, Intruder alert! Intruder alert!

I'm on my second drink now since this flight to Puerto Vallarta will take several hours. "The only regret I have…." I pause for a dramatic ending, after telling the exciting pool story to the couple on my right – Rick who is in the center seat next to me listening intently, while his wife sitting by the window is desperately clutching his arm as if she should protect him from this crazy passenger telling such an obviously ridiculous tale. Two flight attendants are hanging over the seats facing me, all ears, thrilled to hear a new story to add to their collection. I've even captivated the elderly grandmother across the aisle, who had been snoring earlier. I take a deep breath, hold up my cell phone and wave it in the air as if it is evidence, "Yep, my only regret is that I left our fancy closed circuit security cameras on."

Fighting back a wicked smile, I ask innocently, "Was that wrong?"

In Search of Rain

The chocolate smudged-faced little girl stood on the porch steps and waved goodbye to the car backing out of the driveway. A tear trickled down her cheek and landed on her lip. She licked it off and tasted the ice cream the nice man had given her. When the car disappeared from sight, she turned to the woman sitting stoically on the chair swing behind her and asked, "Is he coming back, mama?"

Her mother's frown softened when she saw her child's hopeful face. She let out a breath that she had been holding until she saw the car turn the corner and said, "No, Phoebe."

Phoebe defiantly turned away and stomped back inside the house. "You run everybody off!" she yelled and slammed the screen door behind her.

Men were often in and out of Phoebe's young life. They would come and go like Christmas day; entering with spar- kling gifts and tender smiles, leaving with empty hands and sad eyes. Most of them left with civility, hugging Phoebe and kissing her mother on the mouth long enough to make Phoebe turn her head. Those who left with anger, made her the sad- dest, because they seemed to be the ones that really put their hearts into this single-parent family. No kisses goodbye, just big hugs that forced the breath out of her, but none for her mother, Naomi. Phoebe recognized the hurt on their faces. They wanted to belong, and she wanted them to belong. She had no idea what her mother wanted.

She was twelve when the last man stepped over their threshold. He was an ex-basketball player who set up a hoop in the driveway and every time he visited, he and Phoebe played HORSE. By the time she had mastered the game, he, too, was gone, and the next four years held no other prospects.

The year was 1989: the Berlin wall came down, Madonna was at the top of the Billboard charts and Phoebe had grown to five-foot-eight, the tallest girl in the tenth grade and quite skillful on the basketball court. She was trying on lipstick for the first time in front of the bathroom mirror, when seeing the immediate transformation, it occurred to her how much she had changed. She puckered her lips and thought to herself, I don't know why I'm just now seeing this, except Mom says many changes are happening at my age, and soon I'll have more responsibilities and could even get a summer job. She looked down at her size A-cup breasts. "If only I didn't have to wear a bra!" She vigorously wiped off the lipstick when her mother entered the bathroom, her arms loaded with towels.

"I know tomorrow you're turning sixteen," Naomi announced, "but unfortunately my doctor has rescheduled my surgery, nothing major, just my ovaries, so you have to stay home for the weekend with Linda."

"That lady who smells like sour lemons? Bummer!" Phoebe huffed. "There goes my birthday! This is supposed to be the biggest of all birthdays, you know?" she yelled, charging down the hall, slamming the front door on her way out to the bus stop.

Phoebe's mother had left four days' worth of food, including store-bought casseroles in the freezer. "A successful attorney does not have time to prepare fabulous meals," she had heard her excuse for her limited cooking skills more than once. So, Phoebe was not looking forward to frozen dinners or following Naomi's strict instructions she had made painfully clear: after school come directly home from basketball practice and wait until Linda arrives. Any outside activity will have to be approved by Mimi, her grandmother. If all went well, Naomi would be home on Monday. Phoebe didn't like the words, *if all went well*, much less the word, *surgery*. Now, she wished she had hugged her mother before she left for the hospital.

That afternoon, Phoebe opened the door to an empty, but well-lit house. Matter of fact, every single light was left on for her entry. She locked the door behind her, as instructed, and dropped her gym bag in the middle of the living room floor. She felt a rebellious grin stretch across her face when she nonchalantly stepped over it, kicked off her shoes, leaving them right where they landed, and headed straight for the kitchen without looking back.

In the corner of her eye she saw something on the counter. Neatly tied up in a bow was a white bakery box, next to it a card. "Happy Birthday, Phoebe!" She recognized her mother's slanted handwriting with a drawn heart hovering like a balloon over the letter "i" in the word, *birthday*. The middle "E" in *PhoEbe* always capitalized; Naomi's clever little way of making the name easier for the reader to sound out.

She stood staring down at the neatly arranged box and card, and although she wanted to open it right then, she wondered if it would be impolite not to wait for Linda. While she pondered the idea, the phone rang. How funny, it was the sour lemon lady on the other end.

"Um hum, I understand. Oh no, don't worry," she spoke into the phone, stretching the cord far enough away from the mirror on the wall so that she couldn't see herself tell the lie. "My grandmother is back from the hospital, and I can stay with her." A quick pause and Phoebe answered, "Yes, Linda, all weekend and until my mother comes home." She felt her heart beating faster and the phone cord she had twisted in a knot was now strangulating her finger. "No, I'm sure. She's actually on her way over right now to celebrate my birthday."

There was no way in hell that Mimi would leave her daughter's side at the hospital, so Phoebe's weekend plan was watertight. "Best birthday gift, ever!" she whooped, unwrapping the cake box first before reading the card. She poured herself a tall glass of cold milk, cut a slice of the moist chocolate cake and sat down at the kitchen table. After the first bite, washed down by the creamy liquid, a sensation she loved and would forever savor, she opened the envelope. Inside was a card that her mother had made using Phoebe's art pencils. On the front, a picture of the two of them standing at the shoreline, both in swimsuits, floppy hats on their heads, barefoot and holding hands. A week at the beach with nothing to do but sleep, eat and sunbathe was her mother's dream vacation. Phoebe looked long and hard at the drawing. Something was missing, something important, something necessary – a father. She tried placing the faces of all the men she could remember that had floated in and out of their lives into the picture. As soon as she did, they would evaporate, as they always had and always would. She snatched a pencil from a drawer and drew an extended hand holding her free hand, the mysterious long arm drifting beyond the edge of the card.

Phoebe turned the card over and read an added note: I'll give you your birthday present when I get home. "When she gets home? That's three days from now. I bet it's hidden in her bedroom." She scarfed down the cake and dashed off to find out.

It had been awhile since she'd visited her mother's *private abode,* she often called it, when explaining to Phoebe the importance of privacy. She never went into the room uninvited, and suddenly she felt like an intruder standing at the doorway adjusting her eyes to the dark, the thick drapes serving their purpose well. Fumbling around the huge king bed, she found the lamp and switched it on. Scanning the room for a present, probably wrapped in the same red ribbon as the cake, she saw nothing in plain sight. She dropped to her knees and scoped out the space under the bed, finding only an earring that she remembered her mother reporting lost. Placing it on the night-stand, she went inside the walk-in closet, three times the size of hers.

She stood amongst the neat line of shoes, stacked hat boxes and clothing, all organized by color, suits separate from the rest. Naomi was a snappy dresser, just like her mother, never leaving the house without looking like they were headed to a social event or court. Phoebe was only slightly impressed by all the garb. In fact, if it were up to her, she'd wear the same soft flowered buttoned-down shirt, baggy cargo shorts with lots of pockets and her favorite ankle height hiking boots every day. But her mother had suggested that when she turned sixteen, she would want to experience different outfits and that possibility crossed Phoebe's mind as she looked at all the choices around her.

The hats got her attention, and she placed them one by one on the bed. She nearly missed the last hatbox, unreachable and tucked deep in the corner on the top shelf. With the help of her mother's vanity chair, she now had them all at her fingertips.

Phoebe had seen these hats worn by her mother on different occasions. She tried each of them on. The sun hat made her look old, the straw Panama felt confining, the gold wool Fedora was fun but silly. She liked the Cloche and left it on while she rummaged through more. When she lifted the lid on the box that had been hidden, she pulled out a Scottish tweed flat cap. It was woven in blue and gray herringbone. She didn't recall ever seeing her mother wear something this simple. Phoebe placed it on her head and tucked her shoulder length hair behind her ears. "This is perfect. A bit large, but I love it! I'm going to wear it all weekend long!"

Gathering up the boxes, she began placing them back on the shelf, keeping the one that stored the hat she now wore out on the bed. She ran her fingers wistfully along the edges of the flowers sewn in the soft downy stuffed comforter and felt a sudden urge to lie down. Propping her head up on the pillows, she listened to the quiet house, as quiet as the inside of a coffin.

As she often did, and with every birthday since she was five, she thought about her father, the father she knew nothing about. He was a secret, and her mother kept it that way.

When she stretched her body, she accidentally kicked the box, and it fell to the floor on its side. A letter spilled out of it. Phoebe eased off the bed and picked it up. It had been carefully opened with a sharp letter opener and the stamps were nothing like she had ever seen. It was dated several months earlier, addressed to Naomi and it was from Scotland. This much Phoebe knew: her mother had spent her last two years of undergraduate studies in Edinburgh at the behest of her Scottish father. She had heard her mother talk about the wonderful time she had spent in the magical country, but never had she mentioned anyone in particular. She couldn't stop herself from opening it.

The letter began with *Darling Naomi*, and her eyes went directly to the signature, *My deepest love, Rain*. Now, she knew she must read it. Excited, she dove back onto the pillows.

The first line said that he was out of the Army and that he was coming to the States, arriving on the 21st. *That's tomorrow! He must not know Mother is in the hospital.* He gave her the name of the hotel where he'd be staying. He went on and on about missing her all these years with subtle reminders of their college days together. And then he wrote something that Phoebe had to read twice and out loud, "I do hope I get to meet Phoebe. I wish you had told me. It must be wonderful raising a daughter. It does not change my feelings for you, Naomi. I do love you still."

So, her mother had a Scottish boyfriend. "The cap must be his!" she exclaimed, removing it from her head. Turning it over, she ran her fingers around the edges and located the label. Made in Scotland. A strange feeling came over her when she sniffed it. It smelled ancient, like the sea. She stayed on the bed, re-reading the letter until she fell asleep; the exhausting question echoing in her head, "Could he be my father?"

The following day, she woke up to the phone ringing – much too early for a Saturday morning. The call was from Mimi giving Phoebe the latest news that her mother would be in surgery within the hour. She was relieved when nothing was mentioned about Linda, as her grandmother detested talking on the phone and was anxious to say only what was necessary – lock the doors, clean up after, and be sure to wash your hands often. Phoebe promised through a yawn, and the call was abruptly ended, not a word about her birthday.

Confident of the plans she had made the night before, she stuffed her backpack with the current book she was reading, a notebook, toothbrush, and the two-hundred dollars that would have gone to Linda. After breakfast she'd make her next move. In her mother's robe, Phoebe made a pot of coffee, a ritual she had watched her mother perform every morning. The familiar gurgling sound as it percolated soothed her. She was not allowed to drink coffee, but since it was her first day as a young adult, she poured a cup, diluted it with crème until it was the color of chocolate milk, buttered a piece of toast and walked out on the porch with the newspaper under her arm.

A sense of maturity struck her with the newspaper opened in her hands, coffee at her side. She skimmed the headlines and went straight to the comic section, skipping over that weird one, *Non Sequitur*, in search of her favorite, *Garfield*. Two sips of the caffeinated liquid was quite enough, and soon she found herself back inside where she showered, dressed, and scheduled a taxi to pick her up.

It felt strange sitting in the back seat of the yellow cab, all alone, watching her house disappear as they drove away. She didn't know why, but she ducked when they passed her school. Behind her sunglasses, she could see the driver looking at her through the rearview mirror. Normally she would have chatted with a stranger, but his expression was sinister, so she continued looking out the window. She was glad when she saw the hotel up ahead and glad to get out of the taxi. The driver grumbled something she didn't understand when she gave him a tip. *Two dollars is quite enough for someone who doesn't even smile!* At that moment she felt just like her grandmother.

She passed through the glass revolving doors and stood in the lobby contemplating her next move. Spring break had started and the hotel was busy. She watched people come and go, families entering with excitement, an elderly couple escorted by a bellboy. She felt her shoulders shrink with every man who walked by, wondering if he was her mother's college sweetheart. Then an idea came to her. She took out a notepad from her backpack and wrote a note to Rain Finlay: "I am in the lobby. Please come down and meet me. I am wearing a Scottish cap."

She kept her sunglasses on when she approached the counter and asked the front-desk clerk to deliver the message. Phoebe walked away and watched the lady summon a bellboy and give him instructions. She followed him to the elevator and slipped in covertly behind him, shoulder to shoulder with guests toting their luggage.

The elevator landed on the third floor. She squeezed out in time to catch the bellboy turning the corner. Further down the hall, he stopped and knocked on a door. "Bellboy," he spoke loudly. The door opened, and a hand reached out to take the note. A "Thank you" was heard from inside the room, but instead of waiting for a tip, he turned quickly, as if he did not want to stay any longer, his head bent, a twisted smile on his face. He brushed past Phoebe without even looking at her.

Phoebe walked timidly toward Rain's room; his door still ajar. She was tempted to peek in, but the door suddenly closed, causing her to jump back in surprise. Avoiding the bellboy, she sprinted down the stairs back to the lobby where she strategically placed herself in view of the elevator door. For the longest she watched people coming and going, none of them a single man searching the lobby for someone. A family with small children filed out of the elevator, the children looking over their shoulders at something behind them. Their parents hurried them along, the mother scolding under her breath, as she placed her hand on her boy's head and turned it forward. "Stop staring, that's impolite!"

Phoebe watched the elevator door closely. A man stood aside holding it open. Just when she thought it had emptied, out walked a man on crutches. He wore a tweed cap identical to the one she had on, a pullover shirt with the sleeves pushed up and baggie pants. Behind his beard, seemed to be a nice face. When Phoebe saw that one of his legs was missing, she winced and hid behind a column. She was alarmed, and she didn't know why. She removed the cap and stuffed it in her backpack.

Afraid to be seen, she stood still and waited, for what, she didn't know. As she pondered her next move, the man walked by. He was scouring the area for someone, and when his eyes landed on Phoebe, he smiled and walked on. Of course, he was looking for her mother, and not a teenage girl. Phoebe watched him closely. His back was strong, and his muscular arms seemed to move him gracefully on the crutches. His dark hair was cut short at the nape of his neck and his beard was nicely trimmed, not scraggly like her science teacher's beard, usually speckled with food from the snacks he ate regularly as he announced to the class that he was hypoglycemic. *Yeah, right!*

The man sat in a chair against the wall amongst people studying the entertainment guides or waiting for others. A guest spoke to him, and they carried on a casual conversation, an occasional smile interjecting their dialog. Although she couldn't hear him, he seemed easy going with strangers.

No others came out of the elevator looking for someone. Phoebe sensed there would not be more. As she watched him, she was torn whether or not she wanted to know if this crippled man was her father, much less her mother's old sweetheart. The thought nagged at her. He continued to look at every woman walking by alone, catching their eye, engaging a smile, then quickly dismissing them. Phoebe spotted an empty chair near him and moved in closer.

A mother and her small son sat down next to the man. The boy, pointing at his crutches, asked him, "Are those stilts? My uncle has a pair of those. They're fun."

"Well, they're sort of like stilts," he answered, patting the boy on the head. "I need them to help me walk. See, I only have one leg."

Phoebe was intrigued by his Scottish accent, and she knew right then that he must be Rain.

So fascinated by the crutches, the boy hadn't noticed his missing leg. "One leg? Oh, like my dog. She got ran over and doesn't have a leg either. Did you get run over?"

The mother looked over at the man and they exchanged smiles. "Well, not quite," he said. "I jumped off a building, and that's pretty much what happened."

The boy frowned and held his finger up to the man's face, "You should never jump off a building, unless you're Superman. My mother won't even let me jump off the bed. Dangerous." Then he leaned over, pulled the man's chin and spoke in his ear, "But don't tell her, I jump off my bed, and see, I still have both legs."

The man and the boy grinned at each other with their secret. "What's your name, lad?" he asked.

"Grayson. And this is my mom." He grabbed his mother's hand and pulled it toward the man so that they could shake hands. Before more could be said, the boy's father appeared and motioned for his family to follow. They said goodbye and walked away.

Watching the man and the little boy bond like that made Phoebe feel ashamed of her fear. She swallowed hard, removed her sunglasses and placed the cap back on her head. Mustering up the courage to say something, she stood and walked toward him. They locked eyes and when the man noticed the cap, he tilted his head and looked as if he had found something familiar in her face.

"I'm Phoebe," she said, more like a confession than an introduction.

The man's eyes opened wide, and large dimples peeked out from his closely shaved beard as he gave her a welcoming smile. "I'm Rain."

Phoebe put her hands to her mouth and stifled a laugh. Or was it a cry? Whatever it was, she was horrified to let it out. She moved in closer to the chair next to him.

"Very nice to meet you. Where's your mother?" he asked.

Phoebe told him about the surgery, and Rain became quite worried. "We should go to the hospital right now, don't you think?"

"I was told to stay home and wait. I should go back. Mom doesn't know I'm here," she faltered, "I, uh, I kind of found the letter you wrote."

"I see," Rain spoke softly. "Hmm, then you know about me and your mother."

Phoebe nodded. The foolish notion that he might be her father made her want to flee. Still, she paused long enough to allow him time to admit it. He revealed nothing, sitting there patiently waiting for her to speak. Overwhelmed with the situation, she nearly choked on her words, "I'm glad to meet you, Rain. But I must go home now. I just thought you should know about my mother." She rose from the chair and went outside to hail a taxi. It was then that she began to cry. From behind, a hand gently touched her shoulder.

147

"May I come with you, Phoebe?" Rain turned her around to face him. "There is much to talk about, and I am anxious, like you, to know about your mother. She *is* the reason I'm here."

Phoebe wiped her eyes on her sleeve and allowed him to help her into the taxi. She hesitated, then moved over to let him enter. He put the crutches in the front seat first before he hopped into the back seat. Remembering the words of love he had written in the letter, she let him console her. It all seemed so strange, but somehow it also felt right.

When they arrived, she made him feel at home while she listened on the answering machine to a message from her grandmother reporting that the surgery went well. Mimi sternly ended the call with, "Next time, Phoebe, I expect you to pick up the phone."

Both Rain and Phoebe were relieved that the surgery was over. So relieved, she shared with him that today was her birthday and offered him a piece of cake.

"Your birthday is today?" Rain chuckled. "Mine is tomorrow."

Phoebe was flabbergasted, and took that as a sign. They sat at the table and enjoyed the cake with milk. "Is this cap yours?" she asked, handing it to him.

"Tis," he smiled, handing it back to her. "You wear it well." Rain took that opportunity to tell her all about how he had met her mother. Phoebe in turn answered his questions concerning school and sports. He was so easy to talk to, and no longer disturbed by the missing leg, she was able to study his face and see his nice features. She wondered what he had looked like in college.

"You know, I'd like to take you out to a special dinner for your birthday. My treat," Rain offered. "And then after, we can go to the hospital and visit your mother."

The thought of not having to heat up her dinner on the stove sounded wonderful to Phoebe. She had already crossed over the line by lying about Linda, and then the taxi ride, and now bringing a complete stranger home with her. "Yes, I'd love that!" she blurted, grinning from ear to ear. "My favorite pizza place is not far from here. And, I have the key to my mother's car…I mean, well, I don't have my license yet, but you…"

"Probably be best if we took a taxi," he maintained. "I don't want your mother upset with me, especially on your birthday, and besides, driving on the right side of the road could be a bit challenging. You know, it's different in my country."

Phoebe had not considered any of those things, only whether or not he could even drive a car with only one leg. The concern lingered on her face.

As if he could read her mind, Rain released her from her thoughts, "I really shouldn't drive until I get my prosthetic leg, which I'm getting very soon. Then, I can put *my* basketball skills to the test. I used to be pretty good."

Trying to picture Rain playing basketball with a fake leg was more disturbing than imagining him driving a car. The odd feeling stirring up inside her dissipated at the sound of the phone ringing. Knowing it was probably her grandmother again, she dreaded having to tell her another lie. With her back turned, she cupped her hand around the mouthpiece and said, "Yes, Linda and I are coming to the hospital." She ended the conversation knowing she would have to deal with all these falsehoods later. But for now, it was time to celebrate, not only her birthday, but Rain's, too. She thought better of wearing the cap to the hospital and left it on her mother's bed next to the letter.

At the restaurant, Phoebe and Rain matched each other in the number of pizza slices they consumed. Rain told more stories of his childhood in Scotland and Phoebe eagerly listened. Not much was said about the army, nor did Phoebe ask how he really lost his leg, or why he hadn't seen her mother all these years. Neither wanted to spoil the party.

On the way to the hospital, he insisted that they stop for flowers. Remembering that he gave Naomi tulips while in Edinburgh, he decided to bring her the same. He bought Phoebe a small bouquet of wildflowers.

They were quiet during the rest of the ride, until Phoebe thought to ask, "Rain, do you have children?"

He looked directly into her eyes and answered, "No, I have never been married, plus I have been in the army most of these years. No time for children. Do you?" he grinned and elbowed her in the side.

"Ha, ha, funny guy," Phoebe laughed, elbowing him back. He had managed to take the pain from his disappointing answer away before it even surfaced.

At the hospital, they walked in silence down the long hall, speaking only to the nurses offering to assist the handsome handicapped man all the way to her mother's room. Rain suggested that Phoebe announce his presence. He would follow with her signal after she was sure that Naomi was ready, or for that matter, even willing.

Phoebe entered slowly, and saw her grandmother first, sitting next to the bed reading. Her mother was also reading, her face made up with lips effectively painted her favorite shade of red. No one would have guessed that she'd had surgery that day. The scene was quite pleasant until her grandmother spoke, "Well, look who's here, Naomi." Looking behind Phoebe, she asked, "Where's Linda?"

Phoebe ignored her and went directly over to her mother. "Mom, how are you?"

"Oh, honey, I am fine. Everything went well." She shot a look of warning at Mimi.

Phoebe caught the look. "So, you *are* okay, and can come home on Monday?"

"Yes, of course, but hey, happy birthday, my girl!" She tossed the book on the bed and reached out for a hug.

"Be careful there, your mother has stiches," Mimi cautioned.

Phoebe released her mother and turned to kiss her grandmother on the cheek. Mimi had established that greeting method early on, preferring a peck rather than a hug. Phoebe preferred it as well, because her grandmother's hair always smelled thick with hairspray, and hugging her made her want to sneeze.

"Mom, I have a surprise for you. I'll be right back." She ran out into the hall where Rain stood leaning against the wall chatting with two nurses. She gently eased into the conversation by touching his hand, resting on the top of the crutch.

He turned away from his captive audience and asked, "She's expecting me?"

"Not quite, but I told her I had a surprise. Come on."

Nodding a goodbye to the ladies, he followed Phoebe back to the room, the flowers now in her hands. She entered first and handed the bouquet to her mother. "These are from an old admirer," she said. "Well, not quite that old."

Both mother and grandmother gave her a confused look as Phoebe turned and motioned toward the doorway. "And may I introduce, all the way from Scotland..."

Rain took several steps in and stood soldierly still. His gaze by-passed Phoebe's grin and her grandmother's shocked expression and landed right on Naomi, who instantly dropped the flowers and pressed her hands together in prayer against her trembling lips.

"Hello, Naomi," Rain said, tears gathering as he stood there motionless, unable to take his eyes off hers.

"Oh, my goodness, it's you." Naomi shook her head back and forth in disbelief. Then her eyes moved to his severed leg, and she began to cry.

Her grandmother stood up and started to say something, but Phoebe grabbed her by the arm and said, "Mimi, I think we should leave them alone for a little while. It's been a long time."

"But I don't believe…" her grandmother began in protest.

"Mother, please. She's right, I'd like to be alone with Rain," Naomi pleaded.

"Well, OK, if that's your choice," she said curtly, blowing air from her nose.

"Hello, Mrs. Ryan," Rain said, as she brushed past him, altogether disregarding his presence.

Following her out, Phoebe reached for Rain's arm. "Grandmother says hello." Feeling especially mature having handled the situation like an adult, she glanced over her shoulder at her mother. Naomi gave her a wink of approval.

In the waiting room, her grandmother bombarded her with questions. Phoebe assured her she would tell her everything later. Although what she really wanted to say was, "This is really none of your business." Knowing better, she kissed her on the cheek and left her before Mimi could make further demands.

"Let me know the minute he leaves," she ordered.

Phoebe gave her mother and Rain another ten minutes before she entered the room. Thankfully, they were both through with the crying and now laughing, Naomi's hand resting naturally in his. They turned and looked at her, all smiles.

"Rain, I need a moment with Phoebe. Could you wait outside?" her mother said, a look on her face Phoebe did not recognize.

When Rain left the room, Naomi said, "Please shut the door, my love."

Anticipating a reprimand, Phoebe closed it and returned to her mother's side. Naomi took her hand in hers, and in nearly a whisper, she said, "I have something to tell you, but before I do, I want you to know that it is all up to you."

What a strange thing to say. Refraining from saying aloud what she was thinking, Phoebe replied with a simple nod.

"Well, I'll just come out and say it. Rain is your biological father."

Phoebe's expression froze. She wasn't sure how to react with her mother's serious look still in place, and the word *biological* sounded so weird.

Her mother went on to say, "And as strange as this may sound, he does not know it."

Phoebe tried to digest the words swarming like bees in her brain, as her mother rambled on.

"My question for you, Phoebe, is do you want me to tell him? I mean, what I'm asking is, do you want Rain to be your father? Because once I tell him, everything will change. Our whole lives will change as we know it now. I'm leaving this up to you."

"Me? Why is this up to me? I mean, shouldn't it be up to *you*?" She sat up straighter and crossed her arms in annoyance. "You're the one who…well, why me?"

"Phoebe, I kept him from you all your life, and now he's suddenly in it, and he's, he's disadvantaged. He may not be the father you have always wanted. And, you don't know him."

"But, he loves you. I read his letter to you. He loves you still."

"I know, you have a lot of explaining to do about that." She gave her the parental look of disapproval. "And yes, he does love me. But, it's not about me, Phoebe. Not this time." Naomi reached again for her daughter's hand. "I will ask you again, do you want me to tell Rain he's your father?"

Phoebe closed her eyes tightly shut and kept her arms folded. She was confused by a number of emotions. Anger took the lead. "Mother, why didn't you want me to know about Rain? I asked you so many times about my father, and you never said a thing. Why, now?"

"Oh, Phoebe, we were so young, he had his career in the army, I wanted my own. My parents were beside themselves and had other plans for my future. They sacrificed much for me. And, we were worlds apart. It just couldn't work. He tried to see me throughout the years, but I refused. I don't know what else to say."

"And you ran off all the other men because of him. Didn't you?" Phoebe offered her hand, determined to understand. Her voice softened, "All these years…you still love him. You do."

"Phoebe, please." Naomi pulled her hand away. "This is not about me. It's about *you.*"

"It's about us, mom. It's about *us.* I know why you're afraid to admit you love him…it's because he's crippled now, and you want *me* to make the decision…let you off the hook. Mom, you can't be *that* shallow."

Naomi put her head in her hands and began sobbing. "I do love him, I always have. I'm afraid…"

"Enough!" Phoebe stood up quickly on her feet. "This isn't a silly fairytale! If this man is my father, he has the right to know. And has it occurred to you that he might not want to be my father? Has it occurred to you that he may go right back to Scotland and live out his life without both of us? We're not the *only* one here making choices."

"It's more than that," Phoebe's mother whispered, unable to look her daughter in the eye.

"What *more* can there be?" Phoebe threw up her hands.

"The surgery I just had was to remove a malignant cyst on my ovary. I have only one ovary now. The chances of more returning are…"

"Don't even say it!" Phoebe insisted. She eased onto the bed and put her head on her mother's shoulder.

"It's fine, honey. I'll have to come in for periodic check-ups, that's all. Nothing to worry about. I shouldn't have told you."

Phoebe jerked away from her mother and bit down hard on her lip. She couldn't stop herself from saying, "Shouldn't have *told* me? You mean, like you didn't tell me about my father?"

With a long face, her mother lowered her head in defeat. Phoebe stood and challenged her. "How many more years do you want to waste, mom?" She pointed emphatically at the door. "There's a man out there who lost you, his child, his leg, and now he's here."

"He is, isn't he?" she sighed. "So, back to my question. Do you want me to tell him or not?"

"It's up to you!" Phoebe turned and stormed out of the room.

"Phoebe!" her mother yelled.

She found Rain leaning over the nurses station. If she weren't so upset with her mother, she would've hugged him from behind. Instead, she tapped him on the shoulder. "I think you're needed in there. I'll wait out here."

"OK, birthday girl, but when the visit's over, let's go get ice cream." He flashed the most charming grin.

Phoebe shaped an OK sign with her fingers and assured it with a vigorous nod. All eyes watched him walk away, and when he entered her mother's room, she turned around and blew out a heavy sigh.

"Birthday?" the nurses said all at once.

Phoebe shrugged. "Yeah, the big sixteen," she said glumly.

"Lucky you. Your mother's going to be fine, and that cutie pie friend of yours wants to take you out for ice cream. You go, girl!" the youngest nurse cheered.

"Whoo hoo!" the plump nurse sitting behind the desk yelled out with exuberance while dancing in her chair; her enormous breasts bouncing in rhythm with her shoulders.

"Ohh, I remember when I was sweet sixteen," one of the interns said, dramatically sliding her body down the wall while dreamily looking up at the ceiling. "This is going to be a *great* year for you, girlfriend."

"You think so?" Phoebe looked around at the smiling women all nodding in sisterly harmony as though they were initiating her into womanhood. The sweet moment of clarity sparked an epiphany: she had already started her journey toward independence that very morning by boldly seeking out what was missing in her life – Rain. Tears filled her eyes, and she knew in her heart exactly why it was going to be a great year. Her father was just a few feet away. My father. My very own father!

Lies, what are they? Truth without meaning,

stars without gleaming, rainbows void of red.

A Simple Lie

Do you know that sitting in front of this almighty monitor writing to you day and night has caused me to see double? Two of everything isn't so bad. Two glasses of wine, two George Clooneys, six chocolate chip cookies. You get the idea. I should thank you for that.

It's 4:30 a.m. Seems to be when I'm going to wake up every morning for the rest of my life, and here I am, in an old raggedy t-shirt left by one of my many husbands, can't remember which one, but it's got a big hole in the back that I made from scratching an itch that won't go away, ever since, well, you know. Anyway.

Can you spare a square? Can't believe I used that line in a public bathroom the other night. The woman sitting next to me said there wasn't any toilet paper in her stall either, so she tore the cardboard tube in half and handed it to me under the wall. I laughed so hard, I blew dry myself off. Ha ha ha!

I miss you. I wish you would write back.

Ending the one-sided chat with 'Love ya', Claudia stood, stretched her arm high over her shoulder to scratch the annoying itch that started shortly after she had told the lie. It was a simple lie, at the time. She had read, according to a study of people who meet online, that nearly eighty per cent exaggerate their attributes on their profiles or they lie by omission – displaying only pictures from the cleavage up or fuzzy action shots while in a life jacket going down the rapids. Harmless it seems, until....

It all started not long after Claudia's fourth husband left to an ashram, somewhere west of Australia. Instead of returning two weeks later, as he had promised, he sent her a picture of himself in a long, ugly brown robe standing barefoot next to a man (or a woman, Claudia could not tell) dressed identically, both with virgin-white, freshly shaved bald heads that looked like halos gleaming under the UV infused sun. On the back of the photo, a farewell note was written, and that's exactly what he wrote, 'Farewell,' along with the number of the attorney that was handling the divorce papers.

By now, Claudia knew the drill well and wasted no time signing the decree, having a garage sale for his belongings, shoving the furniture around to how she liked it, and changing her name. After having been a Howard, a Bishop, a Sanchez and the hardest to pronounce or spell, Costrowski, although she liked writing the initials CC, she decided to return to her maiden name, Claudia Day. Perhaps wiping the slate clean is just what she needed. After all, there were no children from these marriages to offend.

Burying herself in romance novels, sitcoms she thought she'd never watch and relying on her beagle to listen to her woes, she was, once again, without a man.

"Some people think I'm ridiculous to have married four times," Claudia told her mother. "I don't get it, I mean, don't we change shoes often, sell our cars for new ones, throw out the dinged-up plates for a brand-new set? I just haven't found the right mate. Trial and error. There's just no other way to know."

But the explanation fell on deaf ears as her mother came from strict Catholic stock and couldn't even begin to understand her daughter's unnatural philosophy, nor did she want to talk about it. She had only one thing to say, "No matter who you marry next, my dear, please don't expect a wedding shower. Honestly, how many coffee makers do you own anyway?"

It was quite obvious that Claudia would not receive any sympathy from her mother, so she decided to search the internet sites for women who have had multiple husbands. It occurred to her that she couldn't be the only one and decided that perhaps through others, she could learn more about herself. She stumbled across an article called "Addicted to Marrying" where she read about a woman named Pebbles who made it her mission to get wifed-up again and again. As she plunged through the words, she began to feel sick inside. The woman confessed to her addiction: the high from falling in love, the jewelry, the trips, the unbridled sex, being shown off, and finally the thrill dying within months after the wedding.

"I'm not like that at all!" she yelled, startling her dog who began to wail. "You don't agree, do you Apathy?" she asked the beagle who tilted his head as if he did. "Wifed up, that's not me. Not me at all!" But the more she thought about it, the casual excuse that marriage was simply about trial and error began to sound absurd. Could she really be addicted to marriage?

She had to talk to someone to approve or dispel her latest theory. Her girlfriends over the years had slowly evaporated– her mother not blaming them, "I mean come on girlie, they don't want you eyeing their husbands next." That thought never occurred to Claudia. For heaven's sake, four husbands or not, she had scruples!

Closing the site of Pebble's confession, she searched for a chat line to talk to someone, anyone, about her dilemma. Skimming through the various topics, she found one that suited her: Healthy Minded Men and Women Discuss Divorce. Claudia sank into her chair and thought about how to start. She wanted certain anonymity, so she knew she must use a fake name. Conjuring up different ideas, it occurred to her that she could go in as a man. Women are more apt to share with a man than another woman, she decided. Ramone, too Spanish. Michael, way too common. Lance, kind of feminine. Fred, her obnoxious uncle's name. Henry, yeah, Henry, an honest name. Nobody would ever think that a Henry would lie.

Signing in as Henry, she boldly entered the chat room. The conversation was lively, and as Claudia scrolled down, she spotted a woman who seemed to have good things to add to the conversation, and when she said she had been married three times, Claudia knew she was the one.

Henry: Hi Lane, I'm Henry. I'm new on here.

Seconds rolled by and for a while, Henry's space sat idle with no response from Lane. Finally, words appeared.

Lane: Hi, Henry. Welcome to our chat room. What brings you here?

Henry: Just need to talk, I suppose.

Lane: LOL, that's what we do on here. Well, sometimes we get someone who wants to sing, and they blast the pages with lyrics from songs that express how they feel at the time. I guess that's some form of communication. But, please, I'm not encouraging you to sing. Ha Ha!

Henry: Not to worry, I don't know all the words to any songs, except maybe 99 Bottles of Beer on the Wall.

Lane: You're funny. Tell me about yourself.

Claudia ran both hands through her hair and tied a handful into a knot, something she often did when she was thinking hard or hardly thinking. Recently she had found random strands of grey hair on the keyboard or on her chest. It always reminded her of death, something she had rarely considered until she turned thirty-five. She shrugged off the morbid thought and began typing.

Henry: I'm 6'3", handsome in an ordinary way, and old enough to know better than to be on here chatting with strangers.

Lane: Cute, aren't we all? I'm 5'6", not short, but certainly not considered tall. But honestly, Henry, we get to the point on this site and discuss things like that after, if we choose.

Relieved that she didn't have to conjure up more lies about her looks, Claudia moved forward.

Henry: I have this need to talk to someone about my four marriages. I saw that you've been married three times and since we have that in common, maybe we can share insights.

Lane: Interesting that you should bring up that topic. I was considering my fourth marriage just this week, and I'm feeling weird about it. Are you married now?

Henry: No, not anymore. Single and hunkered down in my home, just me and my Apathy.

Lane: Apathy?

Henry: My dog.

Lane: You named your dog Apathy? Hmmm…

If Claudia had not disguised herself as a man, she would have told Lane that it was her third husband who gave the dog that silly name; the one who left her because he suddenly realized that he didn't know what love meant but learned later when he got engaged to a stripper from the *Bounce an Ounce.* That would have gotten a good laugh. Instead, knowing that a woman simply cannot resist a man with humility, she continued the ruse.

Henry: Anyway, the poor little beagle came that way. Just like I came with the dull name, Henry.

Lane: Aww, that's not a dull name. I find it very charming. Matter of fact, I know a Henry, and he's a very nice man.

Henry: Let me guess. Your grandfather is named Henry.

Lane: OMG! How did you know?

And from that moment on Henry and Lane created a private chat room where they chatted through that night and every night thereafter like clockwork. They shared their fears, their likes and dislikes, poetry, prayers, their closeness in age, no children and the horror of experiencing difficult mother-in-laws. Most importantly, they came to realize that they were not addicted to marriage, but were merely loving souls believing that marriage was the highest compliment after telling someone that you love them. Lane made the most sense when she explained: when you find yourself in front of God vowing to love forever and ever, you really do mean it, at the time. She reiterated, "at the time." Then she said something that really made sense to Claudia: a human has no power to control how another human being loves. And who would want to?

Claudia's affection for Lane grew with each chat, and when her online friend finally confessed that her name was not Lane, but really Jordan, and that she had changed it to protect her anonymity, Claudia could not admit the truth. Instead she thanked her and continued the masquerade.

Henry: Well, my name is Henry, you can be sure. No one in their right mind would use that as a pseudonym. Maybe Mike or Rob, but certainly not Henry!

As the days went by, the conversations turned to more talk of love, and before Claudia knew it, while sitting in her sparsely lit bedroom on her fluffed-up bed linens, legs crossed, wine nearby and the laptop propped up by a designer pillow, she had become Henry – Henry, the MAN. The kind and patient man that wanted to confess to Jordan, the sweet and deep philosopher who spewed words of wisdom, that he was falling in love. Now that Jordan had broken up with the current man in her life, Henry thought that Jordan might be feeling the same. And the longer they shared, they both knew that the time would come when they would finally want to meet. It would not be Henry's idea.

Two months passed and both Jordan and Henry were now ending their chats with sentiments like, 'See you in my dreams', or 'I'll be thinking of you fondly and your funny socks while at work tomorrow', and then the granddaddy of all, 'Love you.' Claudia froze when the letters in sweet flowing italics first crossed the screen. Thinking it was one thing, but writing it? She quickly unplugged the computer. She needed to think. Later, she would simply tell Jordan that the computer froze.

But, the next time Jordan presented the word "love" at the end of their nightly talk, Claudia wrote, 'Love you, too.' And she meant it.

Not long after, Jordan suggested that they finally meet. Since they lived in the same town, but at opposite ends, they agreed to meet in the middle at Angelo's Restaurant with the promise that if either felt uncomfortable, they would simply part ways.

Lying in the pitch black, her brain racing, Claudia could not believe that she had agreed to a meeting. As wonderful as it had been to love Jordan as Henry, it was a lie. It was the worst kind of lie. Her skin crawling, she jerked the blanket off and leapt out of bed. Reasoning with herself in front of the bathroom mirror, she wondered if she could possibly pass for a man. She tied her hair back as tightly as possible and studied her bone structure. She wasn't all that pretty without make-up, she bargained with her reflection. Jordan would probably laugh at the harmless 6' 3" lie. Could I pull this off? What about my breasts? My smooth hands? She held her brightly painted fingernails up in front of her and slapped both of her cheeks harder than she intended. "Snap out of it! You're crazy! You must tell her. This is so wrong!"

She argued with the red-faced insane woman staring back at her until Apathy showed up at the door and began howling. "I'm pathetic, girl, I'm pathetic. I'm also in love. And worst of all, I think she's in love with me. Oh Apathy, I must tell her. I have to tell her soon."

Claudia could barely think at work the next day and left early, feigning an oncoming cold.

Relieved to be back under the covers, she opened her laptop and proceeded to locate Jordan. Scrolling through the chat room, it occurred to her that all she had to do was cancel their Saturday date. But she'd have to continue cancelling, and all this would do is postpone the inevitable. She didn't want to lose this wonderful friend, this wonderful feeling and just before she signed off, a message popped up from Jordan.

Jordan: Now just how did I know you'd be looking for me? The same reason I'm looking for you?

Claudia watched the innocent words dance off the screen and into her ears where she imagined Jordan's voice with a soft, Southern drawl unlike her own. She wanted to say something sweet, something clever, but she knew better. The truth had to be known.

Henry: Hi there. Actually, I was looking for you to tell you something.

A long pause.

Jordan: Oh, are you going to tell me that you don't want to meet?

A longer pause.

Henry: No, no, I wasn't going to say that.

Jordan: Oh good. I was hoping, well, anyway, come to find out, I can't meet Saturday. Something important has come up.

Claudia blew out a long breath of relief and threw herself back onto the pillows. "I don't have to tell her yet," she reported to Apathy, who looked up at her dubiously.

"Don't you look at me like that. I can buy more time, maybe a month more. I don't want to lose this. It's too important."

Jordan: Hey, are you still there? Please don't be mad at me. We can reschedule.

Henry: Sure, we can. But I can be disappointed, can't I?

The second Claudia wrote the words, she knew it was wrong.

Henry: Jordan, I have to tell you something. It's hard, it's so hard, I don't know how to say it.

A pause – much longer than any pause before.

Jordan: Oh no, don't tell me you're married, or going to be married

Henry: No, no, no. Actually, worse than that.

The daddy of all pauses.

Jordan: Well, don't keep me in suspense.

Henry: I'm NOT Henry.

Jordan: Oh great! Thought it was something serious. I wasn't Lane either, remember? Let me guess, John, Paul, George or Ringo? Oh wait, what about Bob?

Henry: None of those. I'm…I'm…shit!

Jordan: Your name is shit? LOL

Henry: My name is Claudia.

There, it was. Done. Now what? Wait for the yelling or rather the exclamation marks. Claudia peeled her longest finger nail down to the quick and painfully watched the screen.

Jordan: what do yu mean youre claudia???

Oh no, the lack of capitalization, the missing apostrophe, the shortened pronoun — a sign of true confusion and disappointment. A moment of truth, the walls were down, when even correct punctuation doesn't matter anymore, and oh, the three question marks!

Henry: I'm Claudia. A female. A woman. A daughter, a niece. A failure in marriage, not one time, not two times, but 4 times!

Before Jordan could type anything, Claudia quickly apologized.

Henry: I'm sorry. I'm very sorry. We can still be friends.

Then, poof, Jordan was gone.

4:30 a.m. on the dot. Claudia walked hypnotically toward the computer, glanced at the empty chat box and instead of typing

her thoughts to her online buddy, she went to the kitchen to start the coffee. Nearly three months had passed since Jordan disappeared from her life. And during all that time, Claudia had written to her every day, telling her everything, like she was writing in her diary, and without one single lie. Today, she had decided to give up. With a cup of hot coffee resting in her hand, she deleted Jordan and Henry forever.

The urge to begin another romantic relationship weighed heavily on Claudia's mind. New Year's Eve was approaching, and she refused to be alone on such a romantic night. It was a Saturday, and the coffee shop near the mall was always packed with single people sipping on a latte, reading their electronic devices. Claudia took a chance and slid into her favorite jeans that lifted her butt cheeks higher, threw on an emerald green sweater that hung off one shoulder, and headed determinedly to the coffee shop.

She entered the shop with a laptop under her armpit. Purchasing an Eggnog Latte, she scanned the room for a place to sit. Noticing an empty chair next to a man playing with his cell phone, she slowly walked over. "Umm," she cleared her throat, "is this seat taken?"

"Not at all," the man said, looking up, acknowledging Claudia with a nice smile.

Ah, straight teeth. Check that off the list. She turned her body slowly around, being extra careful not to spill the coffee while maneuvering her bottom onto the chair. Leaning seductively toward the man, the sweater slipping further down her shoulder, she whispered, "This place sure is crowded."

"Always is," the man put his cell phone back in his shirt pocket and turned toward Claudia. "I'm here every Saturday. Don't think I've seen you before."

"I used to come here a lot, but I've been too busy until lately."

He leaned forward, put his hand out and introduced himself, "Glen Glen Burrows."

"Claudia Costrow...oops, I mean, Claudia Day." She felt her cheeks flush, remembering she had gone back to her maiden name.

"Recently divorced?" he asked calmly.

"Well, not quite a year. Is that considered recent?"

"I don't know. My girlfriend dumped me about four months ago. Guess it depends on how long it takes to get over it."

And that was all it took. Both strangers with something in common, and before they knew it, they had agreed to meet for dinner the next evening. And when that dinner went well, Claudia accepted Glen's invitation to a New Year's Eve party on the second floor of the swanky Driskill Hotel.

When they arrived, every plush seat around the bar, in nooks and crannies, near the band and even out on the balcony was taken. Standing room only. Glen held Claudia's hand and pulled her through the crowd. After ordering drinks, they stepped up to an elevated area and scanned the partiers below.

"Looking for anyone in particular?" Claudia finally asked, as Glen studied the guests.

"Well, my ex-girlfriend might be here, and I was kind of hoping to avoid her. Heck, there she is," he announced.

Claudia followed Glen's eyes to a group of women chatting in a small circle. "Which one?"

"The blonde in the red dress. The one with her hair pinned up."

"Oh, she's very pretty." Noticing a sad look on Glen's face, she asked, "Why is she now an ex?"

"She left me for another man. A man she met online. Can you believe that? The girl's obviously crazy. And to top it off, she's been married three times. Probably a good thing we're not together. Anyone who'd marry that many times must be really nuts."

"Oh," was all Claudia could muster up.

"And you know what else? I think the guy must be old, because she said his name was Henry. No one has that name anymore."

Claudia nearly choked on the Gin and Tonic she held tightly to her mouth. Through watering eyes, she stared down at the woman in red. "Where's Henry now? I don't see any men around her?"

"That's the weird part. Turns out that she never met the guy. He was her online fantasy. She said that one day he just disappeared. Still, our relationship is over."

Claudia could barely contain her excitement. Observing Glen silently pining over the lost love, she put her hand on his arm to console him. "I'm sorry. Break-ups of any kind hurt."

"Yeah, well. Will you excuse me? I have to go to the men's room."

As soon as Glen was out of sight, Claudia walked down to the party below. She squeezed through the beautiful bodies of men and women dressed to the nines and stood very close to Glen's ex-girlfriend. She listened quietly to her talk to the others – her voice a soft Southern drip of honey, just as she had imagined. She had a hearty laugh and seemed to be enjoying the company. Eavesdropping, Claudia waited curiously for names to be exchanged.

"Oh my, look over there. Isn't that your ex?" one of the women in the group declared.

All eyes turned toward Glen who was now walking toward Claudia.

"Good Lord, he's coming over," the woman in red grumbled, bowing her head.

When Glen reached Claudia, he looked over nervously at the ladies and said, "Hi Jordan, um, ladies. Have you met my friend, Claudia?"

Claudia's eyes opened wide when she heard the name. Everyone greeted her with a nod and only Jordan reached out to shake Claudia's hand. Both women locked eyes when their palms met, as they silently acknowledged each other's identity. The awkward pause was timely interrupted by a man on stage announcing the band.

Jordan turned toward her friends and excused herself. Claudia stood watching the woman she was now certain was her online lover briskly walk toward the outdoor balcony. Glen sighed heavily as he watched her leave. He started to follow, then realizing Claudia was standing next to him, he stopped himself.

"Well, that didn't go too badly, did it? She at least gave me eye contact," he scoffed. "But did you notice that odd look on her face when she shook your hand? Do you think she is jealous?"

"I don't know. Are you hoping she is?" Claudia looked up at Glen with lifted eyebrows.

"Maybe so. Maybe so. I guess I would like that."

"Well, didn't you say earlier that she'd been married three times before, and that turned you off?"

"Yes, I did, didn't I? Thanks for reminding me. I won't ever get involved with a woman who changes husbands like she does her underwear."

"Glen, I've been married four times," Claudia announced, holding up four fingers in front of his face to make her point. "Four."

"WHAT?" Glen's face contorted into a grimace, and at that moment he looked very unattractive.

"Yeah, four times and if you'll excuse me, I think our date has just ended." Claudia stuffed the half-empty glass into his hand and walked toward the balcony. She spotted Jordan leaning over the railing, looking down at the street below.

Claudia stood next to her and looked up at the moon. "I lost a good friend not long ago. I sure would like to have her back in my life," she spoke softly.

"I've missed you," Jordan whispered, without looking up.

"I know."

"Do you think we can get past this? I mean, it was a lie what we had," Jordan said.

"Just a simple lie, nothing really harmful. We became friends without even being together. It didn't matter what our gender was. The way I see it, we're the kind of people that fall in love easily anyway. You could've been an eighty-year-old. I could've been a pervert. Instead, we're girlfriends."

"Yes, but I really was falling in love with Henry," Jordan sighed and turned her direction.

"And I fell in love with you."

With that confession, they looked into each other's eyes and deeply considered one another, until Jordan playfully grimaced and Claudia suitably recovered with an explanation for both of them. "Look, I think we're just addicted to love after all, Jordan. So, what? I can think of worse things to be addicted to. One thing I do know is I needed a friend and so did you. We found each other and what were the odds we'd finally meet? I mean, come on, meeting Glen and coming here, and...."

"Crazy, isn't it?" Jordan chuckled, looking toward the crowd. "Really crazy."

Claudia turned Jordan around and hugged her tightly. "Well, one thing for sure, I'm glad I'm not six-foot-five," she laughed, standing back, her hands on Jordan's shoulders.

"And I'm glad you're not really a man. The odds that a man can be a woman's best friend is nearly impossible," Jordan said convincingly. "I guess it's better this way. At least we won't get married again. Ugh, I can't believe I even said the word."

Claudia rolled her eyes, recalling how her friends used to roll theirs at her when she said she'd never remarry. "Come on, Jordan. Look around. There are plenty of gorgeous men at this party. Let's just do what we do best. Let's be like Pebbles. Let's go fall in love again!"

"Pebbles?"

"I'll explain later. Meanwhile, I've got dibs on that hunk standing by the bar."

As Long As You're Here

"As long as you're here, Marshall, make yourself useful. Pick up that basket and take it to the laundry room, and along the way, shut my bedroom door, it gets too cold in there with the door open, and if you can remember on your way back, pick up my house slippers, my bunions are freezing. Last time I was this cold I lived in Wisconsin. That was sure a long time ago, and little did I know I'd end up in this Texas hell-hole where my ex-husband abandoned me!"

I dropped the basket in the tiny laundry room. Spotting my grandmother's bras and panties draped over a pole, I winced and turned so quickly, I tripped over a broom used to hold the door open. Sitting against the wall, waiting for my knee to stop throbbing, I could still hear my grandmother rambling on about the grandfather I've never met, the dirty old bastard that left her alone in this very same house with a belly full of her only child, my father.

It's hard to feel sorry for the old gal when she's ranting. She could've had a different life, remarried a nice man, but she was determined to stay independent, occasionally allowing a man-friend to visit. No one would have ever known except for the scent of menthol cigarettes they left behind soaked in the slip covers on the hard vinyl sofa where they propped up their

bare feet and watched the one station available out here in the
sticks where Grams says the mold grows faster than weeds, and
cobwebs clump up everywhere like the brown spots on her
arms, thighs and butt.

"I was so bored one day," she rambled on, as if I were right
in the room with her, "I took a pen and drew dot-to-dot to
every brown spot I could see on my wrinkled old body. It took
me two weeks to get it to fade after my doctor said I looked
like a tatted motorcycle slut, and that is not what a lovely
grandmother of seventy-four should look like. Hey, Marshall!
Come see the state of Florida. It's still on my thigh. Everything
else is faded...much like my life."

I'm a writer, well, a freelancer, that is. I've been published
a few times. They actually paid me for my stories, but not
enough to make a decent living, and not enough to get a respectable book agent to take me seriously. I'm also an editor on
the side, but I haven't had a solid job in some time. So, here I
am at my grandmother's home. It's small and smells like her,
but it's a place to rest my thirty-year-old weary head. I'm told
I'm too young to be weary, but I am.

The idea of looking at my grandmother's thigh with the
faded map of the sunshine state made me shiver. It's not that
I can't handle old people's decay, it's just that I know my
grandmother doesn't really want to act this way, vulgar and
angry at the world. She's always been a little rough around
the edges, but I liked that about her. She used to be a more
active, loving woman. She's changed since then, for reasons
I don't like to think about. But now that I'm here, it's un-
avoidable. You see, her son, my father, well, he was killed. I
never really knew the true reason for his death, but people
whispered behind cupped hands whenever they'd see me, like
they knew what I wasn't supposed to know. Fortunately for

me, I was struggling through my first year of college and left all that behind.

I couldn't hide out in the hallway all day, so I told my grandmother I'd see the map another time, kissed her on her rippled forehead and drove toward the city to the nearest bar, promising to bring her soup and a six pack when I returned. It's then that I'll drop the bomb on her that her only grandson, Marshall, is a failure and needs a place to stay for just awhile, just long enough to….

Austin has changed into a frenzy of folks trying to recover from the recession. It's now so saturated, I find myself on the outskirts looking in, when once I hung out on Sixth Street surrounded by writers, musicians and old retirees with fat wallets trying desperately to rediscover their youth, bobbing their heads to 60's and 70's cover songs that our generation had recycled. There's still an old saloon just off the main road that has managed to remain completely intact, nestled in a small community of run-down houses without deed restrictions. I swear every time I go there, I see the ghosts of popular Austin musicians, Stevie Ray Vaughn, Doug Sahm, Townes Van Zandt, standing in the shadows tapping their feet to the music with a bottle of whiskey in their withering fingerpicking hands.

The bartender there works seven days a week. He's saving his money to go to Istanbul with a detour to Thailand where he is certain he'll find a better life and never have to return to this materialistic country ever again. John, Frederick, Sam, he gives me a different name every time we meet. Says it keeps him from going insane. Tonight, he's Steve, and he's wearing a

Tommy Bahama shirt that's as faded as the old Austin I used to love. His shorts look as though they've been handed down one too many times. I'm afraid to bend over the bar and see his feet.

"Written anymore stories?" Steve remembers to ask me, although I haven't been in this bar for months.

"Sure, lots. None published though. Guess it's my subject matter," I answered him honestly.

"Ah, still trying to make a political stance, are you?"

"Yeah, with a touch of anger and bitterness, just enough to make the reader want to either throw up or write the editor and complain." I took a gulp of beer, so cold, so refreshing, I chugged half of it down. "Ah, this Thirsty Goat is one smooth beer."

Steve put his elbow on the bar and leaned in, tapping me gently on the forehead with a yellow pencil that matched his yellow smoke-stained fingernails. "Why don't you try writing about real people, you know good folks like me, people with dreams and obstacles, kids, dogs, and all the fears that are wrapped up inside that brown paper package we call life."

I drew back on the bar stool, away from the teeth-marked pencil and smiled warily at the poet standing before me. "You, you want me to write about *you*? Um, no offense, Steve, but I can't imagine a bartender's life being all that noteworthy to write about."

"Oh, I see." Steve leaned in closer. "You'd be quite surprised about my life. You'd be surprised about most people you meet. There are stories inside of all of us. Good ones, too. Just hidden there like fancy feathers, waiting to be plucked. All you have to do is ask and dig a little deeper into our souls. Maybe, into your own soul."

I thought about what Steve said as I watched him high-five a hefty woman with a crew-cut dressed in army fatigues pouring her a shot of tequila and one for himself. Their laughter filled the bar – a signal that the party had begun, and everyone at the tables began to talk louder.

The second beer took longer to drink, as I pondered all the people I had met in my life and what stories they might share. I left half of the third beer on the counter, waved goodbye to Steve and walked into the cool December night. On the way to my grandmother's I remembered that she wanted me to pick up beer and soup. I guessed at what she might like, based on the smell in the refrigerator and the empty bottles in the recycling can, so I picked up onion soup and a six pack of Lone Star.

The old gal was sitting on the front porch when I arrived. She was listening to vinyl records spinning on an ancient turntable. A small cigar was burning in a ceramic ashtray shaped like a lizard, next to it a tall plastic glass containing melting ice.

"Got your soup and beer," I said, carrying two cold ones outside and using my foot to stop the screen door from slamming.

"You're a good boy," she replied sleepily, accepting the beer and looking up at me with gentle eyes; eyes void of bad thoughts. "I've missed you, grandson. It's really wonderful to see you."

I was relieved to see the face of the grandmother I used to adore, the one who taught me to peel an apple in one long piece, how to drive stick shift in my great grandfather's old Chevy, and who introduced me to Mozart and Haydn and books that inspired me to become a writer. I patted her on the head, pulled up a chair and stared into the night; Nat King Cole singing from within the old house I barely knew anymore.

We sat silently for a while. I drifted off to places I shouldn't go, and only when my grandmother took a drag from her cigar and said my name did I remember she was sitting on the porch with me.

"Marshall," she said, while I watched the thick smoke swirl lazily into the night air, "I imagine things aren't so good for you now, since you haven't had anything published in a while. Why do you think that is?"

"Writer's block, maybe. I don't know."

"Fear, maybe, fear of the unknown?" The old gal cocked her head to the side and lifted her eyebrow.

"Oh, I guess you know about my financial state. Been talking to my ex-wife lately?"

"Well, we did chat a bit. I saw her in the hardware store yesterday and she said you might be coming to visit. She looks a little scrawny these days. That new boyfriend of hers doesn't seem to keep her fat and happy. Maybe she shouldn't have…"

"Please Grams, please don't start on Sherry. She's not the reason I'm not doing well. I take full responsibility."

"OK, I'll be quiet. But you know Marshall, it seems to me that you don't want to hear much about anyone's life. Your writing is, well, about stuff that doesn't really make a difference. It's good writing, don't get me wrong, but there's so much more you can offer your readers. Take my life for instance."

"You're not going to start ragging on your ex-husband again, are you? Isn't there a statute of limitations for holding a grudge as long as you have?"

"Well, if I didn't stay angry, I'd be crying all the time. Life hasn't been all that good to your old grandmother." She paused to suck in a mouthful of tobacco smoke.

I started to feel uneasy. I know what hurts my grandmother. It hurts me, too. That's why I won't and never have talked about it. But I haven't popped the question about living with her, so I decided I'd better let her say her piece.

"I can tell you one nice thing about your grandfather. When I married him," she began slowly, her rough voice softening, "he was a jewel of a man. He opened the door for me, even in the house. Can you imagine that? Even in the house." She rested her head on the back of the rocker and smiled at the sky. Seconds later a scowl appeared across her face. "Then he moved me to Texas for a job. Always promising me that it was only for a few years until we could save enough to move back to Wisconsin and start a farm. He inherited two-hundred beautiful acres." She hissed under her breath, "Son of a bitch."

I pretended not to hear that last line but saying something nice about the rotten grandfather I never knew threw me for a loop. I was sensing what I thought might be the calm before the storm.

"You know he traveled a lot," she continued in a serious tone. "Sometimes he'd be gone as long as a month. The first year was hard, but after that, I got used to his absences, looking forward to his return because he always came home happy and never empty handed. It was in our third year that I learned he had another wife back in Wisconsin. Bet you didn't know that part, did you, Marshall?"

I perked up and lost control of my jaw. Snapping my mouth shut, I answered, "No, Grams, I didn't know that. Holy cow, he was married to two women at the same time? How awful. How awful for you."

"Yes, it was. I made a huge fuss and demanded a divorce. I mean, please, it's against the law to have more than one wife in our country. Besides, I also learned that they had three children. It only made sense that I give him up, or he'd end up in jail and leave those poor kids without a father. It was the right thing to do, I think."

"But Grams, you also had a child – my dad."

"Well, yes, I did. He was in my womb at the time and I didn't even know it. I was so hurt, so devastated, so angry.

When I found out I was pregnant, it just made me angrier. But when your dad was born, beautiful, strong willed, with that gentle spirit, I replaced all those bad feelings with my love for him."

We both sat silently slipping into a respectful reverie for my dad, who was all those things and more, but the questions wouldn't let me stay there long. "I never heard my dad mention his father. Is that because he didn't know about him?"

"He knew only a little of him, Marshall. But, because I didn't want to hurt him about the other family, I couldn't tell him the rotten truth. Eventually he found out. Seems someone spilled the beans. Your dad was very unhappy with me for a long time. Then he went to meet Jim face to face. That's his name...Jim."

"No kidding? When did all this happen?" I started trying to piece together my life while my dad was alive. "I never heard anything about that or anyone named Jim."

"That's because, because, this happened when, well, right before my son..." Grams stopped cold and couldn't say the words that even to this day, I can't say out loud. Murder comes off the lips like the word suicide; ugly and bitter tasting and when it's said, it hangs in the air like the smell of decaying road kill.

Grams wiped her eyes with the back of her hand.

"Truth is, if he hadn't known about his father, well, he'd be alive today."

"What are you saying?" I jumped up from my chair. "What are you saying, Grams?"

"I'm saying...I shouldn't have told him. It's because I told him...I caused my son's.... "

"My God, woman! How did YOU cause it?" I yelled into her face, suddenly losing my temper over something that happened twelve years ago. Where did this anger come from? I collected my wits and sat back in the chair. Softening my tone, I asked again, "How did *you* cause it, Grams?"

"After your dad learned about his father's bigamy, he became very upset and demanded that I tell him where he lived. I didn't want to tell him. I mean, what good would it do? But, I couldn't lie anymore, and your dad deserved the truth...and so do you."

I've never wanted to know the truth about anything. Writing conveniently helped me hide from it. Maybe it's time I did. With some reluctance, I gave my grandmother permission to continue. "Go on, tell me the rest."

"Well, your father, determined to seek him out, drove himself all the way to Wisconsin. I was a nervous wreck while he was gone. Your mom was beside herself, but she understood and didn't try to stop him. Guilt runs deep in this family, Marshall. Deep."

The suspense was mounting within me, and her pause after that remark sure didn't make this conversation any easier.

"So, what I know is that when he got to the farm, at first, he didn't get to meet Jim, but he met one of his adult sons. According to him, Jim's latest wife had recently died giving birth to their fourth child. The child died, too. There was also another woman living there. He said she was a sheepish young thing who locked herself in the bedroom when he arrived. As he was leaving, she ran out to his car and gave him the address where Jim was staying part time with another woman in a nearby town. Then she told him that she was married to Jim. It was all so confusing, all those wives. Can you imagine such a thing?"

I couldn't imagine anything she was saying. She took my silence for an answer.

"But instead of just coming back home and leaving it alone, your dad was so outraged, he decided he had to find him."

I found myself perched on the edge of the chair sitting on my hands, her trembling voice nursing the sick feeling festering inside me. She could see I was trying not to run away.

"Yes, he found him alright. But what happened wasn't like something in the movies, the typical scene, father and son meet for the first time, teary-eyed, hugs and all. No, nothing as nice as that. When he met Jim, the other wife was with him. They had twin babies sitting in a playpen in a small apartment near the college campus. Your dad said he was so upset, he couldn't stop himself, and he told Jim that he knew everything and even went beyond that and told the new wife about the other families. She started crying. The babies started crying and before he knew it, Jim threatened to call the authorities, and your dad ran out of that place driving like a bat out of hell down an old farm road until he ran out of gas. He called me from someone's house. He didn't know where he was. He didn't make any sense. And that's the last time I would ever hear my son's sweet voice again."

My grandmother put her face in her hands and wept. I bit my bottom lip until it bled. I knew at that moment I should sit next to her and comfort her, or at least say something soothing. But I couldn't do it. I sat there on my numb hands, completely dumbfounded. The questions rushed at me like a pack of dogs, but only one stood out. "Grams, did Jim kill my dad?"

She composed herself and sat up straight, as if crying had become second-nature since that horrible day. "We all knew he was killed on that road, but we don't know how it happened."

"Haven't you always wondered?"

THE JUICY PARTS AND OTHER QUIRKY STORIES

"Yes."

"The man had multiple wives and multiple families and lied to everyone. And he never cared about my dad. It seems to me that he would be capable of anything. Was he questioned?"

"Of course, he was. I told the police everything, but he had a solid alibi. One of the wives claimed he was at home with her when it happened."

I shook my head in disbelief. I had known my father had been killed by a blow to his head and that there were no witnesses or clues. I gave up wondering about that when I left for college. Lots of pot and beer and an overload of classes kept my mind busy. But now, that ugly question is here to haunt me again. This time with a name. Jim.

"Marshall, Jim died of a heart attack while in prison a year after all that happened."

"Oh?" That statement took me a few minutes to register. "Why was he in prison?"

"Bigamy. It *is* a crime. You could say I got my revenge after all. But, just imagine, if I had not told my son where Jim lived." My grandmother turned her head in shame. It was then that I realized she was not only sharing, she was purging, confessing.

I can't control these horrible thoughts running through my head – that she is right, if she hadn't told my dad about his father, he'd be here sitting next to me right now, patting my grandmother's hand while I laughed at his silly jokes. All would be well with the world. I would feel whole again. I wanted to hate her for what she'd done, but when I looked at the agony in her face, the hardened wrinkles around her sad eyes etched from years of mourning and the burden of carrying that awful guilt, I began to feel a deep sadness for her. I'm not a parent, but right now, I am full of empathy, imagining how she must feel, losing her child, her only child and blaming herself. While she held back her tears, mine began to flow.

"Oh, Grams, I should have been here for you. I should have helped you through this. This guilt you're carrying is unjustified. It's made you bitter and robbed you of your sweet life. You have to let it go. You just have to." Where these words came from, I do not know, but I felt as if something had burst inside me.

And when I sat close to her and held her hand, I felt like I was eighteen again. All the pain I had stuffed since my dad died surfaced. I cried in my grandmother's arms until my voice became a whimper. The gentle patting of her hand on my back soothed me to a stillness, and in that humbling moment, she spoke the words that would help set us free. "God, grant us the serenity to accept the things we cannot change, the courage to change the things we can, and the wisdom to know the difference."

I knew then why I had come. It was easy for me to ask if I could stay awhile, because now, I didn't just need to, I wanted to. "Grams, may I…?"

"Yes, of course, you can stay. I got your room ready yesterday, silly boy." She pulled me toward her and kissed my cheek. Her lips were as soft as I remember them years ago. "Now, go unpack that car before my neighbors call the cops. It's so full of shit, it looks like two Sumo wrestlers are stuffed in the back seat."

I'm on my way back home from delivering my latest story to the Texas Gazette, who I have been steadily writing for this past year. From there my stories have been published in various magazines across the country. The one that got my career going again was one I wrote about my grandmother. From then on, no one has been a stranger, and my stories are rich with their histories. I'm not a big success, but I'm busy and can handle my bills much easier, not to mention, my own life. And even Grams has made some changes, including no more cigars and cheap beer, but the cursing habit she says may take some time, so now she's spelling out the cuss words instead. Kind of cute. We actually enjoy living together. Seems we needed each other more than we knew.

On the refrigerator is a note from my roommate:

Will be back in a couple of days. Off to visit an old friend. Left two steaks marinating for you and that new girlfriend with the funny spelling name. As long as you're here, make yourself useful and take out the garbage and for heaven's sake, change the sheets on your GD bed! Love, Grams.

When I was a young girl, I didn't quite understand eccentricity, but I learned to respect it, mostly because my own family was pretty darn quirky. Now, I understand it completely. Just so happens, I follow a somewhat different orbit, too.

Old Paul Elly

Not many people would smile at old man Paul Elly. Sitting near the curb slumped over in a plastic lawn chair wearing his dark blue house robe and worn-out army boots he could have easily been mistaken for a rusty yard ornament. I don't know why it is that one day I felt compelled to greet the broken-down, gray-haired geezer that no one acknowledged. I tend to do things like that, off the cuff. Something deep within drives me that way.

Everyone in our small suburban cul-de-sac knew Paul Elly as the crazy old grandfather visiting the Connors', whose household consisted of two ill-mannered teenagers, parents that both worked and yelled a lot, and an ugly dog that barked incessantly until what started out loud and bold at the break of dawn, ended in a wheeze by dusk. The other families steered their children away from the paint-chipped house on the corner, quickly picking up their pace every time they walked past the unkempt yard.

I was a tall and gangly eleven-year-old living next door to the Connors with my younger sister and older brother, a two years' difference either way. Our mother was the kindest woman you'd ever meet. She refused to talk badly about anyone, and I swear I never heard one cuss word come out of that beautiful mouth. Never. It was my capricious and witty Irish father with the hypersensitive skin that cornered the market on profanity.

The first time I saw Paul Elly was on a late Saturday afternoon, seconds before dark, returning home in our 1961 Plymouth sedan after spending the day at the YMCA. There he was, buck-naked showering under the garden hose in the front yard of the Connors' home. My mother turned off the car lights and entered the driveway slowly, so as not to disturb him.

"Mom, he doesn't have any clothes on!" my little sister shrilled, while I pressed my body against the back seat, holding my breath, squinting, trying not to look, as my brother leaned out the window, his eyes practically popping out of his square head.

"Quiet now, kids. Give the man his privacy, and when you get out of the car, don't say a word and go directly into the house." Our mother's soft and velvety voice made us want to follow her to the moon.

Somehow, I knew my mother was right, and even at my young age I didn't quite understand eccentricity, but I learned to respect it, mostly because my own family was pretty quirky. My silly dad wrote funny jingles while sitting on the toilet – he said the bathroom was an inspirational place to create. And my mother tried, in vain, to teach her clumsy daughters how to tap dance in the garage, while my brother raised pigeons, a raccoon, a rooster, and for one short week, a pony that had wandered into our small backyard. My chubby sister loved to sing like Ethel Merman and her sturdy voice would resonate throughout the entire house. Me, well, I sat in trees like a monkey for hours on end contemplating my small world and sometimes allowing my thoughts to venture beyond the rooftops. We were anything but ordinary.

Occasionally, unusual and interesting family members from all over would come to visit. Like the time my little Aunt Alma, who was a mere four-feet-six-inches, (my mother said her growth and intellect was stunted from lack of oxygen when she was born) came from Kansas with her seven-foot-tall boyfriend who would hold her on his lap while they sipped beer when visiting with my parents. They looked like a ventriloquist act. I can't explain that unsettling feeling I had seeing the giant man frequently lean down and kiss my tiny aunt.

When my grandmother from Oklahoma visited, she brought along her sister – a disturbingly obese woman in thick pancake make-up and bright red rouge, who huffed and puffed just to get across the room. She would insist that one of us rub her fat, aching feet with a dreadful whine that would send us kids and the dog flying out the screen door not wanting to return until we were called in for dinner, or she drove north, whichever came first.

My grandmother was just the opposite, kind and lovely; she wore furs and expensive jewelry and a hat with a tiny feather. She looked odd sitting on our old, brown, vinyl couch in her stockings and leather heels. When I hugged her, she smelled like a gardenia doused in a sweet liqueur that made me a little nauseated. I asked my mother about the powerful scent, and she said that elderly people liked to wash their clothes in some kind of sweet perfume concoction – they did it to hide the old people odor. I didn't understand what my mother meant until later.

Angelina, my mother's cousin, resembled and longed to be Carmen Miranda, dubbed the Brazilian Bombshell, a famous singer that wore fruit on her head in the 1940's. Angelina came to visit our simple home one summer toting a cornucopia of fruit-laden hats in the trunk of her car. That night my mother shoved all the furniture against the wall and cleared a path for her to give us a special performance. There she stood in our tiny living room with my family sitting erect, hands in our laps watching this vulgar woman shaking and swaying her body, snapping her fingers and trying not to trip over our German Shepherd while holding the fruit bowl on her head in a comical attempt to entertain us. My father nearly fell off his chair laughing, and my sister and I sang "Chica Chica Boom" for the next two weeks until my mother begged us to stop.

So, seeing Paul Elly showering in the yard, just feet from my bedroom window, didn't make me feel all that uneasy. I think he did everything he could to stay outdoors; avoiding the terrible occupants living inside. That evening while tucked in my bed, I listened to him whistle lullabies as he whittled away at a stick with a knife. The delicate tunes lulled me to sleep, and I dreamed that I could whistle just like him.

On Sundays we always had waffles and stacks of bacon and sausage and the smell of all those things mixed with coffee brewing seemed to make the whole family happy. No one spoke at the breakfast table about the strange incident – a naked man showering in his front yard was not nearly as important as who would get the next waffle.

After everyone ate, and I helped clean up the kitchen, I went outside to see what the day held, while my stuffed and content siblings lounged in front of the TV watching the

Dallas Cowboys game with our father. He was the ruler of the
television set, and we all knew better than to ask him to change
the channel. Our time would come later that evening when
Disney came on, and mom would make a special dessert just
for that occasion. We'd sprawl out on the floor holding a big
bowl of ice cream with a brownie on the bottom, sometimes
with a banana and a cherry on top, and we'd never take our
eyes off the little black and white screen. It was a magical hour
that we'd carry throughout the rest of our lives.

Outside it was a warm, but windy day, and with a full
belly and the taste of maple syrup still on my lips, I felt like
the world was all mine. I sat down on the cracked pavement
and watched ants struggling to carry things bigger than their
bodies across the wide driveway. Their determination reminded me of my mother and how hard she worked each day
to get the house clean, the ironing done, and dinner ready
before my dad arrived from a hard day welding ornamental
iron. She adored him and did everything to make him comfortable. It was the same for her children, but we knew that
dad always came first.

The neighborhood was quiet. I guessed they were all
mostly at church; not crowded around the television like
my family. I thought I had the cul-de-sac all to myself until
I heard whistling to my left. Under the pretty Spanish Oak –
the only nice feature of the Connors' place – sat Paul Elly. He
was looking down at something in his hand and whistling up
a storm. I didn't know the song, but it was charming, and it
circled around my head and lured me toward the old man.
"That's a pretty tune you're whistling," I said, standing just near
enough to make sure he had on all his clothes.

Paul Elly tiredly raised his head, almost as if it was too
heavy to lift, while fumbling for his shirt pocket where he

stuffed the photo that he had held in his hand before he slowly smiled at me. The teeth in his mouth seemed very tiny for his face, but his smile was nice just the same. He had the bluest eyes, nearly as blue as my little sister's, only his were small and half hidden behind flaps of drooping eyelids that made him look sad. He twitched his mouth back and forth, as if he were winding it up to talk, then he said, "Like my whistling, do you?"

"I do. It's really nice. I try to whistle like that. Sometimes I sit up in that big tree over there and practice." I pointed to the grand oak whose limbs stretched across our entire backyard and on windy days, lightly scraped the roof shingles.

Paul Elly turned to look behind him and said, "Oh yes, that's a great place to practice, right up there with the birds." Then he asked, "Can you whistle me a tune?"

I bit my bottom lip and felt myself smile, an awkward smile as if he'd just asked me to perform in front of my entire fifth grade class. "I, uh, well, I've been practicing, but I can't whistle like you. But, I sure do want to."

"Let me hear what you got." Paul Elly slowly lifted his gnarly hand and wiggled his index finger, signaling me to start.

I pursed my lips and out came a tiny whistle that sounded so bad I had to muffle a laugh. I tried again, and a little more sound came out. This time I couldn't hold back the laughter, imagining my lips sticking out like a chimpanzee, my eyes bulging. I'm sure it wasn't a pretty picture.

"Hmmm," he moaned, studying my face and waiting for me to compose myself. "Put your tongue behind your bottom teeth. Don't press hard, just let it stay there and try again."

I did as he told and after a few blows, I made a better sound.

"Now what's one of your favorite songs?" He bent over to pull up his sock that had inched its way down into his old boot.

"Oh, let's see. I like Raindrops on Roses and Whiskers on Kittens…On Top of Old Smokey all covered with cheese… and my favorite that my mom sings to us is Que Sera, Sera, you know, the one that Doris Day sings."

The last song made the old man perk up and while he shifted in his chair, he directed me to sit down. I sat not far from his feet, folding my legs underneath me in an Indian style, the thick Augustine grass tickling my ankles.

"Que Sera, Sera is a good start, because the notes aren't too high for you," he began. "You want to start with a comfortable song first."

I'm not sure how long I sat there transfixed, listening to Paul Elly teach me to whistle. His words were simple but made so much sense. He said that when he was a boy he had learned to whistle from a black man that sang the blues. The stories he told about his childhood in Louisiana made me laugh. Then he asked me if I had homework and told me I should go home and do it now so that I had time later to climb the big oak before dark and practice whistling. I did what he said, and I stayed up in that tree until my lips were chapped from licking them too much.

It had been the perfect weekend, and I felt good whistling on the way to school the next day. My little sister, watching me in awe as I held her hand to cross the busy street, eagerly waited until I was finished to ask me how I did it. When I told her that it was Old Paul Elly who had taught me, she was horrified.

"Don't be silly," I scoffed. "He's a nice man."

I couldn't wait until school let out so that I could show Paul Elly what I had learned. When we got to our house, I was pleased to see him sitting in his lawn chair in the same place by the tree. My little sister ran past him, nervously glancing over her shoulder, anxious to get inside to the safety of our mother's arms, not really knowing why. I stopped at the curb and waited for Paul Elly to lift his head. When he didn't, I slowly approached him and cleared my throat to wake him.

"Sir, sir, it's me. Are you awake?" I said softly, not wanting to startle him.

He slowly lifted his head, just as he did the day before and gave me the same smile, only a little wider.

"Here for your second lesson?" he asked.

"Yes, thank you. I did really good up in the tree yesterday. My mom put lots of Vaseline on my lips before I went to bed. I think I licked them a little more than I should have."

"Can't do that. You have to rest in between, or it'll become work instead of fun."

He whistled an Irish tune for me that sounded like the one my father sang while puttering around in the garage. I sat down in the same spot and waited patiently for his next instruction. When we finished, we whistled a tune together just before my brother called me in.

That evening while doing my homework on my bed, I heard whistling outside my window. I got on my knees and peered out, and beyond the bushes I could see just a little of old Paul Elly's lily-white bottom while he showered under the garden hose. He seemed really happy, and I thought about how great I felt playing under the water sprinkler during the summer and how good it felt to whistle, and it occurred to me that it wasn't weird at all that old Paul Elly was doing something he liked, only with less clothes on. I smiled and went back to my homework, knowing that it was disrespectful to spy, even though my sister and I did that once when my brother had a really cute friend over that we just couldn't help staring at. He was the closest thing to Ricky Nelson we'd ever seen, except for the limp, and for years after, my little sister told everyone with certainty that the famous singer had visited our home. There were times I actually believed her.

∽

I really like Tuesdays. I can't explain why. Just the name alone makes me happy. It's like having two days in one. So, when I got home from school, I was already in a good mood before I walked over to visit Paul Elly. He sure does sleep a lot, I thought, tiptoeing up to him so as not to scare him.

"Mr. Paul Elly," I said softly. "Mr. Elly," I said again. Then I tried, "Paul Elly, sir." He didn't move, so I cleared my throat and plunked my books loudly onto the ground. He still didn't move.

I don't know why I didn't walk away and just let the man sleep. Somehow, I knew he enjoyed my company, so I didn't think it would bother him for me to wake him up. I tapped his shoulder, and he didn't move at all. I tapped it again and then before I did it a third time, I noticed in his hand a black and white picture of a pretty woman standing next to a younger Paul Elly.

I stood back and studied him, so peaceful, the sunlight shining on his hands, shadows of leaves moving slowly across the faces in the photo. A fly landed on his ear and then walked around to his nose. Paul Elly didn't flinch or even swat at it. When the fly landed on his mouth, I had to do something to stop that filthy insect from carrying germs to my friend. So, I brushed it off his mouth, but my fingers hit his lips, and Paul Elly's head fell forward, and in slow motion his entire body crumbled to the ground. There he lay in a heap with only the sound of the thud left hanging in the air, as the wind carried the picture across the yard.

I ran to pick it up and returned hoping to see the old man sitting up laughing at his silly fall. "Paul Elly, Paul Elly!" I cried. "I'm sorry, I'm sorry, I didn't mean to knock you out of your chair!" His body was stiff, and only the little tuft of hair at the back of his head moved with the breeze. I leaned over him and said his name again, and at that moment I smelled the old people odor that my mother told me my grandmother hid with perfume. It was pungent and strange. I made a sour face and stepped back.

I wanted to pick him up and place him back on the chair, but I tried to picture myself lifting him, like I've tried to lift my older brother, and I knew I didn't have the strength or the height. So, I decided right then to whistle a song for him, thinking maybe he would like that enough to get up himself.

I whistled *Que Sera, Sera*, the best I could, and it sounded so good to me that I knew he'd lift his head and smile at me with his small teeth. Then when I got to the end, I barely sang the words, "what will be, will be", and with the picture still in my hand, I ran home crying to my mother, knowing then that something was terribly wrong.

It seemed like it took forever for Saturday to come. We took our regular trip to the Y and when we slowly drove up our driveway, I looked for Paul Elly, hoping to see him showering under the garden hose whistling a tune. He wasn't there. My mom reached over and touched my hand and said, "He's not coming back, honey. It was his time to go. But don't you worry, he's with his sweet wife now."

That night, the wind picked up and the moon was full, and it filled my bedroom with so much light, I thought I could read by it. Lying on my belly, squinting over an Archie comic book, I calmly listened for a whistled tune beyond my window. When I thought I heard it, I jumped up on all fours and strained to hear more. It turned out to be only the wind, slipping in and out of the chain-link fence entwined with clinging rose vines that my mom had planted neatly along the side of the house. I was feeling restless, so I put on the clothes I had worn that day, grabbed my sweater, and carefully pried open the screen on the window. I had done that many times before during the summer when Mother thought I was napping. Effortlessly, I slipped out into the moonlit night.

It was easy to see the limbs on the old oak tree, and I thought I could've climbed them blindfolded anyway. I had memorized the shape of each knot in the branches that I had used to lift myself higher, and I knew the perfect place to sit and lean my back against the trunk, letting my legs either dangle or rest on the limbs below. From that spot the whole moon was in view, situated between two branches and right where I could watch it without moving my head. I took out the picture of Mr. and Mrs. Paul Elly from my sweater pocket and carefully secured it between my knees. I puckered my lips and whistled the song I learned was called Danny Boy that I once heard stream from Paul Elly's old lips and from my own father's voice earlier that day. When I got to the last verse I sang the words softly just for Old Paul Elly, "I'll simply sleep in peace until you come to me."

Then I whistled the song again, this time for his lovely wife.

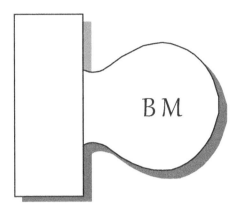

(Bathroom Material)

I came from a one-bathroom family, and there were seven of us! That kind of closeness makes for a whole lot of humor, and one of the reasons I love the bathroom so much and why I dedicated a chapter of short stories to be read in that particular room.

Some are written for those quick trips; others written for those wonderful leg-numbing visits when the bathroom is truly yours and for another thirty minutes thereafter. I really believe that this is where these stories belong – in the only room in the house where we truly let it all go!

At The Bar

"My name is Sondra, but I'd rather be called Eve," the newcomer at the bar said nonchalantly to the man next to her. Then she turned to me, because I was on her opposite side, evidently eavesdropping, and repeated the introduction.

"Oh," I said, relieved to be jolted out of my boredom from having sat alone talking only to myself until this woman arrived, "I like the name, Eve."

Sondra reported, "It's actually my sister's name, but I like it better than mine, so I think I'm going to use it for a while."

"Ohh," I said again and pretended to slap myself. "Of course. Why not?" The bartender caught my eye and stifled a laugh. Already, I could tell this was going to be interesting.

Looking straight ahead expressionless, Sondra took a big gulp of the frozen margarita now at her fingertips. "Oh no! Brain freeze!" she cried, massaging her temples vigorously with all ten fingers. Then she tossed her head back and declared in a deadpan tone, "I've always hated my skinny sister."

I thought maybe now I should find something to do with my mouth before I said something idiotic to the fleshy, apple-shaped woman squeezed inside a skintight polyester zebra-striped dress that wanted to steal the name of a sibling she loathes – so, I started nibbling the dry pizza crust on the plate in front of me.

In a sudden move, Sondra swiveled toward me, lowered the leopard print glasses covering the top-half of her ruddy cheeks and narrowed her eyes. "You kind of remind me of my boss. So, what's your name?" Before I could answer she twirled around and asked the man next to her the same.

"I'm Kira," I offered an insincere toast to the braided ponytail at the back of her head.

"I'm Charlie," the man replied, lifting his beer in the air, and before I knew it, we were clinking glasses.

"I think I'm about to be fired from my job," Sondra announced sullenly, fluffing her hair in the gold-flecked mirror behind the bar.

"Oh, that's too bad," I said, followed by Charlie's "that sucks" remark, and then the bartender chimed in with "yeah, that stinks," while the Hispanic dishwasher nodded quietly in agreement.

Bar patrons understand that there are no rules for conversation or etiquette. It's kind of like sitting at the dinner table with a big unruly family. Everyone is privy to what is said and can jump in at will. I've always liked that about bars – this silent pact between complete strangers to talk about whatever zany topic is introduced. That's probably why we don't give out our last names. I think we secretly hope that while under the influence divulging information that may or may not be true, the odds of running into each other out there in the real world are slim.

"My boss made me cry." Sondra tapped her glass and motioned to the bartender for another one. "Fat people always get fired first," she grumbled.

Ignoring the last comment, I decided to be kind and indulge this woman in a sour mood named Sondra who hated her skinny sister but coveted her name and was about to be unemployed by a woman that she claimed looked like me. "What do you do for a living, Sondra, uh, Liza?"

"I'm a receptionist at a massage center." She twisted around to face Charlie and asked, "What do *you* do?"

"I'm a technical support specialist," he answered blandly.

Showing absolutely no interest, Sondra looked over her shoulder at me. "And you?"

"I write fiction. Short stories," I proudly offered. "But I make my living as a social worker."

"Oh, yeah?" Sondra decided now to give me her full attention and faced me head-on. "What are you writing now?"

"I just finished a book of shorts called *BM*. Bathroom Material. Short stories for folks who love to read on the toilet."

"WHAT?" Sondra shrieked. "READ ON THE TOILET?" She plopped down her drink so hard it spilled over onto her hand. "Ewww, I've never heard of such a thing."

Her unpleasant response was not what I expected. "Oh, come on. You're kidding, aren't you?" I looked at her as if she had just told me she wore a size four.

"I think not! That's disgusting!"

"Hey, Charlie, you're obviously a reader," I assumed, pointing at the faded Einstein on the front of his t-shirt, "don't you read on the john?"

"Never," he said, with a curled lip.

"Never?" I asked, totally blown away by his answer. "Not even the label on a tube of ointment?"

"Absolutely not!"

"See?" Sondra gloated and tapped her glass against Charlie's beer.

Feeling outnumbered, I reached out to ask the new arrival next to me the same question, but the guy was on his cell phone, apparently in a seriously heated conversation. I looked over at the bartender, but he quickly turned away and busied himself. The sweet-faced dishwasher shrugged his shoulders helplessly.

Sondra seemed to be pleased with my exasperation and decided to go in for the kill. "Why in the *world* would you name a book that?"

"Well, I doubt you'd understand since you're not a member of the Throne Readers Club, but I write stories that last as long as the experience on the toilet does. You know, three hundred-word short stories for that quick visit, five hundred-words for when the morning coffee kicks in, and a hundred words longer or so when you want to, say, avoid a guest in the house. Those are timed to end just before the feet tingling starts."

Charlie, looking as if he had just swallowed nail polish remover, elbowed Sondra, and they rolled their eyes at each other.

"Well, my family thinks it's a good idea," I said glumly. "Matter of fact, I was raised with four other siblings, and we had only *one* bathroom. The stories I can tell centered around that are hilarious."

"Spare us, pleaseeee," Sondra begged.

So, I did. But, as I sat there nursing my drink and my pride, I felt more and more determined to convince these two nonbelievers that they had the wrong attitude. I just can't imagine anyone with a sense of humor not reading on the toilet, or at least appreciating a book of short stories timed for the ultimate bathroom experience. I was not about to let this go. "You know, there are books about far…well, flatulence that have sold millions. My favorite is a cute little book called *The History of Gas* that's sitting on the back of my toilet right now. Makes my book seem tame compared to those," I explained, turning on my barstool to catch their reactions.

"And your point?" Sondra asked with arms tightly crossed.

I tried not to roll my own eyes and turned back to the bar. "There *is* no point," I said. "There's just people like you and Charlie that don't have a sense of humor for my kind of writing."

"Well, did you read Fifty Shades of Grey?" Sondra asked me.

"*I* did," Charlie inserted his answer instead.

"You *did*?" Sondra batted her eyelashes.

"Oh, yeah…twice."

Emboldened by Charlie's confession, Sondra boasted, "I read it twice, too!" Then she turned back to me. "Did *you* read it?" She pulled her glasses down to her nose again and waited for my answer.

"No, I'm really not interested in that subject matter, but I guess I'm beginning to get your point." I think I would have said almost anything to end this ridiculous conversation that was going nowhere with people that will most likely never cross my path again, much less buy my book.

The guy next to me grumbled, yanked the earbud from his ear and complained to the bartender, "Can't a man get a drink around here?"

Eager to focus on something else, I offered my wisdom to the cute thirty-something year old, "The bartender's name is Nick. I bet if you ask him nicely, you'll have a drink in front of you in no time at all."

"Sorry, I just broke up with my girlfriend…on the cell phone. Not feeling too good about it," he said, scoping me out with his glazed-over eyes. "Well, um…not yet, anyway."

"Oh, that's too bad," I reacted sympathetically, softly patting his arm while taking in his gorgeous profile.

"That really sucks!" Charlie lifted his glass to the situation, as Sondra clucked her tongue, and the bartender stood silently offended at the far end of the bar, while the dishwasher, scrubbing like mad to get a lipstick smear off the rim of a wine glass, vigorously nodded.

"I'm Kira. This is Sondra, uh, or Eve, and that's Charlie," I introduced us all in one fell swoop.

"Gregg," he said, gloomily.

"Hey, Gregg," Sondra prodded, leaning in and invading my space, "any chance you read on the toilet? Kira, here, is taking a survey."

The sarcasm in her tone made me squirm.

Gregg looked at me and hesitated, and I knew right then I was about to be thrown to the wolves. But to my delight, he said, "Sure, I actually have a small library in my bathroom. Why are you asking?"

Sondra shrunk back and rolled her eyes again at Charlie, this time with a little less smugness. I flashed them a grin and repeated the same spiel that I gave them earlier, this time with more enthusiasm.

Gregg laughed heartily. "I'd love to read your BM book. Is it published?"

"Self-published, for now. I made a hundred copies for friends and family. Would you like one? I happen to have a few in my car." Actually, I carry a couple dozen in my trunk just for times like this.

"Sure," Gregg said excitedly, while Charlie and Sondra openly sulked.

Sliding off my seat with a whole new mindset, I sashayed toward the door, and what popped in my head made me turn around and say to Sondra, "Hey, Eve, save my *stool*, will you please?"

When I returned I handed the book to Gregg, and I slid two more down the bar to the skeptics. "Just in case you change your minds. You never know." I threw in a cocky wink and tossed one to the pouting bartender. I couldn't resist the dishwasher's soft brown, pleading eyes, so I reached over the bar and placed one at his elbow.

Thinking it was the perfect time for an exit, I bought a round of drinks for the three of them and bid my farewell. "As much fun as this has been, I do need to run. I've got to get this new stuff in my head down on paper. You all are simply inspirational." I patted Sondra and Charlie on their backs and gave Gregg a warm hug. "You know," I whispered in his ear, "someday I'd love to see your library."

He hugged me back and whispered, "That could be arranged."

I felt my cheeks instantly blush, and all I could think to say was, "Toodle-oo."

"Toodle-oo?" Sondra and Charlie sneered. Gregg's eyes followed me as I exited, and then he settled in to read the book, laughing out loud at the first paragraph.

That night I began a new short story. It ended like this: Sondra hid the stopwatch and the new bestseller by Kira Sheffield in a towel and rushed past her pencil-thin sister, quickly locking the bathroom door behind her. Charlie's feet began to tingle as he sat on the commode engrossed in the book the sexy and beguiling writer at the bar had forced upon him. Meanwhile, Gregg finished the book smiling, and the following morning he dialed the phone number on the card that he had found so cleverly tucked between the pages and called the illustrious author to congratulate her and, of course, to discuss the skillfully written stories over a long, romantic dinner.

Well, a girl can dream, can't she?

Twinkie in the Pantry

I knew I had stayed too long on the throne. The first warning sign was the tingling of my feet. But I was so deeply engrossed in what I was reading that I just couldn't wait hours later to finish it. Captivated and captive in the small windowless bathroom, I continued reading in ultimate privacy. The story was about an older man who had fallen for the owner of a restaurant simply by watching her from the table where he sat eating dinner six nights in a row. He decided he wanted her and set out to win her heart. In his silver years, he wasn't sure if love really mattered anymore – companionship was the necessary component. And it did not matter to him that they were both married.

The writer took the story somewhere I had never anticipated, and it left me thinking for days after. That's not the best place to leave me – my imagination runs amok and that's why standing here at this New Year's Eve party I am slowly waking up to the world I'm in. Especially after watching Marie lean against my husband, Joe, and whisper in his ear, her glossy red lips lingering just inches from his freshly shaven neck. It isn't the act that is really bothering me. It's that Joe had closed his eyes with that dreamy look on his face that I haven't seen in years since the time I spoon fed him my *Better than Sex* cake. That's not a look one easily forgets, but Joe and I have been a little off-key lately and after twenty years of marriage, things are becoming a bit fuzzy.

"Charlene, come taste my artichoke dip. It's wicked!" Helen's raucous voice pulled me from my trance.

Oh sure, that's exactly what I need, another calorie to add to the rest that had settled in my midriff and lately shifted to my arms. *Wattle,* I was told it was called: a fleshy lobe hanging from the neck, but in my case, from under the arms. I remember my cousin complaining about hers while holding her sleeveless arm up and shaking the loose fat just to annoy me. "You'll get yours, just wait and see," she promised me, the look on her face just a tad shy of evil. I had scratched her name off a party list I was planning for Joe's fiftieth birthday, only later to pencil it back in after my mother insisted that I was being too sensitive and a little cruel – she had to tell me this right after she showed me her *own* wattle.

Helen plopped a big chunk of dip onto a wheat cracker and fed it to me. I could barely keep it all in my mouth and had to use my fingers to direct it. "Wow, you are right. This is scrumptious," I said, licking the remains from beneath my bottom lip. "About as scrumptious as Marie looks tonight," I added facetiously with a hint of sarcasm, certain that Helen would love the chance to gossip. I pointed to the vixen with only my eyes and without turning my head – a skill we women have perfected over the years.

"Oh, yesss," Helen cooed, disguising her expression by placing her shiny orange fingertips lightly over her mouth. "She's quite the package tonight." Then she looked around the room for Marie's husband. "Hmmm, looks like Burnie isn't here. Better warn the wives," she giggled, elbowing me in the side.

"Why?" I attempted to look innocent.

"Haven't you heard? She and Burnie are on the outs. Word on the street says that she's got another Twinkie in the pantry."

I hate when Helen talks like that. Why can't she just tell it like it is. It's almost as if she is afraid she'd make it real if she did. It was like when I was a teen and my mother would say, 'Watch your p's and q's,' as I was heading out the door to a party. It took me years to figure out what she meant, and I don't think pints and quarts was what she had in mind.

"Oh, too bad. I like Burnie," I said. I generally root for the underdog, especially if they are short and bald and their wives are that attractive.

"You know Twinkies have a very *long* shelf life. It's all the *sugar*." Helen eyed me warily. "They may be headed toward the big D."

I didn't like the sound of that. Marie and Burnie had been married a few years longer than me and Joe. People divorce all the time, I knew that. But giving up after twenty years? I looked over at Joe again and felt a sadness overcome me. He caught my eye, cocked his head and lifted his eyebrows as if to ask if I was alright. Or maybe he was asking me if I wanted to leave. I didn't know, but I was suddenly glad that he had seen me at all. We'd been there nearly an hour and not once stood by each other. The moment we walked in the door, he went one way and I went the other. Now that I think about it, it's been like this for several months, probably longer. I've had my head in books lately, and he's been buried in work.

I started toward him, just when Marie walked up and handed him another glass of Scotch. Joe looked quickly away and took the offering from her with a nervous smile. I turned my back and continued talking to Helen. "Hmm, I think I might head home early tonight. I'm a little beat from planning Joe's party."

"Honey, it's not until next weekend. What are you doing, remodeling the house?" Helen laughed between sips of wine.

"Well, kind of. I hired a band and set up an area to dance. I've also been making my own hors d'oeuvres. I want it to be very special. After all, it is his fiftieth."

"Yes, I agree, it should be very special. You're pretty sweet to make such a fuss. I know he didn't do that much for *your* fiftieth." Helen avoided my eyes and looked down at her sparkling shoes.

"No, I guess he didn't," I said, trying to remember what exactly he did do six months ago to celebrate my half a century on this planet. "Oh yes, he took me to dinner at Bartlett's and...."

"And, he went back to his office to work afterwards," Helen jumped in. "I recall how upset you were, but you also knew that he was on a big project with a short deadline, so you understood. That's what we wives do best...we understand." She rolled her eyes and then quickly flashed a fake smile at one of the guests nodding her direction. "I'll be right back, love. Stay put. Have another one of my heart'a'chokers."

I glanced at the dip in the shiny silver bowl and then I looked over at Marie. She had on a sleeveless dress and when she lifted her arm to take a sip of her drink, I noticed hardly any wattle. My eyes followed the outline of her body, and I saw exactly where the wattle had gone, straight to her hips, her gorgeous Italian hips. *Baby making hips* my father used to say to my mother before they had a half dozen children and before she woke up one day with a double chin and a pound of wattle. With that image still clear in my mind, I turned my back on the dip and eased through the crowd toward my husband.

"Hi honey," I said in my softest, most sultry voice, looking directly into Joe's eyes. I quickly turned before he could respond. "Nice to see you, Marie. Where's Burnie? I hope he doesn't have that awful flu that's going around."

"Oh no, he's uh, well, he's not up for parties these days," the she-devil said rather awkwardly.

"Well, if he tasted Helen's artichoke dip, he'd change his mind. But maybe he's just not up for a new experience. Why don't you check it out yourself, Marie? It's really good." I found myself taking her by her wattleless arm and leading her toward the table.

"I'll be right back, Joe. Pour me a glass of wine, please, sweetie," I said over my shoulder, followed by a slow wink. Helen saw me maneuvering Marie toward the spread of fancy appetizers and excusing herself, she quickly ran to my aid. "Ahh, are you tempting our guest to try my incredible dip?"

"Of, course. I can't keep this secret all to myself." I picked up a cracker and Helen scooped a glop of the creamy artichoke, carefully placing it on the center of the thin wafer. "Brace yourself," I warned Marie and crammed it all in her mouth

She chewed heartily with eyes opened wide and reached for a napkin to dab her mouth. "Oh dear, this is really good." And before she could finish wiping Helen had another one heading right toward her. Marie instinctively opened her mouth wider this time. "I cull eat deese all day," she burbled in between chews.

"I'll send home the recipe so that you can make it for Burnie. It's too bad he didn't come to the party." Attempting to disguise her curiosity with concern, Helen paused before dragging out the next question in a slow singsong voice, "Is everything alright?"

"Well, yes," Marie stalled, the look on her face revealing that she knew Helen knew what she had not thought anyone knew.

Helen put her hand on Marie's shoulder and said gingerly, "I've heard differently, dear. How are you holding up?"

I stood there watching Helen magically weave her web, luring her guest into her confidence. Marie didn't once look my way, but kept her eyes fixed on Helen's as she told her that she and Burnie were sleeping in different beds. And before Marie knew it, Helen had managed to pull out of her that it had been nearly a year since they had sex. She even had the nerve to ask Marie if she had a Twinkie in her pantry. Marie looked at her as if she had just spoken Chinese. Then Helen, in her own evasive way, explained what she meant, while Marie turned three shades of red and stuffed her mouth with more dip. I knew then what I thought I already knew and quickly excused myself before anyone else knew what I didn't want them to know.

"Where are you going?" Helen raised her voice over the crowd.

I grabbed my husband's arm, and trying not to draw attention to myself, I slowly and silently mouthed, "We're going home to clean out the pantry."

Poor Owen

They had not seen Owen for nearly a year when he popped up unexpectedly one morning at their table in the sleepy little mom and pop Cajun restaurant where they were feasting on fried eggs and potato chunks surrounded by sautéed collard greens; the Cajun hash, Zeke's favorite. All the way from Minnesota to Texas, and soon to be fifty-one, with a little more scalp exposure and wearing that same expression that said, "*I didn't do it*," Owen still held his own, and one would guess by his swagger that he was quite single.

"Well, I'll be darned, it's Owen," Zeke said, genuinely glad to see the Minnesota man towering over him. Zeke is from the Midwest, too, so the camaraderie was automatically set in place, for who could not be happy to see one of their own directly from the nation's breadbasket?

"Yes, I'll be darned," Jill mimicked, only in a higher tone. If they had said it in unison, it would've sounded like June and Johnny Cash. Jill and Zeke had been a couple for half a decade and although they lived together, they still felt like they were dating, and they liked it that way. That's what you do when you're over fifty, sleeping in separate rooms, doors unlocked, and declaring your independence after having been married before to another for twenty-something years. *Knock three times,* was their motto. They liked each other a lot, and their love was one of deep respect, and they were determined not to make the same mistakes they made when they were younger.

Just midway through their breakfast, Owen decided to join them and immediately ordered his own. While the men were recapping the Packer's last game, Jill sat quietly recalling the first time they had met Owen.

They were waiting for their table at a very popular restaurant, and the wait was projected to be over forty minutes. Owen was alone sitting on the bench next to Jill, fidgeting and arguing with himself about why he had chosen to wait when there was a perfectly good McDonalds right across the street. Jill, unable to resist talking to strangers, started up a conversation. They chatted casually for a while and seeing that the man was completely open, honest and vulnerable she began her magical probing.

"So, Owen, did you leave family behind in the Midwest?"

"Well, yeah, I did. My parents are still there, and," his smile dropped, looking up at Jill with trusting eyes, "and, also the love of my life."

"Oh, want to talk about it?" Jill patted his hand, stopping him from thumping his thigh and looking at his watch every two minutes.

"You don't want to know." He pressed his lips together and pouted.

"Of course, I do. I understand love on all its crazy levels. Tell me about it." She mimicked his position, uncrossed her legs and slumped over, elbows placed on her knees, hands clasped, like a man sitting on a bench whittling away at a piece of wood. Leaning in, she was all ears for Owen. Zeke slid further down the bench and reread the menu.

"Well, Misty is the love of my life. We were engaged to be married, but then the company I had started bombed, and I lost all my savings and frankly, I was broke and had to start all over again. This didn't suit her at all. She wanted fine things, a big house, a Mercedes, you know the stuff that makes women happy," he paused, anticipating an interjection.

Jill closed her eyes tight and managed to fight off a grumble.

"Anyway, I had planned to give her everything, but when my business went down, she broke off the engagement. And can you believe this? She did it on the day of the wedding…just before we walked down the aisle. Boy, was I ever devastated."

At this point he paused to scrunch up his face in regret and to swallow a big gulp to stop himself from crying. He looked so pitiful it was painful for Jill to watch this nice thick-necked man with large capable hands in such a wretched state. She knew right then that meeting him was meant to be, and that she could possibly help him.

"She just left me. Just like that," Owen seemed compelled to say more. "Wouldn't take my phone calls, wouldn't see me at the door to her house, wouldn't even answer my letters. I don't know what happened to all the wedding gifts. She didn't want me, and there was nothing I could do about it."

"How did you end up here in Austin?"

"I read an article about this being the number one city in America to live in, so I was so miserable and humiliated, I thought, well, why not. Besides, I'm pretty sure the whole town hated me."

Jill wanted to say, *I doubt that*, but small towns, she understood, were much like big families. She'd watched enough Mayberry episodes in her day to appreciate the simplicity of it. "So, I guess she's moved on, too?"

"Yes, I think she has someone new now. But she's still the love of my life, and I can't let go of her, even this far away."

Her intention, and Jill had made it quite clear that night when Owen joined them at their table, was to help this lonely man find some women friends, not necessarily lovers, which was none of her business what direction it took, but the most important thing was that he make friends. Because friends have friends and those friends introduce you to more friends, and before you know it, you've got a community of friends. Seems like Owen wasn't capable of that kind of worldly thinking, and like the men from his town, you either stamp your women on the forehead with *Mine* or you leave them on the shelf for the next shopper. Men just did not have women friends. Period.

Jill was determined to broaden his thinking, so, she arranged with Owen to meet her at their local restaurant where she would introduce him to her single girlfriends. And because they were both from the Midwest, Zeke would be there to take up the slack.

Turned out the ladies liked him, and dates were set up. Later the reports came in, and it seems Owen dominated the conversation, whining mostly about his lost love, and the biggest complaint was that he ate too much while on their date. He ordered appetizers, entrees with sides, dessert, and girly drinks afterwards, and even picked food off their plates. By the time they left the restaurant to go dancing or whatever dates do after dinner, he was bloated and lethargic and ready to watch a movie with popcorn and Milk Duds. None of the women wanted to hurt his feelings, so they asked to remain friends. But as Owen would stay true to his convictions, there was no in between, and he moved on, missing a wonderful opportunity to have female friendship. Jill suspected he had gone back to Minnesota after that because they never saw or heard from him again.

But now, here he was, energetic and talking up a storm. Jill was anxious to know about his dating world and when the perfect pause had finally arrived, she leaned over Zeke's plate and said, "So, how's your love life now, Owen?"

Zeke dropped his shoulders in surrender, knowing Jill was putting her spell on the man again, and soon Owen's emotions would spew out in between bites of French toast and Cajun grits and any chances to talk sports would take a miracle. She gingerly patted Zeke's knee to remind him that this was bound to happen and that he should just reap the rewards from listening. Zeke ordered another coffee and prepared himself for the long ride.

"Oh, you don't want to know," Owen said, pouring more syrup on his toast.

Well, that was an invitation if ever there was one, for Jill had heard him say this before.

"Of course, we want to know. If you want to share, we can handle it," she said assuredly. "Right, Zeke?"

"Yes, yes, I can handle it."

Owen held a generous bite of French toast in the air not far from his lips and began, "A woman I knew back in Minnesota came here for a convention, and we hooked up for dinner. Her name is Jackie…she's single."

Jill's mind trailed off to a scene: Owen at a restaurant with platters of food filling up the entire table, sitting across from a cornfed female stuffing rolls in her overall pockets for later, both talking over each other with mouth's full about the folks back home. She had to suppress a laugh.

Owen carried on. "We got things going in a hurry and next thing we knew, I convinced her to move to Austin and we'd be a couple. She went back home to arrange everything, and it was moving along really well, but guess what happened?"

Jill looked at Zeke, and Zeke looked at Jill. Zeke, known for his occasional one-liners, couldn't help himself now, the set up was just too perfect. "Let's see, she got hit by a bus on her way to you, won a big lawsuit against the bus industry, went back to Minnesota, bought a bus station and married a bus driver?"

"I wish!" Owen cracked up laughing. Zeke sat back in his chair, quite pleased. Jill hid behind her coffee cup.

When Owen finally composed himself, he asked Jill, "Do you remember me telling you about Misty?"

"I do. The love of your life, right?"

"Yes!" His eyes lit up when seeing that she remembered the most important thing in his world. "Well, Jackie was all ready to fly back here," he paused to add an important detail, "I paid for the ticket." He looked over at Zeke, "Would've been cheaper if I had put her on a bus."

"Ha, ha, ha!" Zeke blurted, snapping his mouth shut when he caught Jill's scolding eyes.

Owen slowly sucked the Bloody Mary through the thick straw and let that painful thought sink in before continuing. "Everything was planned for her to move in with me, and she was flying down to look at jobs. Not that she needs to work or anything, because I can take care of her and all, but she wants to. Well, guess who calls right out of the blue?"

Zeke and Jill whispered at the same time, "Misty?"

"Yeah, Misty. Can you believe it? She calls to tell me that she's made a mistake, that she misses me and wants me back. We talk it out and one thing leads to another, and before I know it, we're planning on *her* moving here."

"You're kidding?" Zeke raised his hands in surrender and smiled impishly, his bushy eyebrows askew. "Holy mackerel! You have *two* women moving in with you?"

Jill threw a napkin at Zeke and turned her attention back to Owen's goofy grin. "What about Jackie?"

"Well, what was I to do? The love of my life wants me back. What else could I do? I broke it off with Jackie."

"Oh, man," Zeke moaned, shaking his head. Jill dropped hers in mourning for a woman she has never met but can imagine is crying her eyes out over a gallon of ice cream in front of *Sleepless in Seattle*.

Upon seeing the couple bowing their heads, Owen confessed, "So, yeah, I broke Jackie's heart. Really bad." He took that moment to finish up the grits in three huge bites, and before he swallowed, he said, "So, I cancelled Jackie's ticket and bought one for Misty."

"Wait, wait, wait!" Jill is now beside herself. "So…you tell Jackie that you've changed your mind, and now you bought *another* ticket for Misty to come here?"

"Yeah, last Thursday."

"Last Thursday? Let's see…this is Sunday, so, where is she?" Jill looks around the restaurant and under the table for dramatic effect.

Owen looks at Jill like she didn't get the punchline in time. "She didn't come. She sent me a text the night before, a long, long text, explaining that she couldn't be with me after all."

"A text? After all that, a text?" Jill is clearly upset and sorting things out, she senses something is mighty fishy. "Owen, tell me, does Misty know Jackie?"

He looked at Jill like she is about to punch a big hole in his story. "Well, yes, uh, Jackie lives not far from her. It's a small town. I'm sure they know each other." Finally putting down his fork, he made a dramatic display of looking up at the ceiling with squinting eyes as if a vital clue was hovering over his plate. "You don't think Misty just did that to stop me from seeing Jackie, do you?"

As if he'd been left out of the loop, Zeke stares at Jill's cocky expression and waits for her to uncover a mystery.

"Owen, please. It's obvious. Look at the timing, it's the perfect answer," Jill says with complete surety. "You haven't seen or heard from Misty in over a year and wha-lah, she's suddenly on the phone right when you have a chance at happiness?"

"I thought about that, but nah, I just can't believe someone would do such a thing."

"Me either," Zeke said.

"You can't?" She looked at both men like they had lost their marbles. "Well, I can't believe that Misty left you because you lost your business, but she did, and right at your wedding with everyone watching, including God!" Jill's hands flew up in disgust.

Now, Owen and Zeke stare at each other with a dumb-founded look, and if they hadn't been two guys over fifty, they would've probably said, "Duh!"

"Gentlemen, I hate to run down my own kind, but history is filled with vindictive women, catty and cruel. Why do you think soap operas became so popular? I'm sorry guy, you've been sabotaged."

Owen, now trying to pick up the puddle of syrup with his fork says gloomily, "I kind of knew that, really, I guess."

Zeke uttered in a soft, sympathetic voice, "Poor Jackie."

"Yes, poor Jackie," Jill echoed his sentiment.

"I know, poor Jackie." Owen sucked on the fork.

For the first time during the entire conversation, they were quiet. Jill noticed the couple at the next table had been eavesdropping, and she could see that they, too, were feeling bad for poor Jackie. Jill was determined more than ever to save the day.

"Well, Owen, do you think you could try to make it up to Jackie? I mean, I know she probably doesn't ever want to talk to you again, but if you still want her, women love to be pursued."

"Really?" Zeke asked, doubtfully.

"Really, Zeke," she said, slightly irked. "OK well, maybe after Jackie rolls over him with her car once or twice."

Silence. Jill drove her point home. "And maybe, Owen, maybe she'd understand your addiction to Misty. You know addictions *can* be cured."

Owen flippantly waved his hand in dismissal at her idea, jabbed his straw into the ice, and searched for the last sip of the Bloody Mary. He deliberately turned toward Zeke, "Hey, did you see the Viking's game yesterday?"

Zeke eagerly responded, "Yeah, that second touchdown was…."

Watching them skillfully move on to another subject that completely excluded Jill, her first impulse was to throw water in both men's faces. Instead, she walked outside for a breath of fresh air.

Perplexed and feeling strangely ostracized, she stood looking at them through the plate glass window. The lady at the table next to them came out and stood by her side. Lighting up a cigarette, she said to Jill through a puff of smoke, "You're kidding. Poor Jackie?"

"What do you mean?" Jill asked the stranger.

"Well, come on, Misty didn't set that up. Owen did."

"You think?" Jill looked back at Owen animatedly talking with Zeke, happy as a pig in mud and ordering another Bloody Mary. Considering the woman's remark, she restructured her thoughts. "You mean, he wanted to make Misty jealous and so, he went after Jackie, called Misty and told her about it and got the reaction he was looking for?

And in his own sick way, he thinks that's love and now his addiction has been fed! "

"Yep, and after *all* that, he still walked away empty handed."

A conspiratorial glance passed between the women. With drooping shoulders, heads nodding halfheartedly, they sighed deeply and simultaneously lamented, "Poor Owen."

Gertrude

You've never had a massage?" Barb shrieked, plopping her groceries onto the kitchen counter and eyeing her friend in disbelief.

Three days later, Monica found herself stripped to her panties and lying face-down on a hard stretcher, her head buried in what looked like a toddler's training potty. *I can't believe I'm doing this. Thank goodness it's a woman massage therapist. I don't think I could handle a man's touch...it's been so long, I'm certain I'd have an orgasm!*

It was a new kind of intimacy, skin on skin, trusting a complete stranger to find her weak spots and knead a year's worth of anxiety out of them. She never dreamed she'd find refuge lying naked in a dimly lit windowless room under nothing but a sliver of fabric.

Before she knew it, Monica had booked another session. This time it was with Gertrude, a sixty-year-old woman who claimed she was a master at Swedish massage, Chakra Balancing, Acupressure, Body Wraps, Energy Healing, Aromatherapy, Intuitive Seeking, and Therapeutic Touch. Then she added – if that wasn't enough – Lay Counselor for Trauma with an Associate Degree in Dental Hygiene.

Gertrude whispered in her ear, "Do you want me to put you out?"

"I, I, uh, just what do you mean?"

"You know, put you in a sleep state, knock you out. I bunce you're extremely stressed today," she explained, her eyes wide with anticipation. "It won't hurt at all, I promise."

"Maybe, uh, maybe next time. I'm really not stressed today," Monica gave a nervous laugh and settled in for an hour of quiet bliss.

Ten minutes into the massage, Gertrude began chanting under her breath. Monica strained to hear what she was saying and could only make out a few words. *My goodness, it sounds like she's praying!*

After she hummed a few lines of "Amazing Grace," Gertrude divulged, "You know, I've crossed over twice."

"What do you mean by that?" Monica heard herself ask, and wished at that moment she hadn't responded, but had pretended instead to be asleep, as Barb told her she does while in the nude under the influence of a stranger's hands. She said it makes it easier to look them in the face afterwards if you don't get to know them.

"I died twice, and it was a fantastic experience. Once when I was a young girl I drowned, and it was so peaceful where I was going, I was actually mad at the lifeguard for saving me. The second time I nearly died from oysters. I'm allergic to them, which I found out the hard way, and dying this time wasn't pleasant at all. An angel stood in front of me and ordered me back to this life and said that I wasn't finished here. I had to believe him. He looked like John Travolta! He also said that I would be a messenger for good from now on, so that's why I'm here instead of cleaning teeth."

"Um huh," Monica moaned and forced her attention on the knots Gertrude had found that she didn't even know she had. *Just be quiet, and I bet she'll stop talking.*

Minutes in silence passed, and Monica began to let go. Just when she was entering that sweet state of euphoria, Gertrude jolted her back to reality – jamming her elbow deep into her shoulder blade. "I can't believe how mad my boss is at me for taking off a week. A lousy week! My dad is really ill, and I'm heading up north to care for him and take him back and forth to the doctor."

"Ow, ow, ow," Monica mumbled into the potty seat, "that hurts."

"Tell me about it. My boss is such a hurtful woman, but I don't care, I'm going anyway. Besides, they need me too much to fire me."

The massaging and the talking abruptly stopped. Glad that the torture was over and hopefully the nutty masseuse had run out of air, Monica stared blankly down at the tile floor. There was only the faint swishing sound of polyester pants rubbing together, and when orange painted toenails nervously jiggling up and down in shiny, green sandals appeared in her view, she snapped her eyes shut.

Reluctantly opening them she saw, just inches from her face, Gertrude kneeling down and peering up at her through the donut hole.

Monica's eyes popped open wider as Gertrude exclaimed, "I'm a LIAR!" Then she stood up and resumed massaging. "I'm a liar, yep I am. I'm not going to care for my father, I'm going to Las Vegas to see this man that I've got a crush on. He's a speaker at a convention there, and I've been nuts about him for years, and everywhere he goes to speak, I follow. Oh, he's dreamy, that one is. When I'm seventy I'm going to marry him. I can wait ten years because by then I'll be tired."

What did she say? Monica raised her head and looked askance at Gertrude who was busily cracking her knuckles. She quickly repositioned her head in the hole, realizing that she was not only jittery, she had completely lost her inner peace.

"Okie dokie, round two! Now, turn onto your back," Gertrude ordered. "I'm not looking, and I'll keep the sheet over you."

Certain that she didn't want to meet eyes with the oddball masseuse, Monica kept hers tightly closed and rolled over. When Gertrude applied pressure to her chest, she let out a loud croaky burp.

"Goodness, honey, you are *so* full of toxins. I can even feel the tension in your clavicles, but next time, give me a warning when you're about to belch," she insisted, fanning the air with her hand. "Now, where was I? Oh yes, I've been doing massage therapy since ninety-eight, and this is a good place to work because they don't make us do the massage that men come in here for. You know, those ads in those weird newspapers?"

What? Don't answer, don't you dare answer.

"Well," Gertrude leaned in whispering, "those ads are for men who want to get that *special* massage." Jerking back, she declared, "NOT ME, no thanks, I don't want *that* job! They can fire me for all I care. I had a guy pull the sheet off once and there it was, erect as a steeple, and he just looked at me like I knew what to do next. I covered it back up and stormed out of the room. He got mad, got up and left. He actually got me fired."

"You're kidding...aren't you?" *Can't I keep my big mouth shut?*

"Not at all. But I'm not worried if I get fired again, because my psychic told me I had more important things to do than rub down naked bodies for the rest of my life." Gertrude took a three-second breather and announced, "You know, you forgot to shave your knees."

"Your psychic?" The words tumbled out before Monica could catch them. *And my knees are hairy?*

"Sure, I have two mediums. One I go see, and the other I call on the phone. That second one doesn't even ask me questions; she just makes the predictions right after I say hello. She's about eighty per cent right most of the time. The one I visit in the institution wears a purple turban. I call him Ali Baba. He uses cards to read my future. You know like poker cards, with the King being the man I'm going to meet, the Queen is about me, and …," from there she went right into song, "and so on and so on and scooby dooby dooby."

Different strokes, for different folks. Oh dear lord, I'm singing with her. Act like you're dead!

"Well, anyway, Ali Baba was right about one thing," Gertrude raised her voice in proclamation. "He told me that someday my lies were going to make me rich. He said that I would probably have my own talk show, you know, like Oprah Winfrey." The louder she spoke the faster her fingers moved through Monica's scalp – rubbing so vigorously Monica imagined her head being mauled by squirrels. "People from all over America would be asking me for advice and the lies I would be telling them would be good lies, you know, harmless lies that make folks feel better about themselves or make them want to change their ways. Kind of like an evangelist, I suppose. You know, I'm a messenger for good now. That's my job for the rest of my life."

Afraid to make any sudden moves, Monica felt her face contort, and she let out a sound like someone passing a large kidney stone.

"For heaven's sake, you *really* do need to relax," Gertrude chided. "Poor thing. You know, it'll be really easy for me to put you into that sleep state I offered you earlier. It won't cost you extra. I've seen your kind before. I bet you're in the middle of a nasty divorce. Most women can't relax while going through that. They just lie here with their nerves all bundled up, and here I am working like a dog to get them to a peaceful place where they can let it all go. It makes you wonder why they come here at all. Why did you come here, anyway?"

"Maybe I came here for that *special* massage," Monica grumbled, too irritated to appreciate her own witty comeback.

"Those are for men, silly," Gertrude chuckled. "Well, I remember my divorce like it was yesterday. By the time I was finished with Max, he left the country with only a suitcase full of underwear. And as calm as I am with all my fancy degrees, I still couldn't stop myself from taking a hammer to his precious bowling trophies and shaving his longhaired cat. Believe me, he deserved more. But I've got my sights on Las Vegas now. There's a man there I'm going to marry. He's doesn't know it yet, but…"

With gritted teeth, Monica slowly raised her weary head. Her hair stuck out in all directions and her face was drained of color. She lifted her chin to the ceiling and let out a disturbing guttural growl, so horrible sounding anyone within distance would have thought she was a demon possessed.

Gertrude jumped back, her hands in clenched fists on her hips, and with one eye squeezed shut, she stood there sizing up the very distressed client. "Gee whiz, honey, you are the worst case of tense I've *ever* encountered! Sure you don't want me to knock you out?"

Me and Shirley

I am going to Ireland with Shirley Valentine today. Before you know it, we will be knocking around the pubs, drinking beer from tubs and kissing strangers on the dark side of the street. We will leave our mates back in the States in their comfy recliners watching their favorite sport and wondering who will retrieve their next beer. Only then, will they notice that we are gone.

I packed lightly – I always do, for I'm dressing for no one, except me, and maybe for those one or two nights at a bar full of merry Celtic folks when I will dance until my feet ache. I bought a simple, emerald green wench's blouse, cut slightly below my adequate cleavage and gathered where it accentuates my waist; below that, tufted fabric fans out to move seductively around my hips, while my black flowing skirt twirls when I am being whirled around by the men who have bought me more beer than any respectable woman should drink. I'm salivating, just thinking about the whole outfit, and the pair of black pumps that can be easily kicked off.

Shirley packed heavily. She has much more bosom than I could carry around on my small-boned body. She wears layers of clothes that frame her ample cleavage, and when you see her coming toward you, you see it first before you see her big flashing smile, and finally those incredible luminous eyes. I like her. I like her a lot. She's the kind of friend that a woman finds once in a lifetime.

I won't tell anyone this, but Shirley has a wall that she tells everything to and holds nothing back, like I do when I write in my journal. Best of all, the wall doesn't criticize her, chastise her, nor does it agree with her or patronize her on those moody days when she could use a little pretense. It simply listens and echoes back what she has told it; keeping Shirley balanced without applying too much practicality, but just enough common sense to help her make decisions, like going to Ireland. She likes her wall. She feels lucky.

Now that our children are grown, we are left alone with our thoughts. Thoughts that have been kept locked up in a vault so thick, only dynamite could break it open. Once the last child left the nest, and there were no more clothes to pick up off the floor, big meals to cook or stories about bad teachers and rotten girlfriends, the house became strangely empty. The men sitting across from us at the dinner table began to take unrecognizable form, and it occurred to us that they did not know who they were. Yet days of routine and nightly dinners went by for months on end until Shirley found her wall and I found my writing tablet. It was then that we realized that it was not only the men who had changed – we had changed.

The taxi picked me up promptly at eight. My husband stood at the door frowning, his head bent as he looked at his ugly, brown house shoes, my very first Christmas gift to him many years ago. I entered the cab and rolled down my window, waiting for him to say something kind or valuable, or a simple,

Have fun! He just continued to stare at his shoes and stayed that way until the taxi rounded the corner, and he was no longer in sight. I wondered how long he stood there, and I hoped that this sad image wasn't the way I would remember him from then on.

During the cab drive, I took the time to recheck the contents of my oversized backpack – passport, lipstick, driver's license, comb, credit card, breath mints, Kleenex, nail file and a cheap paperback novel that my neighbor said was a 'must read'. Seven pairs of undies, two bras, running shoes, four cotton shirts, three pairs of shorts, socks and that lovely green blouse and skirt with the slip-on heels. Most importantly, my journal and a brand-new pen, easily accessible in a side pocket. Anything else I needed, I was wearing, including a light sweater that was wrapped around my waist. I was essentially hands-free.

I giggled thinking about what Shirley would pack and imagined her lugging the biggest roll-on bag they make – a bright red one so it could easily be found. She would never think of carrying an ugly backpack on her back, unless it was decorated in rhinestones. I'm certain that her essentials are quite different from mine and include a large bulging make-up bag, a set of hot rollers, an outfit for every day with matching shoes, a travel iron and a first aid kit, all crammed neatly inside. If she could have, she would have packed her wall, too. But she made it clear that there would be no talking on this trip, just playing. I'm kind of cheating by bringing my tablet, but I can't help myself – there will be so much to write about.

The airport is especially crowded this time of year when school is out, and folks are either vacationing or sending their kids off to camp. I'm not fond of crowds and tend to find the quietest spot by the windows to watch the magnificent planes being prepared for their next flight. The idea of that large beast carrying 250 passengers across the mighty ocean for nine whole hours without stopping never ceases to amaze me. I admire it on the ground and in the air and mostly when it lands me safely at my destination. However, I do not admire the seats and to this day I have no idea if first class seats are really better. If I had an extra thousand, you can be darn sure I wouldn't spend it to find out.

The longer I sit, the more I think about my life. The image of my sad husband standing in the doorway has not yet left me. I try hard to remember him when we first met and settle further down in the seat to put my memories on paper.

He was a beautiful man; tall and slender with thick, black hair like my mother's. We met at a party, like many couples did back then. Seems like there were always parties– one every night, on campus, around campus, generally in a rich kid's apartment. We liked each other immediately and wasted no time falling in love. He got drafted, I got pregnant, and we both had to quit college. I saw him only twice in two years while I lived with my mother and raised our little girl. Soon after, he left the Army, started a new company, bought us a home, and we brought two more children into the world. They were simple years. We both worked diligently, and life dealt some hardships, but my husband was strong-willed and determined and we came out shining every time.

And here I am, waiting to board a plane that will carry me thousands of miles away from twenty-eight years of marriage with a good man. A good man that no longer loves me enough to travel with me, nor loves me enough to take me dancing, or bowling, or to parties, like he used to do. A good man that no longer stares at me across the room or shoves me against the wall and kisses me hard, making me feel like his lover, or wakes me in the middle of the night and tells me about his dream. A good man that once thought I was beautiful and funny and once upon a time, would never want to be without me.

The image of my still-handsome husband with his graying hair and strong hands standing in the doorway, afraid to look at me, but finding comfort in looking down at his house shoes, brought tears to my eyes. We both had changed, but I thought I was brave enough to do something about it.

Only thing is, after I roam the green hills of Ireland, close down the pubs with my new best friends, visit cold castles that bring me no comfort, wash down corned beef and cabbage with a pint of Murphy's, sleep on the side of a hill and bicycle through villages with fine names such as Claddaghduff and Killarney, I will still have done nothing about it, and everything will be the same when I return home nine days later.

While Shirley was probably already seated aboard her plane with a ten-dollar bill in her hand, waving it at the flight attendant to take her drink order, I sat slumped in the waiting area of Gate Five wondering what to do next. I needed an answer.

Over the loud speaker a thin voice reported that our flight to Dublin would be delayed for possibly three hours. People moaned and groaned, and some headed straight up to the counter to complain, while others surrendered to the nearest bar. I flagged down the next taxi and headed home. Along the way, I shared my story with the taxi driver who sadly confessed after ten minutes into it, that he understood English much better than he could speak it. I told him not to worry, that it felt good just to talk about it.

We passed by my favorite department store, and I asked him to let me run in for a minute to pick up something for my husband. He smiled and gladly turned around.

When we reached our driveway, I saw that my husband's truck was still parked in the same place. I shook my driver's hand, and he wished me good luck. When I entered the house, I was surprised that the television was not on and not even one light. I peeked down the dark hall before heading toward the master bedroom. Entering the room slowly, I saw, nearly hanging off the end of the bed, my husband's size thirteen feet in his favorite pair of white socks, the bottoms blackened from walking outside in them to get the newspaper. He was asleep, or so it seemed, as he had his arm resting over his eyes, and on his chest was our wedding album, opened and gradually rising with each labored breath. I sat down next to him and put my hand on his. He jerked a little and uncovered his tear-filled eyes. When he saw me, he half smiled and said, "I can't believe I let you go."

"I can't believe I let go of you."

Then that husband of mine pulled me toward him and kissed me like the young soldier I married. When he finally let me come up for air, I handed him his gift. With a big grin on his face he sat up, opened it and pulled out a fine new pair of house shoes.

"Does this mean you want to start over?" he asked.

"I do." I laughed, feeling a little bashful like a newlywed, and with the children no longer living there, we left the bedroom door wide open.

Ten Items or Less

The grocery store was not her favorite place. The colorful rows of boxed and canned food, sixteen different varieties of ketchup, jelly, sauces and that amazingly long line of cereal always baffled her. Being single and forty-two, without children, pets or plants, or an ex of any kind, Holly doubted she would ever experience all that the store had to offer. It annoyed her just to think about it.

While she was rummaging through the clearance bin of two-day-old meat, she heard a sudden burst of applause from the other side of the store. Looking up, she saw curious shoppers hurrying toward the sound. She threw back the hamburger patties that were already browning at the edges and decided to follow. When she rounded the corner she saw a very large bouquet of colorful balloons before she noticed the couple standing next to them. The young woman was shrieking with laughter, and the man was beaming, smiling so wide nearly all sixteen of his upper teeth were showing.

"Hmm, I bet they just won a ton of groceries," Holly surmised. "I never win anything," she grumbled to the woman standing next to her who had opened a roll of paper towels to dab at her tearing eyes.

The woman shook her head in disagreement, and in between sniffles, she barely got out the words, "He just…he just proposed to her in front of the *entire store!* Oh, it was so beautiful."

"You've got to be kidding," Holly responded condescendingly, looking back at the excited bride-to-be who was now squealing and had fallen to the floor on her knees, pounding the tile with the palm of one hand, while holding her left hand up high to show everyone her engagement ring. Her fiancé stood frozen in the same spot with the same stretched grin, only now his face had seriously reddened after seeing his girlfriend drop to the floor.

Holly looked around and noticed that everyone watching was either smiling or crying. The scene was infectious, and she started to feel a little gooey inside, too, when suddenly, a very short, obese woman wearing a bright yellow pantsuit and a serious scowl stepped right in front of her. She stood up on her toes and put her round face just inches from Holly's chin. "Her life is ruined now. RUINT!" she boldly declared behind yellow-framed glasses, and then she briskly walked away.

Startled, Holly turned and watched the angry stranger's bulbous bottom bouncing up and down like a deflated beach ball as she exited the store. She wondered how her little legs could move so fast carrying all that extra weight. "Humph," she shrugged and looked back at the deliriously happy couple again, and for a split second she wanted desperately to disagree with the cantaloupe-shaped woman in yellow – but she knew better.

In the checkout lane, Holly pondered the possible reasons for what had taken place at the store. When she couldn't come up with an answer, she asked the young cashier with rhinestone studs in her chin, nose and along the edges of both ears, "Why did he propose in the grocery store? It's kind of weird."

"Oh, not really. They actually met on check-out lane six – Ten Items Only. She had *way* over ten items and he was behind her with only one, a toothbrush. They argued and then ended up laughing about the whole thing, and before they knew it they were exchanging phone numbers. So, I guess that's why," she said, while robotically passing grocery items over the scanner and using her tongue to force a big wad of pink bubble gum under her top lip.

"Well, that's kind of stupid. Sounds like one of those silly scenes in a Nora Ephron movie." Holly let out a sarcastic chuckle, still fighting back her emotions, while the cashier crinkled her nose, looking confused. "You know, the writer. She wrote the movie, *You've Got Mail?*"

"Oh," was all the pin-cushioned teenager could offer, glancing nervously at the cute sacker, as she slid a box of ex-tra-large sanitary napkins his way.

Holly looked over at the boy to see if he knew the famous writer. "Surely *you* know who she is, don't you?" she scowled. The sacker quickly looked down, hiding behind the long bang that successfully covered one eye, and while loading the paper bag, he absentmindedly dropped the box of sanitary napkins on top of Holly's eggs, followed by a bag of tomatoes and a half Bundt cake. Too busy asking the next person in line the same question, Holly hadn't noticed the blunder.

As usual, she had picked a basket with a bad wheel and it squeaked and clunked noisily, reminding Holly of her own crummy existence. The wheel got stuck in a sideways position. Losing control of the basket when she tried to straighten it out, she rammed into the back of a patron crossing her path, nearly knocking him to the floor. She gave him an insincere smile and gestured weakly at the wheel.

Incensed when he didn't smile back, but instead turned quickly and stumbled away, Holly huffed past the happy couple who were now posing for pictures in front of check-out lane six.

Along with her grumbling, the noise from the wobbly basket caused the couple to look her direction. Unable to stop herself, Holly cupped her hands to her mouth and yelled, "YOUR LIVES ARE RUINED NOW! *RUINT!*"

Except for the Bee Gees music in the background, the store became suddenly quiet. Charging forward and without looking back, Holly walked out with a self-satisfied smirk on her face.

Loading the groceries in the back of her old El Camino, she picked up the last bag and the bottom fell out. Broken eggs rolled down her polyester dress and onto her shoes, and the bag of tomatoes landed on the cement. She stood there clutching the remains of the wet sack, holding the sanitary napkins to her chest and the Bundt cake under her chin. Infuriated, she wanted to go back inside and complain, but she knew she would not be welcomed after yelling at the couple.

She grabbed the tomatoes and carried them to the front seat. Slowly driving by the storefront, she leaned out the window and threw one tomato at a time at the electronic sliding door. When the last tomato grazed the store manager's head, she sped away.

Not knowing why, Holly cried all the way home.

Out of Luck

As if there wasn't enough to cry about, Sally's boyfriend moved out like a thief in the night, leaving only a Post-it note stuck to the pillow on his side of the bed: I'm just not equipped for this sort of thing. Sorry.

"Equipped? Are you kidding? Who *is*?" Sally grumbled, standing over the toilet watching the tiny pieces of torn paper whirl around and around until they disappeared into the abyss. Feeling abandoned and dejected, she was in a serious funk. And to make matters worse, it was St. Patrick's Day. A day she had for many years enjoyed spending with her father, the old Irish fart. But not anymore.

She found herself sitting on the floor of the bedroom closet fixated on the tarnished gold buckle attached to her father's worn out boot. Regretting that she had agreed to attend the CD release party for her band, *Under the Bus*, she said lovingly to the boot, "I'd rather stay home in my pajamas and watch "The Quiet Man" with you, dad." The ritual had started in her late teens when she was deemed old enough to discuss with him particular scenes from the movie: like why a man spanked a woman, who paid for the damage in bar fights, and ways to deal with dirty money other than burn it. Remembering their spirited conversations made her smile, but when she closed her eyes, that memory disappeared, and another one began to materialize, slowly like an evil cloaked figure emerging from a thick fog. Once again, she tried to make it go away.

Slumped over, choking back the tears, she didn't hear the knock at the door. Whoever it was continued knocking until Sally finally heard, through the thin apartment wall, her neighbor yelling, "Answer your damn door!"

With a sudden sense of relief, she remembered Jen was on her way over. She picked up her father's boot, moved in slow motion and opened the door just when her friend was attempting to pick the lock.

"Hey, I almost had it!" Jen exclaimed.

Sally shut the door and taunted her from the other side, "Oh yeah, show me."

"No, no, no…it's OK, I already broke a nail!" Jen wiggled the doorknob and finding that it easily opened, she entered with a frustrated grin. "And darn it, it was the only long nail I had left. How else will I clean out my ears now?" she said jokingly with her rough Texas drawl. Seeing that Sally had been crying, she changed her expression to one of concern. "Oh, dear…how's my favorite depresso?"

"You know, same ole, same ole. I'm sorry it took so long to answer the door." Sally managed a semblance of a smile. "I was in the closet visiting with my dad, and you know how he can talk," she said much too casually, as if talking to the dead was an everyday thing.

Keenly aware of her friend's fragile state, Jen played along. "Oh, yes I do. Next time tell the old bastard hello for me and that he owes me a beer. Oh, and I'm sorry about your break up, darlin'."

"I'm not."

"Hmm, well…OK, then. We've got twenty minutes to make you look halfway decent." Jen gently took the boot from Sally's grip, grabbed a handful of her tangled red locks and swept them away from her face. "I brought my make-up bag, but girl, you're on your own with *that* hair!"

When they arrived at the venue, the music had already started, and the place was packed. Jen pulled Sally through the crowd and propped her up on the only empty stool left at the bar, gave her the *stay put* finger and then scurried off to tell the band that their songwriter had graced them with an appearance.

The band was at its best, and Sally perked up hearing the lyrics she had written floating across guitar notes and bouncing in and out of drum beats. The next song was her favorite, accompanied by a flute; a sappy and dreamy Celtic piece that always made her tear up. Sally couldn't believe they chose that very moment to spotlight her with a long introduction to the audience. When the clapping began, she hid her face from the lights, slipped off the stool and fled the scene. Jen was backstage too busy flirting with one of the sound men to see her leave.

Through the light steady drizzle, Sally ran down the busy city street brushing past cheerful people dressed in green – hats, t-shirts, hair, here there everywhere, huddling under umbrellas or dancing openly in the rain. Without looking back, she rounded the corner and signaled for a taxi. Bent over at the waist, her chest heaving, she tried to catch her breath. A cab pulled up beside her and waited patiently for her to recover.

"Thank you, thank you very much," she said, sliding into the back seat. "Phew, I haven't run like that in a while!"

Sally noticed immediately that the driver had on a classic green, Irish tweed cap, and when he turned around to speak to her, his smiling eyes sparkled in the city lights. "Good evening, miss. Tis a fine St. Paddy's day."

His unmistakable Irish brogue caught Sally off guard.

"Oh! Are you Irish?"

"I am, indeed, born and raised." His smile broadened with the claim. Handing her a napkin, he eyed her quizzically. "What, may I ask, were you running from?"

Sally lowered her head and meekly answered, "Me, I think."

"I do that all the time, and I always catch up with me self." The old man's grin lifted his thick eyebrows to the rim of his cap. "I mean, *myself*. Old habits take long to cure."

Wiping the rainwater from her face, Sally gave the driver her address. As he drove, she sat quietly listening to him sing an Irish tune, so low, she had to strain to hear it.

"That sounds like a song my father used to sing to me when I was little," she said, solemnly. "He's Irish, too. I miss him so much."

"Oh, but if he's back in Ireland, he is surely celebrating with the finest."

Sally swallowed hard. "I wish. I could live with that, but... he, he died...not long ago." And when she heard those words come from her own trembling lips the tears fell as easily as the rain.

The cab driver pulled off the road and ran around the car to open the passenger door. "There, there, lassie," he said, consoling her. He put his warm hand on hers, holding it there until Sally's sobs subsided. "We're almost to your home. Hang on a wee bit longer, and I'll get you there safely."

By the time they reached her apartment, Sally and the rain had calmed down considerably. She tucked her damp hair behind her ears, blew her nose and in between sniffles, she apologized to the man behind the wheel who was no longer singing a sweet Irish tune, but keeping an eye on her through the rearview mirror. "I'm so sorry, I seem to burst out crying a lot lately. I'm OK now. What is your name, sir?"

"Eamonn Connolly, and yours?"

"Sally Walsh," she said, leaning over the front seat and reaching out to shake Eamonn's now familiar hand. "Would you mind seeing me to my door?" she asked with pleading eyes.

"Of course, I will. I am most pleased to assist a lady in distress." He quickly exited the cab. Watching his head bob up and down as he did a little jig in front of the car lights made Sally giggle. Then opening her door, he removed his cap and took a deep bow, as if she were exiting a chariot. She was utterly charmed.

At her apartment door, Sally looked down at the small man, at least a foot shorter. His presence and natural concern for her wellbeing comforted her. "Eamonn, could we visit for a bit? I can make us a cup of hot cocoa."

"It would be my pleasure," he said, and he tipped his cap again.

Sally motioned to her guest to sit at the kitchen bar. She resisted helping the little Irishman as he struggled to reach the top of the tall stool; relieved when he settled in.

"I always bake something special on St. Patrick's Day. How about some oatmeal cookies?" Sally asked.

"Sounds delightful." Eamonn rested his elbows on the counter and settled in to watch the pretty lady pour ingredients in a bowl. "I have a niece, about your age, back in Ireland.

She bakes marvelous cookies and sends me a dozen every year on my birthday."

"That's so sweet. Is all of your family in Ireland?"

"All but my daughter and my grandsons. They're the reason I moved here. After my wife passed, my daughter Emma asked me to come live with her. She has two strapping teenagers that could use a bit of their grandpappy's wisdom. It has been quite an experience."

"I bet." Sally placed a tray of cookie dough in the oven and offered the mixing spoon to her guest to lick the remains. He easily accepted. "I'm really sorry you lost your wife." She inhaled a deep breath in an attempt to squelch any further emotional outbursts.

"Shauna was quite a gal. But if I may say, I don't think your father would want you to be this distraught."

"I know he wouldn't. But, it hurts, and there's this guilt I can't…" Sally stopped from saying more.

Eamonn seemed to sense her uneasiness with the topic and carefully began telling her of his own experience with the ghosts of guilt. "Yes, I understand. Let me tell you a story. When I was a young lad, oh, about nineteen, my mother, God rest her soul, was working for the local bakery in Galway, not far from where I was raised. Times were difficult, but we managed to find the joy in our daily living. The green of Ireland can fool you into feeling mighty fine, and then of course, there are the beautiful ladies to distract you, as well." He smiled, eyes half closed, looking far beyond the room at a fond memory.

"It was a rain-threatening day, not unusual for the season, and my mother had hurried off to work at the break of dawn to begin preparing dough, just as you are." He paused, eyeing the bowl eagerly, seeing that it could use a few more swipes from his spoon. Sally quickly got the message and passed it to him. "Folks in our town loved vanilla curd cakes, and my mother made the best, adding a secret ingredient that she even kept from the shop owner himself. I was in love with a girl that also worked at the bakery, and that morning, seeing the dark clouds approaching, I noticed that my mother had left her umbrella behind. It was a grand excuse to see Shauna and get the first bite of fresh pastries, too, so I quickly followed just minutes behind her. It was a good twenty-minute walk, mind you."

Eamonn took a deep breath and ran his finger down the palm of his weathered hand. "As I remember it like I do me own hand, it still hurts to speak of it." Collecting himself, he looked up at Sally who was now leaning over the counter waiting attentively for his next words.

"I was across the road when I spotted my mother and Shauna standing in front of the shop. I yelled a hello, and they both turned quickly to walk toward me. I yelled again for them to wait, that I would come to them, but Shauna started prancing across the muddy road, eager to see me, she was. My mother followed closely behind."

Adjusting his cap, Eamonn cleared his throat and twisted his lips, as if preparing for the climax. He lifted his chin and continued. "Then the worst thing happened. Old man Jefferies came out of nowhere in the gloaming, slapping the whip to his horse and buggy in a terrible hurry. Seeing that he was heading straight for Shauna, my mother charged toward her with all her might and shoved Shauna out of harm's way. But my poor mother was trampled to death…right before my eyes."

Sally uttered, "Nooo," followed by a deep sigh.

"Yes. It was the worst day of my life, and for the longest I blamed myself. Until…"

"Until, what?" Sally urged, praying that he had something valuable to say that would ease his pain and perhaps even hers.

His frown eased toward a smile. "Well, I married Shauna, and we had a baby girl the following year. I was happy, but still tormented over my mother's death. We named our daughter Emma, after my dear mother, and when she was five years old, we took her to the forest for a picnic. It was a most lovely day, and while Shauna and I rested on a blanket, Emma went looking for flowers which she brought back to us, one by one. She was gone a bit too long after the fourth flower, so I got up to look for her. I found her not far away sitting on a log looking into a sunbeam, her eyes wide with curiosity, the sweetest smile on her face. I was captivated watching her. It was a beautiful thing."

"I heard her say, 'This is for you Maimeó Emma.' She handed a flower to the sunbeam, and lo and behold, the flower floated up and disappeared above the trees. It was a most amazing thing, and I started to cry believing that my little girl was talking to my own mother. Emma rushed toward me, so excited she was. She put her tiny arms around my legs and looking up at me with such tenderness, she said, 'I just talked to Maimeó Emma. Please don't cry, she is very happy. She said to give *this* to you.' And in the palm of my baby girl's hand was a beautiful glass marble. 'To remind you that she loves you,' she said."

Eamonn took the marble from his pocket and held it out for Sally to see.

"It is beautiful." Sally held it up to the light and admired the emerald green swirls captured inside the glass. "And you carry it with you, always?"

"Not always. There are days I feel the need to be closer to her…like today."

A teardrop landed at the top of Sally's lip as she turned to look at the picture on the wall of her father holding her in his arms when she was about the same age as Emma. "You are very fortunate to have had that message and delivered by your own daughter. I can only hope for such a message. You see, like you, I saw my father die, and I want so much to believe that it was an accident…and, that he forgives me."

Eamonn braced himself on the stool with his small, rugged hands. "Go on, please."

"We were just leaving a Celtic event and walking back to the bus stop. My father was in such a cheerful mood, telling me again about his life on the Emerald Isle, how he'd met my mother, his fights with his brothers and stories he's told me since I was a child. The day before was my birthday, and he suggested that we celebrate before going home. He always found a clever way to get behind a Guinness."

Adding an Irish accent, Sally quoted in a deeper voice, "My daughter is now the fine ripe age of twenty-five…'tis time to share a pint with the old man." Eamonn laughed and nodded his appreciation.

"So…," Sally went on, "we slipped into the nearest pub and downed a few beers. I wanted to go home, but once he starts drinking, well, he *loves* to talk. He often dredges up old memories that make him melancholy, and it goes downhill from there. He said the demons descend upon him, and he has to fight them off. But once he does, he returns meek as a kitten. *Do as I say, not as I do*, he'd tell me."

Sally had never shared this with anyone until now. Was it a sense of relief or betrayal she was feeling? She chose not to let these confusing thoughts interfere with a chance to share her story with a kindred spirit.

"When I finally convinced him to leave, we went out the back door, because by now I was certain we couldn't go out the front without causing a scene. I so wish I hadn't."

Eamonn nodded empathetically. "I know, I do understand regrets."

Sally placed the marble on the counter and focused on it. "The back of the pub was in a dimly lit alley. We had only taken a few steps when a man approached us with a knife and told us to give him any money or jewelry we had. My father pulled me behind him and said, 'Mister, if I had any money, would I be wearing *this* awful garb?' He pointed to his clothes and lifted up his boot and laughed. He had worn those ugly boots as long as I can remember. They had a big brass buckle on the side, and he would kick up his heels and tell me they were his lucky dancing boots. But that day…we were out of luck."

Feeling an unexpected rage well up, Sally balled up her fists and lifted her eyes to the ceiling. Angrily she blurted out, "That crazy father of mine kicked that man in the stomach and knocked him to the ground with such force his boot flew off! I grabbed him and tried to pull him down the alley. He yelled, 'I can't leave my lucky boot!' And then he shook free of me and went back. The robber was struggling to get up. The boot was lying between his legs. When my dad reached down, he tripped over the man."

With eyes now tightly shut, Sally said almost in a whisper, "It all happened so fast, I didn't know…" She allowed her fingers to loosen and rest upon her heart. "I'll never forget the look on that man's face…staring at me as if he was completely in shock. He started crying, 'I'm sorry, I'm sorry' and pulled himself out from underneath my dad. It was only until he ran away without the knife that I understood."

Sally lifted her heavy eyelids and ended the story. "It pierced his heart."

"Oh, my," Eamonn exhaled and shook his head in sorrow.

Right on cue, as if the angels had been listening, the ding of the oven bell lightened the tense air, and at the same time the marble began to slowly roll off the counter. Before Eamonn could catch it, it rolled off the edge and landed in the pocket of his jacket draped over the stool next to him. Reaching inside the pocket, instead of pulling out the marble, he pulled out something else that brought a smile to his face. "Ahh, thank you, Mother," he said in a whisper.

Sally turned around to see the old man's hand stretched out, offering her a piece of paper. He said, "The passenger before you put this in me hand tonight. Now, dear Sally, I am quite certain it is meant for *you*."

Wiping the tears from her cheeks, Sally couldn't help but smile watching Eamonn's eyes twinkle when she reached for it. He encouraged her to read the words out loud, and as she did, he said them softly along with her. "No man ever wore a scarf as warm as his daughter's arm around his neck."

Where Are You Now Eleanor Bean?

Did I mean to let you go? Back then. Back when we were youthful, fertile, learning by chance, and wisdom seemed so far away.

We had both married young to our high school sweethearts. I had a child with Brent, you had none with Nathan. You and I nurtured our new friendship with long walks late in the evenings after the suffocating Texas heat finally yielded to the unbound night air. Under many waxing and waning moons, we gradually exposed our vulnerabilities. During one of our walks, followed by several glasses of wine on your back porch, I learned that you longed for a child but were not able to conceive because Nathan decided he didn't enjoy sex anymore. "With you?" I asked, wishing I had not been so blunt. "Yes," you replied sadly through a soft whisper, "with me."

After that powerful eye-opener, I could sense you were sinking in humiliation, and it seemed as though I had deliberately thrown you under the bus with my blatant assumption. I felt the need to make it up to you, to even the score, so, I divulged something I had told no one. Brent's infidelity. In all honesty, I had not intended to dump that on you or anyone, yet I insisted on expounding even further that he'd been unfaithful from the very beginning. Strangely, I found comfort being under the bus with you.

Days later, in a tender moment, we sat on a curb in the dark, and I admitted I was no longer in love. It was painful bringing the words to life. You sat still and soundless as a dead tree, while I looked for an answer in the stars. Finally, it crept from your mouth that you have never been in love. We were silent on the walk home. Lying next to Brent's warm body that evening, I was sorry I had said those words out loud. Were you?

We refused blame and judgment for all those intimacies we shared that summer. It made it easier that way. A friendship bonded by secrets extracted from our own private hell, promising to never tell.

Then, out of the blue, my uninhibited cousin facing divorce decided to make an impromptu visit, testing our resolve. I saw in his demeanor an immediate attraction to you – a spurned man bent on screwing any woman he could. I saw in your eyes a hunger to reciprocate – ripe for the picking.

He was a complete fool, flirting openly, shamelessly, and when I told him you were a teacher, the teasing intensified. "Oh, Mrs. Bean, you're my *favorite* teacher." You were coy with a reticent drawl, beckoning approval, emboldened by my silence. He insisted on joining us on our walk.

Later, when I saw the two of you slip away into the night, and he returned without you, flush with sex, sweaty, gloating like a cocky teenager who had guiltlessly stolen whiskey from the liquor cabinet, I knew.

You avoided me week after week. I left you alone with your conscience. Me with mine. I convinced myself it was a necessary reprieve. Did you?

In my spare time I made stained glass – piecing together a slender lady in a snug fitting red gown, hand on her curvy hip, the other in the air – Audrey Hepburn, your favorite. You always wanted to be like her, I remembered you saying.

You dropped by unexpectedly one morning, avoiding my eyes with small timorous glances. Our visit was shortened when I decided to give you the stained glass, introducing it as *Audrey in Red*. "No one has ever...." Your confession through tears, although utterly sincere, could not bring me to tell you that I was pregnant. Little did I know that you were, too.

The day after, I ran into Nathan. "She went to her mother's for a while," he said, blandly.

You never returned from your mother's. Later, I saw a SOLD sign in your yard. I drove away with a sense of gladness mixed with sadness. A bittersweet surrender. "Where did you go, Eleanor Bean?

I knew nothing of you until roughly eight years later through your letter, more like a memo. I saw it like this:

- You were divorced.
- Your mother had died.
- You were teaching elementary students.
- You had a seven year old son.

You ended with, "I hope you still enjoy the little things." No return address.

Twenty more years have slipped by. I am alone. Brent is married to another, and our children are grown. The sun is shining through the steady rain, overwhelming me with nostalgia. Rummaging through an old box of mementos, I picked up a very small, delicate book, *This Morning I Held a Rose: the little things that bring us happiness.* On the first page, your inscription, so perfectly handwritten, the consistency of the letters made my back stiffen. The Palmer method, a teacher's curse, was my first thought. I had to read it twice.

I could not remember you giving it to me. How could you have? You were long gone by then. The slim book, foreign in my hands, had me completely mystified. Again, I read your words: "You are often in my thoughts. Please remember, you're an important individual, too. I think you tend to forget that."

Am I an individual? Am I important? I forget.

What I *am*, is an expert at putting up walls. Impenetrable walls, the higher the better.

Then it hit me like a ton of bricks, and my wall of self-preservation came tumbling down. From the rubble, a chapter of my life I had purposely concealed began to surface, and there was nothing in the way to stop the memory from flooding my brain and piercing my heart. That year, shortly after you walked out of my life with the stained-glass piece and pieces of me, everything fell apart. My marriage was crumbling, and we were too young to know how to fix it. Then, as fate would have it, it repaired itself. Brent had been seriously injured, hospitalized, and in that blurry nightmare, I was told he might not survive the night. I made a promise to God in those most humbling hours: Please let him live, and I will honor my vows with or without his love.

My prayer was answered. Nothing else mattered. Not even you. Could it be that you reached out with this little book of kindness when I was too blind to see?

Only just now my eyes have opened, and I'm realizing I lost a dear friend. Where did I go wrong? We were at a crossroads, it seems. You left, I stayed. Our secrets were safe, shackled by courage and fear.

Who is the father of your child? Do you still have *Audrey in Red*? Are you lonely like me?

Please save me from drowning in regrets and questions long unanswered. Help me find happiness in the little things again…like a walk with a friend.

Where are you now, Eleanor Bean?

Well, the book has come to an end, and I found that I have not used that "infamous" word in any of these stories — a word that has so many meanings, yet seldom misunderstood, is so ugly, yet so poignant and fundamental that when used at the precise moment, it can silence a room instantly.
And the strange thing is, it's even more powerful in print.

It's Over

The garage door opened slowly and efficiently as it did every time she pushed the tiny button on the visor of her car. Gilda watched it rise through the pouring rain, and at that moment she never thought she'd count her blessings for something as simple as an electronic door opener offering a safe haven for her BMW convertible and her new hairdo. She slowly pulled forward and located the tennis ball that hung from the ceiling, stopping just as it touched the windshield, preventing her from running into the sheetrock wall like she often did before Doug came up with the ball idea. Her boyfriend was always doing thoughtful things like that for her, until lately.

For the first time that week, there was nothing to carry into the house, so she entered the back door quickly and unburdened. Doug's voice trailed down the hallway as loud and friendly as she had heard it many times before. She knew he was sitting in his small office with his big hairy, bare feet up on his massive, cluttered desk, unaware of the world around him. He loved talking on the phone, and it didn't matter to whom. Sometimes after a long conversation with someone, she'd ask, "Who was that?" He'd answer, "Oh, just a solicitor." But this conversation was clearly not with a stranger. His playful laughter bounced off the walls and carried throughout the house. Gilda stood with the door opened and listened. She was certain that he didn't hear her come in until she shut the door behind her and suddenly the laughter stopped, and his voice dropped to a low decibel.

Gilda tossed her purse on the bed in the guest room that doubled as her office. Usually she would go about her business, plopping down in front of the computer and going straight to her personal email first before checking on her business account. But this time, she found that she was quite interested in her boyfriend's conversation, so she stood perfectly still and cupped her ear his direction.

"Can I get back to you on that?" she heard him ask, followed by a pause and then something incomprehensible and then silence, indicating that the party at the other end had hung up.

Gilda hurried to her desk and began opening email. "I'm home!" she sang, as she usually did when she entered the house that she and Doug had shared the past two years, only this time her voice cracked.

He predictably answered, "Welcome home!" as he sprinted down the hall, the bottoms of his sockless feet slapping against the laminate floor, greeting her personally, wearing the cutest grin on his round, fat and tireless face.

"You're home early," he said, bending over to kiss her on the forehead.

"Early? I didn't tell you I'd be home any particular time," Gilda smugly pointed out, pulling away dismissively.

"Oh?" Doug stepped back, bracing himself for an impending fight. "Well, then…excuuuse me!"

Rotating her chair to face him, she remarked, "You're funny."

"No, *you're* funny."

"You're funnier," she snarled.

"You're funniest." He stood taller.

"Fuck you!" Gilda snapped, and usually when she said that word, she wasn't smiling. This time she was. Only the smile was weird and meant to make Doug feel uncomfortable.

"Well…, maybe you should tell me about your day so far. Something *bad* happen?" Doug pressed his back against the wall and crossed his arms in defense.

"Not yet," Gilda mimicked his crossed arms, defiantly tapping her foot on the loopy carpet and glaring up at him.

Doug let out a sigh and turned to leave the room.

Quickly searching her desk, Gilda grabbed a staple remover and threw it at the back of his head.

"Ow! What was that for?" he yelled, turning around to meet Gilda's eyes.

"You know exactly what that was for."

"I don't," Doug scoffed. "I don't have a clue."

"Well, when you figure it out, come back and maybe we'll talk. Meanwhile, *I* have work to do." Gilda turned away, feigning interest in a stack of mail piled on her desk.

Doug rolled his eyes and went back to his office. Unaware that a large bump was rising on the back of his neck, he sunk down on his elbows and stared at the monitor in front of him. He had been playing computer chess earlier before the phone call came in and distracted him. Trying to recall his next move he started whistling – a habit he had when he was in a state of uncertainty. Gilda hated when he did that and yelled from her room, "Please don't whistle. You *know* that drives me nuts!"

Doug whistled louder the tune of "Row, Row, Row Your Boat" while making a bad move on the computerized chess board. "Argh!"

Gilda slammed the door shut and fumed. "Let's get this over with," she whispered harshly through clenched teeth, as she picked up the house phone and looked at the last caller's number. Nervously, she tapped the *call* button and held her breath. The phone rang three times and just when she thought no one would answer a woman's voice spoke, "Hi, Dougie! I knew you'd call me back. Can't resist little ole Marilyn, can you, baby?"

Practically drawing blood from biting into her lower lip, she quickly pressed the *off* button and let out an audible gasp. Her hands began to tingle, and her skin felt clammy from a sudden burst of perspiration. She immediately recognized the familiar sign of an oncoming panic attack. They had been occurring often lately as she began to doubt her relationship with Doug. Dropping her head to her chest, she slowly rolled her head to the side, then back and around. She did this several times while taking deep, rhythmic breaths. When she knew for certain that she had control of the attack, she raised her arms above her head and stretched. She picked up a Sharpie and wrote the phone number, that she had just redialed, down in bold, large strokes, filling the paper from edge to edge. The potent smell from the permanent marker made her sneeze.

"Bless you!" she heard Doug yell from his office.

"Drop dead!" she yelled back, while grabbing another piece of paper and writing the number down again. She held the two sheets up in front of her and then sat them side by side on the floor. The urge to do something asinine grew stronger with the swelling anger. She picked up a stack of paper and began writing the number on several more. Before she knew it, she had written it over fifty times and the floor was nearly covered. Standing over the sea of white, the bold, black numbers shouting inside her head, she began to laugh. "What's so funny in there?" Doug asked from the hallway.

"Come in and see for yourself," Gilda managed to sound cheerful.

Doug cautiously opened the door. In a weak, timid voice he asked, "You're not going to throw anything at me, are…?" With one foot into the room, he looked down at the floor. "What's this?"

"Recognize Marilyn's phone number, Dougie?" she asked with a nasally accusatory tone, waving the house phone in the air as evidence.

Doug scanned the floor and let out a *humph*, followed up by whistling, and he turned around and sauntered back to his office. Gilda followed. She stood posed in his doorway, arms crossed, feet apart and staring at the lump on the back of his neck, determined to wait him out. Despite his talkativeness, he was better at silence than she was, and she knew that hell would freeze over before he'd start the conversation. Fuming with impatience, Gilda cut to the chase. "Tell me about Marilyn."

More silence occurred as Doug sat stoic like a chess piece. Gilda repeated the statement, this time with less demanding. "Please tell me about Marilyn. I have a right to know."

Doug snatched a crumbled piece of paper from the trash can, flattened it out and wrote something in the tiniest print. Gilda leaned over and squinted trying to read it. Just inches from his face, she swallowed a breath when she recognized the phone number of a man she had met weeks earlier at the gym. She stepped back and put her hand over her mouth. They stared into each other's guilty eyes until Gilda's cell phone rang from inside her purse.

Nearly knocking her over, Doug bolted past her, heading toward her room. He picked up Gilda's Prada knockoff handbag and dumped the contents out on the desk. The phone continued to ring. Answering it, he pressed the *mute* button and listened. The voice from the other end was shouting. "Gilda, Gilda, can you hear me? We have a bad connection, I can't hear you. I'm at the gym, babe. Call me."

The papers on the floor stuck to Doug's sweaty feet as he turned to go back to his office where Gilda had remained in the same spot with her hand still over her mouth. He shoved the phone in front of her eyes and watched her face contort as she looked at the number of the last caller. Gilda figured the ball was now back in her court and this time silence was *her* ally. They stood staring at each other and as usual, she knew she would be the first to speak.

"OK. OK. It's over," she said submissively.

"Yeah, it's over," he nodded in agreement.

"Good. Well then, let's celebrate, shall we?" Gilda smiled innocently.

"Celebrate what?" Doug gave her a puzzled look.

"It's over. I'm not going to see that man anymore and you're not going to see that woman either. Isn't that what we meant when we said, it's over?"

"Not quite," Doug huffed. "I meant it's over for me and you. I thought you meant the same thing."

"I thought you meant what *I* meant."

"Well, *I* thought you meant what *I* meant."

"You're funny," Gilda said sarcastically.

"No, *you're* funny." Doug spouted.

"You're funnier," she shouted, practically spitting on his face.

"You're funniest." he snapped.

"Fuck you!" they blurted in chorus.

At a standstill, they were startled when the house phone rang in Gilda's hand, and at the same time her cell phone went off in Doug's hand. Each glancing down at the numbers on the screen, neither could stop the smile from taking over their face. Recognizing Marilyn's phone number, Gilda handed it to Doug. He turned her cell phone toward her so she could see that the man from the gym was calling. Sheepishly, she reached for it.

"Hold on, I have something I need to finish," he said to the caller and held it to his chest.

"Please hold a minute, I have to say goodbye to someone," she said to the caller and pressed it against her bosom.

As if a lightbulb went off in their heads, they nodded a gentle surrender, leaned forward and gave each other a simple peck on the cheek. Gilda turned, greeted the caller in a hon-eyed voice and walked out on the patio.

Doug crooned into the mouthpiece, "Hellooo, again!" and closed the door behind him.

This isn't right. Ending the book using the 'queen mother of dirty words' just to rattle my children. So, I'll leave you with a little story I'd like to dedicate to all the wonderful quirky people I've met and will meet, in the hope that it will encourage you to be who you are and not what you are expected to be.

My Sweet Weirdness

My last boyfriend left me with these final words, "Let me put it delicately…you are an attractive woman, but you're also a bit weird."

Delicately? Weird? What do you mean I'm weird? Like an eggplant? An aardvark? Fine, go ahead, call me weird! You think it bothers me? And by the way, that's no reason to break off a relationship!

Alright, I'll admit, I'm weird. Ever since fourth grade everyone called me *weird*. By the time I was in high school, I had fallen in love with the word. Not only did it suit me, it spurred me on to entertain my friends in a goofy sort of "Carol Burnet" kind of way, and as a result, I landed the zany character roles in all the school plays.

Even my mother confessed that she was weird back in the seventies when it was cool. But now, my very practical mother reminds me that her generation also thought dirty bare feet, bad pot, and Boone's Farm wine was cool. She said she eventually outgrew that silly stage, but I know she still longs for it. Because when I turned twenty-five, through a tearful ceremonious trip down memory lane, my mother gave me her old handmade bellbottoms, a set of beads, and a slightly faded flowered headband. She said, with a wink, the little wooden box filled with crushed incense might come in handy someday, so she kept it for herself. In her own way, she was telling me to be who I am.

And so, I have remained faithful to my kooky self, but now that I'm approaching thirty, I find that I am still under the scrutiny of my co-workers and neighbors, and even my so-called friends make fun of me behind my back. "Can no one appreciate *me*?" I asked the janitor, while sharing a sandwich on the steps of the fire escape in the back of the building where I work. He thought a moment and then answered assuredly, "Austin, Texas would appreciate you. You'd fit right in there."

While considering his advice, I decided to take a break from the "normal" people. Mr. Pinot Noir became my best friend, and together we found comfort in my cracked-leather chair slumping over a computer that I lovingly named Sam where I applied my unusual ideas to poetry, songs, and letters I never sent, filling hundreds of pages and consuming many lonely nights.

Until, after this four-month long hiatus, without warning, Sam died. I sat there feeling numb – struck at my strange reflection in the lifeless monitor, barely recognizing the de-ranged woman with dark circles under her eyes. And what are those deep vertical ruts between my eyebrows? My cousin called those ugly lines a "frownie." She tried to tame hers with duct tape.

Looking closer I realized that this was not the funny girl from high school voted most likely to be in lights onstage. Oh no, this woman sadly reminded me of someone from the past, someone I did not admire. To my astonishment, I had become Ms. Bruel, my fourth-grade teacher!

As my mind wandered back to elementary school, I remembered her sitting mummified at her desk staring at something far beyond the tops of our heads. Even when a double-dared student slammed a book hard on the floor in an attempt to startle the teacher back to her senses, she didn't budge. That was the first time I had ever witnessed someone sleeping with their eyes open. Talk about weird!

It was when several of us were ordered to carry boxes to her car that we discovered empty gin bottles in the trunk. From that day on, the poor comatose teacher in her crapulent state would bear the brunt of many practical jokes. I confess, it was me, in the beginning stages of my weirdness, who found delight in passing out rubber bands to shoot spit wads – many that landed in Ms. Bruel's thickly teased beehive where they remained stuck for the rest of the day. Let it be known, I refused to participate in the thumbtack on the teacher's chair idea, which was a total failure anyway. Nothing could pierce that woman's girdle!

Sadly enough, we found out much later that the old gal wanted to join the circus in her early years, long before she made a career in academia. I wonder what happened to destroy *her* dream? Did her friends shame her into hiding within the thin walls of an elementary school shack where she secretly numbed her portly body with booze and thoughtlessly failed a third of the fourth grade? If so, I sure don't want to end up like Ms. Bruel!

I shook free of that dreadful thought and apologized to poor Sam. Bless his little worn out pixels. And with a proper eulogy, I buried him in the back of the closet under a pile of clothes that used to fit and set out to recapture my sweet weirdness.

I adore balloons. I love seeing them tied to a kitchen chair, in the hands of children who can't take their eyes off them, dancing around in the back seat of a car on their way to a party, and I especially love letting them loose outside on a cloudless sunshiny day. At my age, this is probably a weird thing to do, so in honor of reviving my old self, I drove to the store in my mother's old hippie attire, beads and all. If the manager would have allowed it, I would've gone barefoot. I bought twenty helium-filled balloons. I tied a note on the end of each string. One by one, I released those carrying good messages into the air while lying on the front lawn singing "Up, Up and Away" in my very best voice.

Then, I set free the remaining balloons with messages listing all the injustices that I had endured – including a few exceptionally good curse words. But I didn't dare let those reach heaven, so I shot them down with my nephew's BB gun. Five out of eight! Not bad.

On the corner of my street lives an elderly man whose wife had recently died. It was said that he had a very bad odor, and the latest cruel joke was that the smell was probably the cause of her death. I only knew him by a single wave each time I went for a walk, as he was always on his porch, either reading or writing. I rarely saw a visitor enter his driveway. Even the UPS man would stop cold at the end of the steps and drop the delivery underneath the porch.

I took my usual walk. Only this time I brought a bottle of 16-yr old Scotch and two jiggers with me in my thrifty yellow backpack that I had rescued from the Goodwill pile I had started when I was that *other* woman. When I reached my neighbor's porch, he said, "I wondered when you'd get around to visiting," and he offered me a seat. During our three-hour visit we sipped nearly half of that bottle while munching on fresh roasted garlic, and this remarkable old gentleman told me stories that filled me with wonder.

I'm on a roll now and feeling mighty weird, just like I used to when I trusted my instincts. Weird enough to knock on my ex-boyfriend's door with a stack of my brother's very well-used smut magazines and boldly say, "You'll probably be needing these about now," followed by a sly wink and a kiss that would blow his socks off, demonstrating poise and confidence as I walk away without looking back. Only, my brother refused to part with not even one issue, so the act was not nearly as effective handing over a stack of my mother's *Good Housekeeping* magazines. Still, the look on his face made it all worthwhile. I laughed all the way home.

I ask myself, am I weird enough to tell my managers' wife that her husband is cheating on her with the cashier at the local pharmacy and then offer her the phone number of my ex-boyfriend in case she wants revenge? Probably not one of my best ideas. Instead, I placed a bouquet of flowers on her front porch with a note attached that read these words: *You are so beautiful to me*. After all, every woman needs a secret admirer, even if they're not real.

In the back of my closet is a pair of roller skates that have not seen the light of day since I was a teen. Next to them in a dusty cardboard box is an outfit – tassels, tights and a red, padded shoulder jacket that I wore during my brief stint with the high school drill team. I couldn't stop laughing squeezing into the uniform, but the skates fit just fine.

At the roller rink, it was a gas gliding across the slick wood floor, and I only fell once, and that's because a clumsy little girl trying to find her balance got her sticky fingers stuck in my fishnet stockings and took us both down. The best part was remembering all the words to the *Hokey Pokey* and skating backwards under the reflective disco mirror ball watching the sequins on my skirt twinkle in the dark. I'll be sore for days after, but oh, it was so worth it!

Nighttime brings on a special kind of weirdness that frankly must be skillfully controlled. My imagination is even more vivid in the dark, and since I'm no longer avoiding who I am by hiding out, I will have to act on it. There's no better place to be weird than in your own backyard, especially when the moon is about to burst.

After I ate a stack of peanut butter pancakes for dinner and sipped on a mug of hot chocolate piled high with marshmallows, I climbed into my hammock and let myself sink into its netting. The stars were beginning to flicker and the moon sat directly overhead. There were crickets nearby to add to the enchantment of the evening and a soft breeze tickled the hair on my legs. *No need to shave without a man around.* I could hear my breathing slowing down, and my heartbeat leapt to my ears. I let the night wrap its arms around me and soothe my soul.

The thought of moving to a city where the motto is "Keep Austin Weird" was becoming more and more enticing. I asked the man in the moon for an answer, and when I saw him smile, I knew he had agreed. And then, a rush of warm air circled through my stomach, darted across my chest, and out of my mouth flew a howl that would attract a werewolf from miles away – a loud, prolonged, mournful cry that lasted eight seconds each round and would probably reach the moon by midnight. What a relief! I had completely emptied my mind. And not until I had all the dogs on that block and the next two blocks over howling with me did I finally quit and allow the celestial bodies radiating perfect energy from above lull me to a calm and dreamless sleep.

What a day, what a night! Priceless! I hadn't slept that well in years, and I didn't even need a man, or wine, or Sam, or pretentious friends. All I needed was me. Just wonderful, weird me.

Acknowledgements

How do I thank a person who has spent countless hours reading, inspiring, and editing my work with indefatigable energy? A walking dictionary that can tell me the meaning of thousands of words, even the word, *borborygmi*. A man with a tireless sense of humor that ignites the fire of my imagination and keeps me running to my laptop to write more. I think the best way to thank this beautiful human being, Robert Alan Radmer, is to share my stories.

Thank you, dear Michael Bryer who motivated me to write funny Christmas newsletters with what little energy I had in between raising our six amazing children. My treasured life with you is forever filled with marvelous stories.

A heartfelt thanks to my brother and mentor, Marshall Rea, and loving friend and author, Evelyn Turner. To my sister, Melody, for the boundless memories. And to you sweetie-pies, Patti Mirehouse, Barb Butzen, Rebecca Dickens, Billy Wilson, Michelle Williams, Joyce Brown, and Michael Wyse who read my crudely unedited stories and still encouraged me. Monica Rae Cantu, you are an inspiration. Jackie Yancey and Jeanie Matthews – thank you for letting me twist your stories into my own. Melody, my little sis, thanks for the memories. My children, Vanessa, Jacob, Lucas, Matthew, Zachary, and Charlotte – you are the reason.

Thank you to *You*, the reader who took the time to read my book, in the hope that you will leave it in the bathroom for others to read.

And a special thanks to Daniel Wallace, author of *Big Fish*, whose kindness inspired me to keep writing.

About the Author

Libby Belle lives in Austin, Texas, a city that thrives on weirdness – a perfect place to nurture her vivid imagination. It's also where all six of her beautiful children, ten grandchildren, and a bunch of wonderful wacky friends and relatives reside.

Anytime, anywhere, and especially during the witching hour, she has written over 100 stories, a book of poetry, and a half-dozen songs. "I even write in my dreams," she says. "It's a wonderful curse!"

Her stories have been published in London and New York magazines and Texas newspapers, with contributions to Beyond Art & More magazine.

Also from Libby Belle…

VISIT: www.LibbyBelle.com
LIKE: Facebook.com/LibbyBelle@LibbyBelleStories

Made in the USA
Coppell, TX
02 July 2021